Night Ivy

Night Ivy

E. D. E. Bell

Atthis Arts

Detroit, Michigan

Night Ivy

Cover illustration by Manou Gijsbrechts
Map of Alyssia by Savanna Sheer
Interior Design by E.D.E. Bell
Layout by G.C. Bell

Published by Atthis Arts, LLC
Detroit, Michigan
atthisarts.com

ISBN 978-1-945009-83-9

LCCN 2022932362

First Edition: Published July 2022

This book is dedicated to Gregory A. Wilson,

who helped me embrace my inner bard.

Contents

Preface

Greetings!

This story is all about beginnings, and so, whether you've traveled with me in the past or are interested to see what *Night Ivy* holds, I hope you will enjoy it.

The world of Alyssia is built on magic and exploration, and sewn with the threads of journeys. What I've decided is that I'd really like Alyssia's stories to feel like bard's tales. Like our lives, they wander and bend, they turn on moments, they can be unexpected— They are filled with emotion, and friendship, and the belief that it is not perfection we seek from each other, but sometimes, someone to share the path. Through the small tales as well as the large.

I have been through a lot regarding ideologies in my life. Decades of understanding, time and time again, that what I was taught is not what I believe. People have noted that my stories breathe from joy and compassion, but they sing to burdens, repression, and pulling through.

In all of the changes I have found in myself as I grasped and sorted and forged anew, I was stunned to learn that I was going to be named Eleanor, but because of multiple layers of family boundaries, control, and conservative politics, the name was rejected. Even my very *name* was influenced by these restraints. My wonderful, supportive spouse and kids even offered I could change it now, but I said no, that wouldn't be right for me. What defines us and what restricts us can be complicated, but to me, my names are like my memories and disorders and my tattoos and my triumphs. Part of the Emily package.

However, I could certainly do what a writer could do, and design a character, take a cool name that I might have had, add a bad-ass X to it with lots of fun interpretations, and then mold that character into my soul, so she is part of me and I clearly a part of her.

I am so proud of my magic student, and so hopeful that we can stay doing this a while so we can have more adventures together.

One note. I drafted this book after a devastating year for my mental health and for our small press (yes, that year), so my confidence was… shattered. As I started to write the story, I started to second guess my decision to give the main character mental disorders like mine. I keep typing other contexts and deleting them, so for now I'll just say: I was worried that people wouldn't *like* her. But I kept thinking of all the other people out there who might draw comfort or strength from her openness—and her beauty—and so she stands as she is. Gloriously!

In other words: my life, my struggles, my joys, and my stories are all twisting together into a celebration of pride in who we are. Fierce pride. I hope you will join me in it.

Thanks to every one of you who breathed life into this story.
To: Manou Gijsbrechts, Savanna Sheer, Tessa Anouska, Camille Gooderham Campbell, Catherine Jones Payne, Sasha Kasoff Moore, Laura Johnson, Deborah Reilly, Meghan Cusack, Minerva Cerridwen, Chrissann Maynard, Johnnie Pittman, Chris Bell, and every one of you who made time to hear my words. I am so grateful.

The bottom line on this story is that I had a blast writing it. It exudes my joy and my resilience and I hope you will feel those in your heart. Whether you read this today or someday, then we share that connection. And, to me, it means the world.

Cheers,
E.D.E. Bell
04 July 2022

Night Ivy

To'Grand
Wehj
To'Breath
Vattam
Satta
Iycro
To'Frond
Savanna Sheer

To'Arc
To'Eyer
Mytil
Tam
To'Charm
To'Dust
Sharre
Alyssia

01 – Petition

Xeleanor Du'Tam. You petition before us?

It was always like this. She'd collect her mind to address someone (in this case a room of Spire Mages), and then right as she was ready to speak, some casually tossed item would trip her. Like this inherently obvious question. Which she never knew how to answer without being seen as sarcastic.

Was she supposed to answer no? They were all watching her.

"I do," Xelle said as solemnly as she could. Like a flame-tossed wedding, which was the exact opposite direction she was trying to go.

Yet. Why hadn't they addressed her by title? *Study Xeleanor Du'Tam.* When they must know what she was here to ask? Her heart was thumping now; she knew her voice would shake when she spoke, as though she were a nervous initiate, not a senior Study with solid experience.

"I'm here to ask the Arc Spire for my certification as Mage."

In any normal circumstance, she would offer them standard reasoning. Her unusually extended training, her accolades from the Tower Watchers. They knew all that; she could see the file she'd put together sitting on the table, disheveled as if someone had read it, assuming it'd not just been tickled for fun.

Truly, pulling herself back in, she was surprised they'd agreed to hear her petition at all. They'd rejected even hearing her before, so what had changed? She'd hoped it was a positive sign, but now she was worried she was missing something. She was definitely missing something.

The seven Spire Mages sat around the wooden table with varying expressions of discomfort, an odd juxtaposition to their velvet and metallic-threaded finery. Some leaned back nearly to the vine-carved pillars behind them. Others pressed fingers upon lips. It was as though they already had something to say but wanted to be polite and let her finish. Or, start.

Fira, it was always too much. She didn't need this. She didn't need status and title. Except, apparently she did. She was trying to create new and better uses of magic, and being a Mage, even a base, non-ranking Mage, would grant her access to libraries and artifacts that were not trusted to Studies. She knew this group was heavy on symbolism, so that was the angle she'd planned to take today. They were watching her. Pretending she could see through the growing fog of her uncertainties, she jumped in.

"In the spirit of cooperation embodied by Helina, my lab work has been noted by visiting Mages, highlighted in ranking exchanges, and employed in major projects affecting the populace. With the base rank of Mage, I would better be able to build those relationships, bring the respect that I can to To'Arc, and better serve the populace. I would—"

"Xeleanor, you know how this works." Nainol leaned forward, pushing with him a cup of tea that was comically small next to his bulky figure. "If you'll pledge to To'Arc, then we can consider you. You have strong qualifications, and we encourage it."

That frustrated her in about as many ways as Nainol's vest had gold buttons. Nothing against his buttons; they were stylish, and nothing lavish for a Spire Mage. But the point was she was frustrated. They'd gone right to a binary before she'd made the case they'd waited so patiently for her to begin. Which meant, she supposed, they'd been hopeful she'd agree this time to pledge? That she was bluffing? Throwing a last long shot? Sure, she rather was. But not like that.

She'd made her position clear before. She wasn't ready to pledge. Studying at To'Arc was an absolute honor; she'd made the best friends of her life, and Arc Magic intrigued her deeply, in a way that her brief studies at To'Ever and To'Frond had not. But one shouldn't be pushed into a lifetime commitment to use the good library, or to make others feel proud of one. On top of that, they'd complimented her—practically offered her the position. That was not normal. Some Studies never earned that type of acceptance, ash, some Mages didn't.

So what was going on?

The Mages had all shifted as she'd talked. Or tried to. The Crown Mage, Jehanne, sat in place at the center of the arced table, her wrinkled face set without reaction. Pelir was writing something down. Kern stared distractedly at the side wall, through the circling columns. We'le, by contrast, smiled directly at Xelle, one of those dignitary smiles that holds pleasantry but nothing like happiness. Awayna sat against one side of her chair, her eyes wandering the chamber but completely avoiding Xelle's, and Gloria leaned against eir broad, curved hand as if deep in thought.

What a mess. She had no idea how to read the room; Mages were always strange, but they were acting entirely so. If this had been her lab, she would have called a meeting and said, 'Alright! What is going on?' But it was not her lab, it was one of the Seven Spires of Halina, Crown of Alyssia, and there were still risks Xelle wasn't willing to take.

Meaning, there were some risks that weren't wise to take.

"I am not yet ready to pledge, Arc Spire. I love Arc Magic and plan to make it a permanent study, but I feel that my growth is best served, as well as my ability to innovate, by—"

She did not owe them this. One of the last pieces of advice her parents had given her before she set out for To'Ever was to never let a Mage convince you that you owe them. She'd kept that in her pocket. She let out the rest of her sentence as shaky air, sounding loud in her ears. "If there is no space for my certification, then I thank you for your time."

Awayna lifted a short arm, reminding Xelle of a Grand Mage aiming a wand. "Actually, we have a mission for you," she said, her voice taking a professorial tone. "You'll be less suspicious unpledged, so what if we leave it at this for now and avoid any other consequences."

Consequences. Xelle resented that deeply. With all her dedication to the craft and mentoring of the new Studies, they would imply, what? That she'd be punished for her request? Or maybe already was, by being sent on some errand? Something they'd been trying to sluff onto someone and then Xelle showed up? She wanted to flash them the flame. She kept that to herself.

"Perhaps you'll find it interesting," Gloria added.

She appreciated Gloria getting that last bit had been harsh, at least. Realizing she'd crossed her arms, Xelle uncrossed them. "Yes, perhaps." She nodded curtly.

Several Mages shifted again, in a weird shuffling quiet as their solid chairs did not creak but their robes and sashes rustled in muted chorus.

Apparently she'd done that wrong too. Rank was important to order here, as was respect. She knew that. And Xelle respected people deeply. Enough to know they were still all hu, and Xelle couldn't keep up with getting every gesture right. Her mind tiring rapidly, she tried to stand respectfully and hear what this errand might be.

The thing was, she did love To'Arc. If right now she could change her life and appear in any of the seven Towers, she'd still pick this one. For several reasons. The Magic, her friends, the Region—that was all true. Her lab.

Xelle's understanding of the other Towers was that they were, in different ways, more rigid. Arc Magic was one of the more complex studies (or at least someone studying in To'Arc might say that) but it was based around travel, reach, change . . . transformation. And so an Arc Mage, by nature, tended to be open to change and variation. This was not the worst Spire to try and sway.

Which did make her curious what this mission might be. A mission, right? Why not call it an assignment? If she had listed this morning a thousand things that might happen today, being assigned a 'mission' would not have been among them. Honestly, it sounded silly. She wasn't going to tell them that.

Xelle tried again to look proper, and reminded herself to maybe not nod the Mages permission to speak again. Not that she'd meant it that way, but Fira. She waited this time, trying to stay still.

Awayna glanced toward Jehanne, who must have offered some sign that Xelle could not detect. Her arm now lowered, she spoke again. "You are aware that Crown Mage Jehanne is seeking to retire?"

Well, that got serious. "I am," Xelle answered, trying to keep her responses boringly unprovocative.

"We are in general concurrence that Spire Mage Pelir is a fitting replacement to the Crown." Awayna paused. "Pelir represents the best of our craft." The way she said it made Xelle think there had some debate on that point, but that 'necessary consensus' had been reached. Not that she knew of anything negative about Spire Mage Pelir. She'd only heard good things, herself. Pelir was young, though. Not even 50 if Xelle recalled correctly.

She glanced toward Pelir. The Mage had stopped taking notes, but had leaned back, as if resting. Now that Xelle noticed, xe looked tired. Very tired. (Pelir almost always took 'she' but xe hadn't been introduced, and Xelle knew xe didn't take 'any'.)

"Pelir has been . . . discredited . . . multiple times lately," Awayna went on. "Rumors were spread that were meant to discredit," she quickly amended. "Detection has indicated that an inhalant is being used. Breath Magic. Turned. To influence the Ascension of the Crown Mage. We can counter the effects of any Breath Magic within our walls, but its caster is skilled and we cannot risk bringing more pers into this . . . situation. And so we plan to send you on a standard exchange."

Xelle tried to unpack all that. Quickly, as Awayna was sure to continue. Using an inhalant to, what, compel someone to spread these rumors, or—well Xelle didn't know, but whatever she was suggesting, some type of non-consensual casting, would be a highly violent act; Xelle didn't even know what to call the sort of conflict that would open between Towers. The spoken distrust alone was of alarm, she'd just openly stated she thought someone was turning the magic—on another Tower. Even the tone! Hearing To'Breath talked down wasn't new to

Xelle; at every Tower where she'd studied, To'Breath was thought less impressive, but if they were dancing on a floor with cracks, all the more to consider. Then she'd said 'detection' had indicated, not that Arc had 'cast' detection, as though their own response was innocuous. Beyond that (and that was plenty to go on!), why the ashes was Xelle, a controversially irritating Study, being brought into something with so many serious implications. When it appeared no one else had. Not that she could know that, but it was her sense.

Awayna was continuing. "Pelir is constantly undermined by unimportant pers." She stopped. "Let me clarify. What I mean is that the rumors start somewhere in the Tower, and by the time we hear them we can't determine their source. It's gone on enough that it's already a threat to the stability of our Region, even aside the Ascension. The dispute on metal sourcing, the—" She flicked a hand. "We've had to stop our promotional efforts until the swirls settle. It would add too much risk of inadvertently undermining her."

Promotional? They run ads on Crown Mages? Xelle was really missing her lab. And she had a little pull in her back, but didn't want to twist and look disrespectful again, especially if it cracked loudly, which had good odds.

Ok. Where was she? This sounded serious; she'd look into it too, if she were on the Spire. They were obviously investigating here at To'Arc. Again, great. And they wanted Xelle to investigate at To'Breath? Why her? Where was that coming from? As they'd divulged this startling bit, perhaps she had a little room to work. Except, she'd have to give up on the not getting in trouble part. For the minute.

She twisted her back, and got a half pop.

"If I may, as it would help me investigate, are there any compiled averments to the hypothesis?" Mages thrived on averments. Anyone visiting from outside the magesphere would probably think the word meant candy.

Tight lips. Around the room. Only Crown Mage Jehanne spoke.

"We are not at a stage of logical narrowing, but rather one where we would prefer your senses fully open. As you've noted, your quali-fications for this excel. Yet, as a Study, you will raise less suspicion."

Right. Because nothing about this was suspicious. Xelle had not been to Breath Tower before, or even past Vattam, though they must know she'd traveled a fair amount of Alyssia. Having always been drawn to magic, she'd started her studies at To'Ever because, she now understood, it was so close to her childhood home. After the initial thrill of her admission, Ever Magic: permanence, protection, and longevity, had not excited her.

Unable to reconcile this, she'd traveled to To'Frond, much more interested in the idea of healing. Surely, with her care for others, she was a natural healer. But To'Frond was built on order. Rune tracing required repetition and discipline, in manners she did not have. And their charge of managing those whose harm could not be contained was necessary but not in Xelle's spirit. Desperate to find a home, she had transferred again, to To'Arc, thinking, though admittedly not in the best place for this type of decision, that if she could not find comfort in the magic of change, then perhaps the world held no comfort for her.

These years had gone well. She loved To'Arc. She loved the friends she had made here, especially in her lab; the connections she had forged within herself at the visceral nature of Arc Magic. Its silence. Its depth of thought. Its vulnerability of understanding. She could see herself here. Arc Magic was her, in a fundamental sense.

But there was something missing.

Maybe there would always be something missing.

She drew in a breath. In the middle of the Arc Spire was not a place to sink into the quicksand of her regret. She imagined a small platform under her feet, pushing to make it solid.

From this tenuous platform, Xelle tried to shift her mind. She thought about Breath Magic. From what she knew, it was based in subtlety. Something made to inhale, to drink, to touch to the skin. Sensory. Broad. Which also required connections, similar to Arc Magic, but in lightness of touch, rather than depth of immersion. She wondered what of her studies here would better help her understand it, or if it was yet another world, a world without Xelle.

The quicksand shifted. She reminded herself that the most powerful Mages in the Region were watching her. As they were. She needed to say something, quickly. Continue the conversation. Her heart pulsing and her mind sparking, she grabbed at a thought, and pulled it to the front.

"If To'Arc has been infiltrated by a powerful Mage, wouldn't the first place to look be here?"

Then Xelle realized what she'd just said. Even before the room fell to an impeccable, pin-drop silence. She had lived all of twenty-nine years trying to break the habit of tossing ill-fitting flops she couldn't take back, and she still couldn't do it. Whatever complexity of magic she could learn, this simple precept was beyond her.

Suddenly, the idea that she was being sent to a Tower based around subtlety seemed more absurd than what she'd just said.

What did any of this mean?

As Xelle's eyelids started to twitch, the silence continued to grip the Spire Mages. Some bowed their heads. She had the strange thought whether some might be laughing. But, no, they wouldn't. Xelle avoided looking at the Crown Mage entirely. More than embarrassment, really—she'd practically accused them.

As she considered what to say to possibly correct this, an eclipse darkened the space from the windows around the high Tower room. Xelle wasn't superstitious about eclipses, but some were, and so she waited patiently for the light to re-emerge, her worries and thoughts of the last minute cycling without permission.

The sunlight, whitened and diffused by the swirling snow, streamed back in through the huge window. Nainol finished the last of his tea and leaned forward to speak. As he always had in the times she'd seen him lecture or announce, he appeared largely unbothered. This was at least a bit comforting. He hadn't silently chanted her banishment or anything. (There was no banishment; this is how she started thinking when her mind started to spiral.)

"Study Xeleanor, these are strange days," he said. "We are simply not at liberty to open Spire discussions any further than we already have. As I can see you are feeling along with us, much is uncertain. Paths are not clear."

Pelir lightly rapped on the table with a piece of smooth rootwood that wrapped naturally around her hand.

"I need to know if you will go?" Pelir asked, as if they were at a coffee bar and the younger hu had not yet answered her preference for cream.

Yes, Nainol had said too much. And Xelle thought she understood. They didn't know either. They knew it could be one of them. They were hoping that it wasn't. Xelle, the talented Study whose own uncertainties and lack of pledged loyalty seemed fairly out for view, was a neutral party. Someone they could hope to trust. A compromise. Meant to take some sort of step forward without further splintering To'Arc. Or Arc Spire.

Fira, that was too much to ask. But, perhaps, not too much to give.

"I will go, Spire Mages." She signaled the Arc, hoping it showed, whatever her aims, one was not to cause this home of hers trouble. "I will return with my findings. And when I do, I will report them right away to the Spire."

The Mages broke into whispers and murmurs, and chairs grated, and finally Xelle allowed herself to seek Crown Mage Jehanne's eyes. They were weary. Deeply weary. And they clearly signaled a sign Xelle had learned a long time ago.

Get out of here, they said.

She did.

02 – Cascade

The scene continued to repeat in Xelle's head. While she knew it had been real, whatever piece of her mind tried to reconcile such things hadn't quite settled yet, and so the sequence repeated, in flashes: Nainol. Awayna. Pelir. She was thinking of them by casual names, strange in itself. Perhaps to minimize? This was the Arc Spire. She'd stood in front of the Arc Spire. They'd denied her petition then given her a 'mission'. It had really happened. It even rhymed. And Xelle didn't know if she'd messed it up, but their faces, looking at her—she must have.

Breathing, she walked down the passageways, down the stairs, one after another, feeling like a hole in one of the wide floor stones might open at any moment, drawing her into another world, one where she wasn't sent to the other side of Alyssia with no sense of what she should do there or if they already regretted sending her before she'd left.

"Hey." Ay'tea's arms nearly reached her, but she halted in place, as if by an invisible cushion, stopping her before he did.

This time, she resented the cushion. She wanted to fold forward, into his arms, and tell him that nothing she did would ever be good enough. No matter how good it was. And for the first time, she realized, if she left for To'Breath, she would not be in her lab. Ay'tea, his smile. His wit. Would no longer be a presence like air and light.

Xelle had ignored her feelings toward him, but of late the weight had grown too much, a dark shadow that had fallen around her, like a heavy cloak.

Heavy because she was the one who was weak. A lab partner was a relationship of trust, of profession. Xelle was not some child, who couldn't separate the world. She was a Study with years of experience. A trusted source of the Arc Spire. Apparently?

She had resolved to stay above it, keep moving forward, bask only in the light but never see the sun.

Then, what force of the world put Ay'tea in her path, right when she needed him the most?

The weight snapped.

Her breath was audible; she tried to stay it. *Breath.* She laughed, inside, at the irony.

It was the session with the Spire. It had her out of sorts. She tried to calm. She felt her own fingers. Rubbed them. They were soft. Looked at the walls. Wispy details, thoughtfully carved through the finely cemented lines weaving through the natural stone. To'Arc. She was here.

He lowered his arms. "I could use your eyes on some of the records that have come in. Patterns."

By 'patterns' he was referring to her skill in seeing patterns across information, something she thought he was good at but he thought she was better. At least he often brought it up. What he didn't say? "Are you well? What can I do?" The omission was jarring, as these would be offered in any relationship, even one proper to a lab.

Perhaps he was giving her the solution she needed. Get to the lab for a bit. Work. Settle. "Yes, I'm happy to look at them."

They walked together, in the direction of their lab, now this fog on top of the other. The room was close; she hadn't realized it was the direction she had taken. As they walked, a sense of familiarity returned. Like every day. Today was like every day.

They were both proud of their project. Another irony, as they'd been assigned to it by Mages who held them in low regard. A project based more on analysis than travel or communication magic.

But they hadn't done the project for the Mages. The effort— reworking travel patterns to improve resource distribution—had been consistently revealing as well as rewarding. They'd quantified inequities in health resources, they'd proposed new bridges, new flattenings and crossings. All to make people's lives easier.

And of course there was the incident with the Mytil City Council; she laughed about that to this day.

They walked into the lab and swung the plain wood door shut. No one else was working; an array of worn desks and tables dotted the broad, low-ceilinged room. Today, it only looked like a maze. "I had a strange day." She tried to speak as if it were a normal day.

He stepped back, lengthening the distance between them. "I can see that. I'm sorry." He heaved a tome onto the mid table, his bony hand resting a moment over the cover, before sliding away.

"Are those the reports?" she asked.

"No." He smiled. She loved how his dedication to the work would always overtake whatever else he was thinking, even if a tiny voice now told her it was off, off to avoid her distress. "The reports all came back in different formats. There were sheets, and narratives, and drawings."

"But you sent out a form?" Xelle had checked it over. It was thoughtfully created, designed for pers of different backgrounds and abilities.

"Yes, and everyone ignored it." His smile turned up, still off. "We even got one response etched into reeds!" He pointed to a shelf, where a stack of reeds was neatly arranged, large in contrast to the small leaves that popped out from the vines crawling around it and across the livewall.

She grinned, still feeling overwhelmed, but not knowing what she could tell him. Meaning, of the Mages. "I would have helped."

"I know. I've been compiling them over the last week. You were busy." He patted the tome. "It's all condensed here. Aggregates by category. I'm going to look them over, but you have an ability to look across categories that . . ."

He stopped. And he wouldn't look at her. Just minutes ago, she'd practically stood against him, and now he stood at the other side of the table, as if she weren't there.

Xelle was worn out from the strange meeting with the Spire. But if she was doing something wrong with Ay'tea, she needed to fix it. No, she wanted to fix it. She reached through her scattered mind. "I'd like to look at it. I mean, I was just meeting with the Spire."

He froze, still not looking her way. "Oh, wonderful!" His voice remained cheerful.

"Not really," she rushed out. "It was so strange, 'Tea. They pretended I was important to them, but the fact is, I'm not. It's like this project here, how it doesn't even train in magic. How we've been working it for years, and how we're both unimportant, and yet they—"

She stopped, seeing him twinge.

"That's. Not. True."

He moved toward her, closing the tome and pushing it aside. Impulsively, she reached for the volume, as though to protect it, and he stopped. They were not so close; yet the air hung thick between them.

She couldn't go on like this. Had something happened? Did he understand? She could never tell. And maybe she shouldn't tell, maybe all of this was just bad judgment on her part. Like so often before. What was she doing?

"I'm sure they'll have other projects for you," he said. "Just as I've been working other things, as pers have seen our work. I think we've got this one solidly on its way; there will be Studies scrambling to take on the accolades of finishing what we've started. So instead, why don't we catch up on sign-off? Been avoiding that for a while, right?" He winced.

Her heart pulsed. No, sign-off. They had.

Her mind now whirling like pebbles in a metal spiral, she agreed, and started sorting through the records they hadn't yet finalized, filing each scroll or volume away with a registered code and signing the ledger to certify its verification and source. She kept her eyes on her hands, on the black enamel pen.

As the minutes passed, her space quieted, and she appreciated the task, though less than fun. But not all of her. She felt unsettled. As if

Ay'tea were upset at her, and she hadn't yet realized why. As if she'd done something wrong. A loss.

Xelle'd tried so hard not to mess this up.

She closed the book on the last of the unsigned records, well, signed now, and she realized she could not resolve this today, not with her senses rattled so and her heart beating unwisely. She needed to get back to her room. To sing, for a while. Check on her blooms. Yes, her room. 'Tea was staring down at a ledger. His winter cap in gray, striped with a subtle blue, held tight to his head. Only a pendant that had fallen out, forward from his jacket, showed any motion.

"Ay'tea, I'll be back in a bit," she said by rote, moving toward the door. Why had she said that? She wouldn't be back.

He leaned one way and then another, and because she knew him so well, she knew it was his stance of trying to make a decision. But this was all too strange. Ay'tea wobbling with that look on his face, and Xelle saying things that weren't true. Feeling overwhelmed, she reached out for the doorknob.

Hearing a sound behind her, she turned. He'd moved close. Unusually close.

Normally calm and humorous, his words were now hurried. "Working with you has been one of the honors of my life."

"Oh, Ay'tea. I . . . you have such a strong future. I know that you'll pledge soon." She almost added 'I'm surprised that it didn't happen sooner' but she was trying not to blurt out statements she hadn't yet thought through. It was true, though. He was older than she was, perhaps the oldest Study in the Tower. They hadn't discussed his reluctance to pledge. Thinking of it now, as many and long of conversations as they'd had, on personal and dear subjects, there were some they hadn't had. Some that would have been important. Anyway, she would think about it on her trip. Then, when she got back—

"Obsidian," he whispered. "You. You're obsidian. I see . . . Xeleanor. I'm sorry." He ran his hand across his forehead, almost touching his cap.

Somehow, the intimate gesture of even suggesting the removal of his cap—which he didn't do but the idea got into Xelle's head—erased whatever he had just said to her. His face remained close; she traced every ridge, simultaneously and subconsciously, with her eyes.

She'd never seen his crownhair. But, she would confess to someone whom she *really* trusted, she'd thought about it. Did he shave it, or was it long? Did it grow out, grayed with sadness and worry, like Xelle's, but striped with growth of the brightest colors of joy and expectation, when she— "Sorry, what?"

All this time together, she hadn't thought it could grow awkward between them. He was the one per here she could relax around. Always. The one who understood her. The only one. Every day, a consistency that kept her level. Or—was that true? Or was she ruining everything now? Maybe meeting with the Mages had affected her. Like she had something on her forehead and no one wanted to tell her. It broke her heart that she'd made it awkward.

His response was slow and measured and that soothed her. Deeply.

"There are different ways to travel," he said, almost at a whisper, leaning, so close to her. So close. "You know this. You've studied advanced methods; I have too."

Then again, his tenor changed, like he had suddenly become far away, despite being right here. Xelle could not understand.

"I've really appreciated our time on this project. You're a brilliant Mage" (she did not correct him) "and you can do good things for our world. The bridges we got built alone are making for better nutrition, faster care for so many children. And then you can imagine what those children will do, seeing what it's like to have power used as a lever for equality. It's a powerful lesson."

He droned for a bit about equality, as if that might erase the strangeness. It was a subject of passion they shared, but Xelle couldn't focus. It felt like he was running his fingernails down a wire screen, waiting for the door to open.

Whatever was happening, she couldn't take it right now.

"Ay'tea," she interrupted, almost forgetting she needed to tell him she'd be away. "I might not see you for a while."

His silence was strange.

He stepped even closer, yet his eyes were fixed at the wall. Why wouldn't he look at her? His voice strained as he spoke, each word oddly emphasized. "I will not get in your way. You are too important."

"What? 'Tea, I'm just going to—" She probably wasn't supposed to tell him. "I'm just going on a little trip. We can talk about this when I'm back."

Talk about what? Did she mean that? Her feelings for him had escaped her all at once, but she hadn't allowed herself to consider them. He was a comfort. A constant. An anchor. All at once, a wind was blowing. Something had changed.

And in Xelle's mind, when something changed, something important, it was like a thousand tiny windows opened at once, and her mind twisted between figuring which window held the breeze, and whether she should be scared. Whether she needed to act.

She closed her eyes, pulling her thoughts back in, deciding what she could say to fix things. To put things back to yesterday: two lab partners making good in the world. Or perhaps a friendly goodbye hug, nothing more than friends. She could imagine it. Could she? Would he? She opened her eyes.

Ay'tea was not there.

Xelle rushed out into the corridor. All she could see was the snow whirling outside the wide, low-floor window, thicker than before, like a dense, soft blanket. She stood there, several minutes, staring out into nothing. Searching for something, the shape of the large tree she knew to be there. But there was only swirling white.

Finally, she rubbed her temples, her fingers cold against her skin. Why now? Why today? Yesterday had been ordinary; what had she done to disturb that? Her petition? It had been a whim, to try again.

The loss of ground was distressing.

Xelle needed her room. Her garden.

She wound around again, keeping her eyes down, and wishing she had the authorization for more advanced movement magic, so she could just get away.

"Xelle!"

A familiar voice called after her.

"Xelle!"

She turned around to see Helia hurrying toward her, a tight knit wrap bouncing on her head, and ear chains whipping back and forth. This was, as a side note, why Xelle preferred caps. And didn't like jewelry that dangled. Personal preference; it did always look good on Helia.

"I heard you were with the Spire Mages!" She leaned in.

Offering a tight smile, Xelle nodded. Ever since Helia had pledged, it was simply impossible to ignore the power differential between them, even if Helia acted as though it didn't exist.

On top of that, Xelle had shown less interest in their occasional evenings out. *Shown.* She had *felt* less interest in them. Maybe for reasons she'd just explained. But since they'd usually just seen a show or tried a new dinner spot in Vi'Arc, Xelle didn't know what she would rescind. "We can't go to the fry" seemed a bit direct for a relationship that was never discussed as more than casual.

On top of *that*, Xelle had just had about the strangest interaction with the Arc Spire, then followed that up with an even stranger interaction with her lab mate, maybe the best friend she'd ever had, who'd just left without telling her why, and she hadn't had a blip yet to parse out any of this.

"So?" Helia unwrapped a candy and offered Xelle one. Xelle shook her head.

"I can't get into it, except that I'll be away a while."

Whereas at this point, Ay'tea had evaporated into a cloud of unreadable angst—Helia's face dropped with blatant dismay.

"Away? I mean, that's great. Especially if it's something exciting for you. It's just . . . Xelle, I've really been enjoying our time together." She moved closer, as if inviting Xelle to wrap an arm around her.

Xelle stepped back. "I'm still kind of overwhelmed right now. And you, know, my thoughts. Just on overload." She'd been open with Helia about her disordered mind. Helia might come from so much privilege she thought toilets cleaned themselves, but she was someone you could trust with personal things. She was a good hu.

"Maybe I can help. Take a walk together?" She looked down at Xelle with care in her eyes. Like, a lot of care.

Why had Ay'tea walked away from her?

"It's just not a good time; I need some time to think."

Helia forced a smile. "As always, it's been lovely to see you. I'm sure we'll talk soon." Without waiting for an answer, she gave a cordial bow, then turned and disappeared through a large group of Mages strolling through the larger corridor.

Sure she hadn't handled that well either, but now really needing the solace of her garden, Xelle headed that way, doing a neat dance to avoid crossing paths with a mid-ranking Mage that was always asking about her transportation analysis. Then she avoided one of her old teachers, a very nice hu but one for whom a 'short' conversation required a chair and a tall glass of water. Then she saw two younger Studies, whispering as they peered in her direction. She looked right at them, and they hurried away.

Exhausted, she considered a world in which she'd not just made that firestained petition, and if so, whether everything would have gone back into place.

03 - *Buds in the Dark*

By the time she was outside her garden room—it was a fair walk—she waited several minutes, peering around the unbusy corridor to ensure no one was nearby.

Unlike the rest of today's touchy and personal subjects, this was one she'd love to talk about. And one she'd kept completely to herself. (Despite all the ways that Xelle kept moving on in life, she and Irony had had a long, impressive relationship.)

The project had started when she'd itched to experiment with a rare phyta, one that was so regulated, she couldn't even find the *protocol for obtaining one* without being a Mage herself. Yet, she trusted herself to handle them, more than a lot of Mages she'd had for teachers, for sure.

She couldn't experiment within the Tower; every last tile was subject to cleaning and inspection. The cleaning crews were friendly, many former Studies themselves or with close ties to Mages, and a Study growing regulated phyta behind the bed was often overlooked. But not what Xelle was hoping to attempt. And not with the Tower Watchers on occasional patrol, especially once the cleaners sensed something off. Or a fellow Study with an ant in xyr pants. Wasn't worth it.

So then, she'd needed a space. With a childhood of building forts, and transforming closet spaces or the spaces under tables into little rooms, her senses immediately tuned to finding her own nook. Somewhere close enough to the Tower to be protected (and empowered) by its security and enchantments, but somewhere the Mages would never look.

Discouragement had followed for the better part of that summer;

Arc Mages held an acute understanding of space—the empty ones were not hidden, and the hidden ones were not empty.

She had been entirely beside herself when, after studying the maps for more evenings than she'd like to admit and then finding remnants of an old path on them, she concluded there might be a gap in between an old section of the Tower and a wide ramp connecting a mostly abandoned service building.

Her theory was, the original curvy path had been laid between the treed, uneven ground to a smaller first-floor door. Sometime after one of the old trees had fallen, someone took the opportunity to widen and straighten the antiquated path, cutting it directly toward the Tower. Deciding that a little extra stone work would be easier than wrangling the mix of soil and huge, arcing roots, the slight ramp was built from the raised section of the structure to a second-floor balcony of the Tower, long unused because of its undesirable view, and easily converted to a wide loading door.

One side of the short ramp was secured into the hillside that had likely built up from debris swept off the building's roof over the years (not worth bringing in casters), and the other was supported by a weathered stone wall, topped with a lovingly wrought iron fence for safety. For safety, but actually exquisite. As if the ironsmith were testing a new technique on this short, out-of-the-way stretch.

Once constructed, there would have been no real need to fill in the space; the ramp was plenty sturdy. Yet, without that context, its stones looked like any other garden wall, only dirt behind them. And if there really was a pocket there, she'd reasoned, the ground-level space would have soil and natural moisture, and with its full enclosure, the darkness she needed for this particular endeavor.

As suspicious as she would have looked tromping the uneven, untended area more than once, she'd next approached the space from the Tower's inside, carefully casting to test her theories. Thrilled (!), she found there was, indeed, a cavity, and the size was exactly what she wanted. Well, a little small. But enough.

Gaining entry had taken her months. The clear choice was to create an entrance through the patch of wall under the old curved staircase to the former balcony above. For weeks after weeks, in a block of time each day so she'd have no chance of nearing material limits, she'd meditated under those stairs. With the aid of a potted vine, she'd mindfully and carefully touched each piece of what would become her doorway, conversing with it about the nature of matter and the smallness of one world. Touching—meaning with her thoughts. Feeling the stone in her mind. Understanding it. Feeling that there was, as she'd thought, space within.

This is why she loved Arc Magic. No wands, no potions, no incantations. All of those tools were exciting, but Xelle loved the depth of feeling the world itself, all around. Conversing without words or hu-type thoughts. Deep. Beautiful. Complex. Like the vines that taught it to the simpler mind of a hu.

Touching the world brought calm to her mind. Quiet. It did not erase the rest of her worries, both present and elusive, but it took her away from them for as long as she remained in the cast. The price of Arc Magic, which was generally time and patience, was one she was happy to pay for such immersion.

And yet, what excited her most about her doorway were her own cross casts: the simplest of tools she'd learned while at other Towers, twisted in like hard twine reshaping liquid silver. From To'Ever, she'd cast a base enchantment of permanence (a word that did not mean what it purported) and wound it with a bit of Arc Magic. So with a jar of holly sap, a pinch of gold dust, and threads of travel, she tilted her passage just slightly, so it would only allow her through. (If she were in distress, she could signal someone to break through the wall. Her parents had taught her to think of these things.)

And then, even more basic, a building block rune of Frond Magic, drawn in spored viscous over the stones outside her room, and tied into the strong protection of the doorway. A rune of flow—not creating magic, per se, but easing it along—so that anyone casting detection would miss what she had done. She'd taken the time, day after day, to refocus and draw similar runes throughout the inside space, sewing them in like crochet (which she was terrible at with actual yarn but her mind loved the curves it created), so that as long as her casts were not loud (in nature, not literal volume) she could operate freely inside the enclosed space.

Sure, a skilled Mage who knew something was there could detect it, but what Mage would spend time inspecting the stones under the stairs in an old utility section of the Tower? It was the best she could do.

With a few nerves, for this cast required extraordinary care no matter how many times she'd done it, she thought her way through the stones, and stepped forward, her body and all she carried passing through the solid wall and into the space beyond. She drew a breath.

She stepped onto the partially-tiled floor and flicked on the lamps that she'd saved up over months to have made. Not a trivial task, as she'd had to order the lightpods from Mytil, where they'd be reliably considered part of an art project and not arouse the gossip of Vi'Arc. She'd wanted the dim, colored lights, because inkblooms only grew in the dark. Pure dark—even the moonslit skies of night were said not to be enough.

Yet Xelle could not see in the pure dark, not with her eyes, and she remembered that inkblooms were said to give off a deep blue light when in bloom. And so she hoped that a lamp in a similar hue would just allow her to see the shapes of the alcove, but without upsetting the delicate needs of the rare blooms. That had been the thought, anyway.

There were still no blooms.

She sighed, settling onto the wide seat she'd designed, like a low, circular basket around a smooth wooden surface, set with turning hardware onto the rain-worn top of the old, wide stump, now treated to last. There was a fitted cushion and a stack of pillows nearby, but sometimes when she was upset she preferred the elegant yet direct touch of the smooth wood. She let her hands run over it, enjoying the cool surface, and the subtle ridges of the natural grain.

She swiveled away from the door, toward the dirt-stained block wall behind which the old storage unit sat. Against which she'd built—with difficulty as she'd had to smuggle in the wood, piece by piece—a tall and substantial cabinet. After all, if she was going to have a secret space, she'd certainly store her more personal items in it. Along the floor rested the small metal grates she'd installed to allow air into the space. They opened into the elevated space beneath the building's first floor, but her casts had assured her that the narrow space was so full of rocks and other obstructions that anyone who crawled the whole way back there might as well have burrowed in from below.

And then, the reason why she was here: To each side of the back blocks were stout stone walls. One, already there from the stone supporting the ramp above, and one, leveraging the hillside, which she'd had to spend (more!) significant time reshaping and supporting with natural stones and strategic use of mortar paste.

Up each side wall, the perfect stone and the hodgepodge across from it, rose livewalls that she'd installed with careful taps and lattices, covered now in tiny dots—not even lights, but barely visible glowing points. Buds that did not open, but that whispered the idea of glowing from their wandering vines. Vines she was certain were meant to open inkblooms.

Ironically, it was unclear whether purchasing the inkbloom seeds would have been harder if she were a Mage using proper channels. It had been hard enough, needing to earn the trust of a whole chain of pers through questions and notes without revealing who she was. The difficulty of the acquisition was what had convinced her the seeds were real; no one would put up with *that* much nonsense for a simple fraud. Still, Xelle had been elated when the prolate, oval seeds had sprouted, again when they'd grown, and again when the tiny points of almost-light had emerged. Then, they'd all stalled. Just like this.

Someday, in her vision, the livewalls she'd built up each side of the small space would shine with their own deep light and she would not need the lamps. She couldn't say for sure, as she'd never seen an inkbloom (as she said, this was an experiment!), and any rare illustration of them simply could not capture the descriptions of a uniquely iridescent glow, somewhere in the space where blue, white, and black all intertwined.

Xelle settled into the space around her, but she could not settle. Her mind continued to tap at her, with new worries on top of old. Any string she tried to pull only resulted in more worry, more unknowns, or a closer view of realities she didn't want to see. With nothing to be done for herself for the moment, at least she could try a couple of casts, until she could return from her 'mission'. *Mission.*

Yes, when she returned, she'd take the chance to reset.

Casting around a tapping mind was difficult, and so she leaned into her practice. No, she'd never been able to separate the two, but process was a handle that never gave way, and when she needed, she knew it was there to cling to.

She greeted the tapping like new lab data, and she made herself view each item, sliding it away, down a mental corridor of her mind. She imagined, again, what it would have felt like had her arms met Ay'tea's. What that could mean for them when she returned. The shock of that was raw and substantial, as was knowing that sliding it would only cause it to return with that same shock. She worried how to tell Helia that they wanted different things. She worried for the sadness of upsetting Helia, the uncertainty of the finality of it, of not wanting to lose her, in a confusing way. This slid. What would happen with her lab work. A Study she owed a visit to. She hadn't yet read that book. Knowing this last piece must also be addressed, she saw the Spire Mages. Their 'mission'. Traveling away from her comfort and this space. But with the opportunity to reset. She could reset. It was all so unclear and her muscles began to ache but she slid it away. And breathed.

Her mind temporarily—not clear, but sorted—she stood and walked toward one wall of the buds. Leaning in, she could see the long, point-ended leaves. Though she couldn't see their true color in the tinted darkness, she imagined them a deep green, darker than holly, but of course she was often influenced by having grown up in Ever Region, not near the Tower but surrounded by the same evergreen forests it revered. She gently touched the side of a bud with her finger. It did not seem bothered by her touch. It felt . . . dormant.

"Whatever time you need," she whispered. Even if the blooms had been ready, it's not as if Xelle had considered attempting their magic for this journey. Still, with each visit, each new technique, she hoped that she had done something right. To test her theories. To grow.

She lowered onto the padded kneeling bench she'd built, another like it on the other side. The worries she'd pushed away receded into the far distance as she sank into the realm of thought. Pushed through what crowded her mind.

The storm fell away.

Carefully reaching through threads of connection, she tied herself to the buds, felt the connection of the thin but strong vines wandering between them.

Xelle leaned against the back of the surface, letting it take her weight. With her mind focusing, she sank into the magic. The threads were slightly beyond her skill, like a knitter straining to loop a complex sequence, or, more crudely, reaching for a jar at the back of a shelf while holding four others. Staying with it, she turned the last knot into place with great satisfaction, leaving two threads: one, a sense of her concern, enough that she hoped she might know along on her journey if the phyta were troubled.

She couldn't be sure; she'd not attempted anything like this over such great distance. And the second, a heart thread. A piece of herself, to protect and nourish the phyta, not as soil or water, but something more profound. These were magics that must be used with caution and care, as they affected the Study (or Mage) casting them, but she felt peace that her connections were safe.

Her breath shook, and she realized she'd actually done it. She could feel the threads. Looped, connected. Perhaps even properly.

Despite the rush of a successful new cast, she considered, as she stood, what little it might do over a true protection cast. But pure Ever Magic, over a complex living being—this would be irresponsible to try with her level of skill, certainly without the phyta's consent. The threads would have to do.

Xelle braced as the thoughts she'd sorted slid, with momentum, back into place. One, stronger than the others. Ay'tea's arms, reaching out. A moment that she'd ruined, from not understanding it. She chilled at the strange expression on his face, as he wouldn't meet her eyes. Coldness. Like she'd done something wrong. 'Obsidian,' he'd whispered. 'You're obsidian.'

She sat back onto her seat, whisking her legs up as it began to swivel.

Obsidian. Why had he mentioned it? It was odd, not right. They never created names for each other. He wasn't one for riddles or shaded gibes; his directness was something she liked about working together. Then why such a strange comment?

Obsidian was rare, very rare, at least anywhere she'd been. It was only found in the mountains, which were difficult to traverse and generally avoided by Mages and the populace alike. Xelle hiked them on occasion, of course just an edge climb she could actually reach, but only because the isolation, and perhaps the chill in the air, was settling to her. She would never take anything there; the mountains had a life to them, a presence more than the rest of Alyssia. None of it felt hers to take.

And so she knew little about the mysterious and rare substance except that it could be used as a mirror effect in complex magic.

She stopped. Ay'tea had no reason to think about this rare material while analyzing moveroom patterns and food distribution, something that could be done with a pencil, a ledger, a keen eye, and an occasional confident plea to local government.

Gazing up at her wall, her eyes opened with wonder. A dark mirror for a dark light. It was a complicated reasoning, but she could see it. Yet, how could 'Tea possibly know about her secret garden?

It wasn't possible.

Yet the thought was in her head. One of her parents, Na'Vuia, had told her several times before she'd left their home to study magic: 'When it comes to magic, what is possible is less of a line and more of a limit.'

This had seemed like the worried mutterings of a loving parent, but now she considered it. She could see the logical connection between the darkness of obsidian and inkbloom in the flow of the magic. Mages at Frond Tower had used mirrors in a similar way, to reflect the light for the growth of phyta.

What would it mean to reflect the dark? It was worth a try.

She remembered something her parent, Na'Foose, used to say: 'Sometimes in order to give a lot, one must take a little.' Sure, she could chip at what e was getting at, but she hadn't really understood it. She'd always viewed it as part of a scholar's story, not a path for life. As her chair continued to turn, Xelle thought through the size and angles of the room. What she might need.

Opening the cabinet and pulling out her large backpack, she shuffled around for the right sized empty bag, sorted through her cold weather gear, restocked Essie, and layered all of it into her backpack. After going over the list in her head a few too many times, she decided she was as packed as she would be. Just a few things from the village. She'd need to leave early, so it was best to move on.

Only as she passed back through the wall of stone, she realized that she had not stopped to sing. Well, surely there would be time to sing on the road. For now, she was going to stop for a quick meal, get her room (as in, her assigned room) in order, then get to bed early for what certainly would be a long day ahead.

04 – Leaving, but it's temporary

"Mage Helia, she's expecting me," Xelle said to the steward. Getting backup from the Mage was one thing she didn't need to worry about today; Helia was solid for her friends.

So it was no surprise when Helia gave the steward a friendly wave that looked a lot like 'she's good' or even 'she's always good' and then stood with raised eyebrows as Xelle stepped into her room.

Xelle had not been in Helia's room before, not her Study room nor her new, more permanent quarters. It was as nice as she expected it to be. Neatly sewn cushions and draperies, smooth wood furniture with rich natural grains, even a marbled stone countertop. And apparently, unlike a Study's studio, this was a full suite, as there was no bed visible, and doors led to what Xelle presumed to be sleeping and utility areas.

"I've got a balcony," Helia said, leading back to a double door, which swung open to reveal a breathtaking view out of the main Tower, reaching out over one of the gardens. Various vines wove between and over large columns, a mix of greens and wisps of brown, with highlights of peachy gold in the early morning light, defying even the snowfall, which seemed to largely pass through the living lattice.

"You must enjoy it so much," Xelle managed to say. She was happy for others' fortune; she was. But to Helia, having nice things was just the way it was. Helia would say that she'd earned them, and she had, but Xelle knew lots of pers deserving of such a view who did not have one.

She stopped herself. This was going nowhere good, and what kind of look was it to stand here griping, even in her thoughts. There was a reason she was here. There was a reason her own chosen space was a muddy hole under a service ramp. She had to believe that.

"I do," Helia said, turning toward her, as if ready to listen. She wore the same hair wrap as yesterday, but instead of the trimmed and sewn Mage's robe she'd been wearing to conduct her regular duties, today she stood in bright orange robes, layered under a shawl of deep blue. Across the shawl wandered a trail of richly embroidered flowers, in an orange just enough lighter than the robes to make them look like they glowed with midday sun. Xelle appreciated the deep, celebratory colors, fitted to Helia's curves as though blissfully unconcerned with the deep set of winter shimmering around them on the curved balcony. No, not blissfully. Forcefully, almost.

"So," she started, "I had a very confusing time yesterday. And when I saw you, I was a bit out of sorts. So I wanted to just say hi again, before, you know, before I go." Xelle hoped that worked. She'd felt bad about dismissing her friend (ok, perhaps casual romfriend) the day before, and wanted to try and fix it.

"Xelle, I could tell something was up. When will you be leaving? Maybe before you go, we could—"

"I'm going now, actually. Just—" She almost said that she'd be seeing a few pers on the way out, but that would probably make Helia feel dismissed again. "My bag is in my room; I'll grab it on the way out."

"I hope that you have a pleasant trip." Helia was oddly nonchalant about that. Then she smiled. "I'm glad you stopped by."

"Well, sure. Of course." Xelle almost referenced their fun together or some such thing, but until she could better think about it, she didn't want to set an impression she hadn't worked through. So she tapped her cap, with a smile she hoped was friendly. Not sure if she should just turn and leave, she hovered a moment. Helia seemed to be watching her.

"I got you something." Helia walked back into the center room and Xelle followed. With a grin, she spun around holding a smallish package, wrapped in a metallic red cloth with strands of fine ribbon tied in a neat bow. "Don't open it now, just sometime when you're down."

"When I'm—"

"I know you, Xelle. And . . . if you ever need to talk, I hope . . . I hope that you'll know you can talk to me." Having clouded in expression just briefly, she smiled again. "Then, where are you going?"

One obvious reaction to this would have been to consider that if a Mage somewhere was causing unrest amongst Mages, and a Mage who had been borderline ingratiating herself to an unimpressive Study suddenly started asking questions about the mission—terrible, now even she was calling it that—that one would suspect this Mage of something suspicious.

She did not. One thing Xelle felt she was good at was judging pers. Not *judging* them, like evaluating their actions, not that kind. The kind that knew if a hu was decent, or if one was honest, or kind, or wanted peace for others. Not just hu—every per, from kelucats to elephants (no, she'd never met one), gave levels and tones of light. Hu seeking power just had this capacity to grab the world and *stretch* it, so Xelle had learned to watch her steps.

Helia was a good hu. If she was asking about Xelle's trip, it was because she was curious and or cared about Xelle's role in it. This made things easier, because Xelle could respond to good faith in turn. And she did.

"So you heard I was with the Arc Spire."

She nodded enthusiastically.

"They want me to check something out. But I don't think I'm supposed to talk about it."

Helia nodded slowly and with weight. "They picked well. You're very good at . . . well, everything. You're good at magic, but you're good at populace tasks as well. And yet you won't attract the same attention."

As a Mage, Helia did not add. That's fine, Xelle got that part. She had chosen not to pledge, and she was going to live with the flaming consequences of it. The way things worked.

Helia waved toward the couch. "Here, have a seat? Would you like a glass of wine? I always take a glass before setting out. Assuming your moveroom isn't waiting?"

She hadn't even checked the schedule, but as she started to say so, she realized she didn't want anyone knowing about her diversion into the mountains. Even Helia, who might be put in a tight spot if pressed. It was time to go.

"What if I take a getslip on the wine," she said instead. "I'd like to get some distance before nightfall. I mean, I know it's morning, but the whole trip. It's long. Anyway, I really just wanted to stop by. We've, uh . . . well, thank you for the gift." She gave it a little hug.

Helia chuckled. "I'm sure I'll see you soon, then. Safe travels."

"Safe travels. I mean, I will. Good luck with everything here."

Before she made things worse, she managed to make her way back out into the corridor, glad to see Helia waving warmly. Nodding at the steward keeping an eye on this section of Mage quarters, Xelle gave a final wave before popping into the stairwell.

Next, she wound down toward her lab, a knot growing in her stomach. She'd fixed things (somewhat?) with Helia, now she needed to do so here. A friendly hello, maybe they could forget the strangeness of yesterday. And she could figure out her feelings on the trip. Go from there. She ignored a pounding in her heart, and told herself what she needed to do.

Poking her head into the lab, she saw one of their assistants, a new Study that Xelle hadn't had much time yet to get to know. The Study startled, but adjusted quickly, offering a smile.

"Ay'tea?" Xelle asked.

The Study shook her head. "Not in today. He said you'd be out?"

Oh.

"Yes, I'll be away a bit. I was thinking some more people might be around." She glanced around the room.

"Nope, just me."

"Not at all. You're doing great! The team is doing great. Excellent work here. Don't let my trip slow you down. Anything new you'd like to take on while I'm out, you have my concurrence."

The young Study beamed and Xelle hoped she'd responded

coherently. She bristled at thinking of the young Study as young, well there again, but really she did look young. And Xelle realized, that was perhaps the first time she'd ever thought of someone looking young who wasn't a child. How, then, did the others see her? A 29-year-old Study.

Even as a distraction, she decided not to think about that more. With a quick sign of the Arc, she slid into the corridor. And, forget the pounding, she could not ignore the ache in her heart.

Ay'tea being here, day after day, was such a constant that surely he'd be here now. He wasn't. He hadn't thrown a card for today or she would have mentioned it, so in theory Xelle could ask where his quarters were and say goodbye to him there. But he was normally here. If he wasn't, there was a reason. She had to respect that.

She couldn't just go track down his room, she murmured, pushing the image aside. If he were here, he'd tell her to get on her way. "Talk when you get back," she imagined him saying.

Closing her eyes just a moment, she briefly saw his warm eyes, and the whimsical tilt to his guarded smile. Seeing a caring that she hadn't quite caught before, she twitched. *Peace and Happiness, 'Tea, till I see you again.* Elements of that peace settled back into her own mind—she told herself they did—and she breathed in slowly before setting back out.

Her own room, the assigned one, was a bit stark these days. Essentially anything she cared about had been moved to her room, as in her garden. This room had become so bare, she'd had to visit a swap market in Vi'Arc for a few common items, just so the Study Monitors weren't (more) concerned about her.

Luckily, unmatching and slightly unaesthetic decorations weren't going to catch notice; if anything they would surmise this was the fashion in her small homevillage.

Backpack cinched up and ready as she would be for her journey, she trotted through the Tower until she reached the Arc Atrium, stopping to take one last look around.

As much as Xelle gravitated toward nooks and cubbies, her favorite rooms would always be the Atriums placed just through the entrance suite of each Tower. Huge, and with layers of life and study swirling around their edges, the Atriums gave her a feeling she was both part of something larger yet important enough to be part of it.

The Arc Atrium was the simplest of the three she'd seen, making it even more impressive—in the way she saw things. Tall, patterned windows let the light stream in from carefully selected directions. Smooth, stone columns in shades of white and gray etched with the shadow of curling vines, punctuated curves and arches, like the travel of each speck of air had been carefully considered and given a path to flow. Metal-trimmed mosaics on low walls and benches wound around the huge space in nearly unrecognized beauty, yet invited one to sit, and reflect. In this Atrium, it not only felt like she was important, but everything. Like everyone could be. But in that moment, oneself.

She lingered a while, just letting herself exist in such a magnificent space. (And perhaps giving Ay'tea one last chance to run in and wish her well.) And then, with a sigh, she walked out to the Front Desk.

It was time now for an adventure. And adventures, after all, could be distractions from the issues a hu simply didn't know how to sort.

"The Spire Mages have reserved you a moveroom," the clerk said, checking off something on a clipboard.

"Ah, no thanks," she answered, rattled by this development. "I need to visit the village first anyway, and I'll be fine to catch a ride from there. Hire one, of course."

The clerk did not seem at all concerned with the choice or the clarification, but slid over a sturdy paper. "Great. Regulations require you to check in immediately at the To'Breath Front Desk and present this card. Then check in here when you return. Right away, please. We'll need to re-ac room and assignments, and the Arc Spire has requested a direct debrief." The accompanying look made it clear that was why the prompt check-in was not optional. "Safe travels."

"Safe tr— Have a good day!"

Safe travels. Shaking her head at herself, she pulled her coat tight, walked through the large arch of the entranceway, and out into the snow. While it would have been nice to have a ride down the hill to the village (they'd reserved one just for her?), she was at least grateful that Vi'Arc was so close to the Tower. She knew some of the other Towers had substantial gardens, or just more space between the Mage Tower and the connected village, which kept it fed with supplies, services, and entertainment.

Xelle was always careful—one might say overly careful but she didn't care—about keeping supplies stocked. In a soft, canvas bag, whom she'd named Essie, she kept anything small that she might need. A bandage until she could reach a healer (if one was even warranted). Congealed alcohol in case she couldn't wash her hands. Mints for her breath. That sort of thing. She was regulating menstruation, or she'd have supplies for that, too. But Essie did hold a spare set of underwear, because at the moment this was needed, it would be too late to wish one had thought of it.

Into her backpack, she'd also rolled a thin but effective blanket, her sleep and laundry clothes, and a few compact tools. Even so, her backpack was not heavy, not with its thick, padded straps, and the fresh, winter air kept a smile on her face as she wound down the hill and into the village.

Despite the strangeness of these last hours, walking through the snowy village cheered her up. Vi'Arc, with its stylishly pointed roofs and latticed windows, was undramatic; it went about its business. Sure, she knew that was ash. No one lived without drama. But at least here, pers tended their shops, kept a keen eye, smiled warmly like the smile tank was infinite, and weren't laden with sashes and tokened chains to boast their accomplishments.

Even if Xelle did ever pledge, she had sworn to herself she would not start wearing chains and tokens. She knew, never say never, but the idea of one's past weighing on them in a literal sense felt a bit too on the cap for her. Whether everyone else did it or not.

She did want to buy a few items first, but as shops required money, her first stop would be Post. It would normally be a little too early to stop in for her Basic, but with assignments from the Tower they tended to be flexible. So with next month's Basic in pocket along with the allocation for the trip (they'd already added extra for the moveroom!), she headed toward the market.

Xelle muttered a list to herself, trying to remember what she wanted to get, or more accurately not forget something. A few snacks, as sometimes it was stressful to deal with a new vendor or cook, not knowing what was served and not wanting to offend by asking questions. And the more she'd thought about being sent as a To'Arc Study to To'Breath, the more she thought she should look the part. Xelle dressed nearly the same these days as she had in her village, a forest nook in Ever Region. Arc was used to her. But normally, a Study wanting to make a good impression on a new Tower would wear something finer, more traditional to the role. She couldn't buy a Mage sash, but perhaps some fine-combed cords, or a more patterned cap.

"Can I help you?" a rather harried voice asked. A tall hu, who was probably years younger than Xelle (again, she hid a grimace at this) walked over. Xelle hadn't realized she'd been rubbing her fingers over a particularly soft travel cape, one with a hood, for pers with shaved crownhair, she supposed. She pulled her hand away.

"I'm sorry. I got distracted."

"I know. Tower life can get that way. All the blustering with no bluster." Xe changed tone. "I'm Jaynel, e. And if I can help you with anything, please let me know." Jaynel was already glancing off at a hu tugging three young children, but the hu waved back, as if signaling xe was fine.

"Hi." Xelle tried to smile.

"Hi," the shopkeep answered, raising eir eyebrows.

Xelle sighed. Sometimes when she was caught off guard it was so hard to interact. "Hello, Jaynel, I'm Xeleanor Du'Tam, she or e." Thinking what to say, Xelle sort of stood there.

Jaynel nodded and started to turn away.

"I think I could use your advice," Xelle said. Jaynel stopped. "I'm a Study and I've been given an assignment to go . . . somewhere in another Region. I just dress like this," she waved her hand around before realizing most of it was covered by her coat anyway, "but I think to look the part of an earnest visitor, perhaps some finery in the style of To'Arc would assist."

Jaynel tapped eir lip, as if e emself was casting magic on Xelle to learn the backstory directly. Lip magic? Who knew. "Without either of us having certainty," e began, "I would say that they sent you for a reason. And so, I could sell you an outfit and we could tailor it while you wait, but my best advice is to arrive as you're dressed now. Less acting, more whatever you'll be doing. And less to carry."

Xelle considered this as the shopkeep started back. E wore a simple gown that probably looked darker with all the surrounding drapes closed for the winter. Yet there was nothing simple about eir headwrap, a bouncy fringed, thick cloth with metallic ornaments sewn into the edges. Realizing she was staring, Xelle looked quickly to the side, pushing out, "That's good advice. Thanks." Then realizing Jaynel had just discouraged a sale, she added, "I'll be back here."

Jaynel smiled. "There is never any pressure in this shop. That cape suits you, though. And no, not just because you were touching it. I give my word."

As casually as the hu mentioned it, Xelle wondered if that was sort of a code among vendors. If one declares one's word, then it should be trusted. The thing was, Xelle didn't need it. She could see the merchant was honest. There was a certain nature to em that gave em an air of trust.

Xelle almost laughed aloud. Hadn't that just been what Jaynel was saying?

"It comes with a matching cap as well. Extra warmth when layered with the hood. Snug fit, even with a bit of hair up there. Like a head hug." E shrugged eir shoulders.

Xelle wasn't sure about that, but she thanked the vendor again, and after stepping behind the curtain, she did indeed feel cozier in the matching cape and cap, which didn't cost quite as much as she'd worried.

With her backpack snug again, she made a few stops to add to it a good assortment of snacks, including some long mushrooms soaked in a blacksauce that looked particularly delicious.

Feeling warmer than she had setting out, Xelle made a good show of being seen around the part of the village where one would hire a ride toward Vattam, then she slipped behind a row of sheds and off in the direction of the mountains.

What Ay'tea had said to her had almost slipped past, but now she couldn't get it out of her mind. Often a cycling thought was a terrible curse, but in this case, she was going to trust her partner.

05 - *Thunder*

Even for Mages, magic was forbidden near the mountains. Xelle had never seen this in any formal decree, but any young child growing up on this side of Alyssia knew it to be true. Doubly forbidden for a Study, who was not authorized to use magic around the populace. Sure, Xelle could argue that in the isolation of these hills, no one would know, but the superstitions of restraint and reverence toward the distant mountains were deep in her blood.

When Xelle was superstitious, then she was dedicated to it. Meaning, that depended. When a rule seemed like nonsense, she prided herself on being the first to toss it out. There was nothing wrong with walking under a staircase, whose sturdy structures were certainly not lurking for her passage. She refused to incant over the passing of gas; what an absolutely rude and strange tradition. And she was perfectly comfortable continuing on during eclipses. If one could walk during the night, why not during an eclipse?

Yet when a superstition found root, she was fervent in its care. Xelle remained a believer that for all the history of magic on Alyssia, Mages had only danced on the precipice of what it could do. Perhaps that was for the best! But, still, when something felt ominous, or glorious, and it wasn't clear why, some respect was an advised caution. There was so much they didn't know about the world. That's how she felt about it.

And so she did not cast in the mountains, not to ease travel, and not to search for her way. Problem was, this same reverence near mountains also prevented the emergence of paths through the low hills to ease the travel of cautious adventurers. But it was fine; she liked to climb, and with her coated, warm gloves, new cape and cap, and double-socked boots, the snow did not deter her as the afternoon wore on.

Not for the first time, she wondered what life was like for pers raised in a house with magic. Did they grow up learning things like climbing trees and hills, and how to bandage a cut? Or from another view, was studying magic simply expected for them? Knowing she could become a Mage, but knowing how to build a ladder was an upbringing she could thank her parents for.

Stopping for a rest, she took a clean breath of chill air. Xelle loved it up here, and visited when she could, for peace and meditation and just sometimes to feel truly alone. In warmer weather, she'd even let her crownhair out in the open, enjoying the sensation of it swaying as she walked, but it was cold now—wintery even for the high rim—and she kept her new cap on, grateful for how it wrapped over her ears.

Mottled rocks jutted from the snow above her; she was high enough up now for why she was here. To find some obsidian.

She knew the glass stone was found here; she hoped she could encounter a patch without too strenuous a search. The covering of snow provided an extra layer of challenge, but making her room had been a challenge, and she'd done that. Couldn't know if she didn't try. Perhaps she'd been taken by an impulse, but she also didn't want to fret about it during her trip. Worth the diversion.

Xelle set a boot in front of the other, and pulled her way through up the jagged slopes, seeking out sheltered sections where the ground was not covered by the thick winter snow, or small cliffs, where she'd seen it before.

With this task actively in front of her, her mind began to buzz. Don't slip, look for dry ground, watch for the rare black shine against the rocks, don't take too long because you're supposed to be going the other direction. Her mind grew tired, and in her concentration barely noticed the passage of the sun, until she stopped for another quick rest and noted the length of her shadow.

She tried to settle. And she resumed her hike, trying not to think how short the day was feeling and how she'd seen nothing yet even resembling obsidian. Not even an outcrop of blackrock. She had seen it before, right? Sometimes her nightpaths were vivid and strange, but she did not have them about rocks. The light continued to fade.

It was probably best to sleep. She hadn't brought her small tent (it was a lot to carry on foot), but she had her blanket and could make a fire. She hadn't seen any signs of an old fire pit, so she took the time to fashion one, in a small area between several large fir trees that was mostly clear of snow but still at a safe distance. Perhaps she'd chosen the evergreens intentionally; though a future hadn't worked out for her at To'Ever, the trees of her youth always brought her peace.

Yes, she searched the area for obsidian—half thinking perhaps the mountains would offer her some luck and half thinking how terrible it would be to unknowingly sleep on it after all this—but finding mostly dirt and sticks, she lit a fire and pulled out a small square of waxed tarp on which to sit. A pinch of soup mix into her metal cup, stirred with snow, created a comforting smell and filled her up nicely.

Finding the small tins of creamy oil she'd tucked into Essie, she moisturized her face and hands, rubbed cleaning powder on her teeth, and tapped a little herbal powder onto her chest, reaching through her layers of clothes.

And as the sun wandered on for the day, she curled up into her blanket and tried to block out the light of the moons above her. Glad for the scent she had tapped out, she tried to tell the storm in her mind to let her rest, and instead to relax into the night ivy, through which she could slowly, hopefully, find her way to sleep.

She woke up confused why she was cold. The mystery was quickly resolved, as her eyes opened to a bright morning sun glaring against a distance of snow, only interrupted by the clearing of her small fire pit. Quickly, she covered her eyes.

Obsidian, she remembered. And then To'Breath.

As much as she thought she could conduct this side quest without notice, she did still need to arrive at To'Breath within a reasonable travel time. A day more—that could be dismissed as lingering at the markets or taking the chance to sleep in. But here she was, farther from To'Breath than she'd started and already a full day spent.

She stood and began to stretch. If she didn't find what she was looking for soon, she would have to let this go. For now. The idea felt heavy, unsatisfying. To not have what she looked for and still be late. Motivation for a search. Pulling her stretch over to the other side, she slowly straightened, then bent forward.

Thwump. Crack.

The sensations of deep thunder rattled her bones and her spirit, and for a moment, visions of an avalanche flashed before her. She had folded forward, and her hands trembled against the ground, as her rear protruded upward.

It could not be thunder, not without a storm. Then, what? She waited, a few moments, fearful of a building slide, or perhaps an aftershock of a rumbling of land. Nothing happened, and so, with a push, she unfolded to her feet.

Fira's fury!

She gaped at the being before her. And the being stared back.

This being was smaller than she imagined. A strange thought.

Is this real?

This was certainly real. As for someone following her here to cast such a beautiful illusion, complete with a full ground-rumble, she saw no motive for such a scenario, though admittedly her mind was still cloudy from sleep.

The magnificent being perched on four legs, the front more limber than the back, with skin somewhere between a perfect gloss and a perfect matte. The smooth skin was colored with a base of solid black, but with veins of red and yellow—each varying in hue, the yellow with greens and mustards and grays, and the red with rust and slate—running, without pattern or reason, over the muscular body. Rising above, a pointed head peered down at her, with a closed mouth that extended to almost a bill, tall, sharp ears, and a row of following spikes that traveled downward and out of Xelle's view. In the wonder of this face and in the sharply watching rose-colored eyes centering it, it wasn't that Xelle abandoned fear. It was more like fear . . . abandoned her.

This was a dragon. She had the sudden feeling this was also . . . a child. Not in hu terms, but perhaps among . . .

What term to use? Non-hu pers were often given ae. But that was because those beings were not known to hold hu concepts of gender. This being was complex. Magnificent.

There was a rare term, zhey, used when a gender was unknowable. Not unknown or unresolved, like xe, but unknowable. Until she knew more, that is what she would use.

"Hello," she said, reaching out her hand. "I am Xeleanor Du'Tam, she or e."

The dragon . . . bounced. Xelle felt sure that zhey bounced.

She smiled. As her teeth chattered, Xelle suddenly understood she had stripped down to her shirt and underwear to wrap tightly in the blanket, but now she stood thus bared in the snowy morning light.

And she was *freezing.*

"Give me a second," she said. "I'm not worried about you seeing my rump, but that rump is going to be a block of ice if I don't get some clothes on. Oh, and do you mind if I make some coffee?"

Coffee? Maybe I should ask the dragon why zhey're here? After all, Xelle— you are looking at a **dragon!**

The dragon puffed out a wisp of smoke. It really sounded as if zhey were laughing.

Xelle stopped. She needed to collect herself; see, this was why she didn't do important things right when she woke up. But if this was a nightpath, it was a realistically cold one, and that was not how her nightpaths worked. She looked up again. A dragon. Ok. So they were real. And here. And she should say something?

"Hello," she began, hearing her voice shaking a bit. "I'm honored that you're here, to say hello? I have to admit; I wasn't entirely sure dragons were real. But you are definitely real and, actually, please don't leave too soon or I might start doubting that. It's been a strange few days. I'm sorry; I don't mean to ramble." She looked up at the dragon, wistfully looking down. Curious, if anything. "I wish I knew what to call you."

I'd call zhem Thunder for that sound zhey made landing!

The dragon bounced excitedly. Xelle peered ahead. *It's like zhey understood me.*

Zhey bounced again. Xelle stepped back. She was a Mage, she meant, a Study, she'd seen stranger. "Are you . . . listening to me thinking? I mean, that's fine if you can't help it, what I mean is, can you hear me?" Zhey bounced. But, Xelle was inventing this. Maybe zhey just bounced a lot. With no one here to tell her this was ridiculous, she tried a test. After all, if she was wrong, the test would not be heard and would not be rude anyway. And if she was right . . . *If you can hear my thoughts, and you want me to know it, then move your head up and down.*

The dragon stretched zheir head very high, and then lowered it down to the ground. The look on zheir face was, as Xelle saw it, excited.

Holy Fira. It was . . . I mean, oh, good job! That's how hu say yes. Except do it more than once, and with less motion, like this.

Xelle demonstrated a nod. *And then this one means no, you don't want something, or don't agree with it, or whatever.* She shook her head, this time as she was thinking.

Again, she hadn't entirely been sure that dragons were real. And she'd just woken up. Anyway, dragon. It was always hard to tell with old stories that didn't directly speak to magic. Some were literal, some were exaggerations, some were even meant as metaphors at the time, but some earnest parent in the wake decided they were meant as written and the concept took. She'd heard stories where dragons guarded treasure, where they flew in majesty to symbolize change. That sort of thing. But in none of those old stories, did the hu or the dragons communicate, let alone through thought.

She didn't have much time to wonder why, as the dragon squinted its eyes into a stern expression, shook zheir head, and then laughed, at least that puff of smoke Xelle was calling a laugh.

"Please let me go pee, ok. I'll be right back!"

The dragon sat back against the ground.

Taking that as an answer, Xelle rushed behind a tree, and was doubly relieved (yes) to see that the dragon was still standing in place when she returned.

"So, would you like it if I called you Thunder?" She pulled on her pants, hoping she wouldn't roll down the hill from all the shivering at this point. Fumbling for Essie, she got some soap to wash her hands before she put her gloves back on. "Whew!" she said rather loudly, letting out held tension into a cloudy poof of cold morning air.

The dragon hopped around, making Xelle glad she had not yet set out a coffee, and then, as if remembering, turned to her and nodded zheir head, up, down, then up again.

She pulled on her cape, comforted by its warmth. "Ok, Thunder! If you have another name I should call you, I'm happy to."

Thunder drew back a little.

Xelle felt that. "I know. Not everything can be answered with a nod or a shake. But for now, we'll start there."

For now? Was the dragon going to go live in her room? Then, why was the dragon here? She supposed she could ask.

"Do you need anything from me? Would you like me to leave?" She signaled. "As in, leave the hills?" She normally would have called them 'the mountains' but for a dragon, these low foothills probably didn't measure.

The dragon—Thunder, she remembered—laughed again. That's right; zhey could read her mind. That would take some getting used to. (And there she was again, imagining them together. Love at first sight worked for stories, she supposed, but this was not a feasible situation.)

Thunder's reaction to this question was more stilted. Zhey had a harder time shaking zheir head, for a neck that was built to bob and stretch, so instead zhey more yanked their body from side to side.

Xelle winced. "Is there an easier way to do it? Something you'd prefer?"

Looking excited again, Thunder crouched down, a quick dip, then stood again. To Xelle, it looked like a much harder motion, but Thunder seemed comfortable with it. "Fine, then, the crouch says no. And if I'm not causing any issues here, I think I'll make that coffee now."

Xelle talked to the dragon through her breakfast. "I prefer fresh grounds, but for traveling, I pre-ground them into little sacks. Oh, you want to smell it. Here, but be careful, your sneeze would blow my potato off the mountain. You know, why wouldn't I call them mountains? You're here, so they seem to count." She went on, carefully poking into the warm potato (she'd brought one, as a treat) and sipping the coffee, her metal cup nestled in her small ovenpad as it cooled.

There is a strange thing that happens when something can't be real but it is, that prompts one to simply stop admiring the experience, and instead, accept it. Xelle found emself firmly in this place as e forgot all about timelines or missions or Towers, and spent the morning enjoying Thunder's company.

Yet after a while, Thunder grew restless and Xelle realized zhey must be hungry, or perhaps worried about being in trouble from other dragons. (There must be other dragons.)

And gaining a sense e might be getting a teenage dragon in trouble for being away too long, Xelle decided to get packed up and start off again.

I'll tell you what I'm doing, but if it's upsetting and I shouldn't do it, please just tell me. I'm looking for obsidian to use in a little garden I have. Just a sample or two. E pulled out the drawstring bag e'd brought and tapped it. The morning had been so interesting, Xelle had completely forgot that e was supposed to be looking for the rare substance, though admittedly based only on a sketchy hunch. E could maybe give the afternoon, and if she couldn't find any by then, e'd have to leave for now. She couldn't risk arriving days late at To'Breath and having word get back to To'Arc. (Imagine if they tracked her footprints!)

Thunder stopped in place, and sat back on zheir . . . haunches? Was that the right word? If Xelle had learned Thunder's expressions in the last hours, e had no idea what this look was here. *Should I not look for it?*

Thunder didn't respond, not really. Zhey tapped zheir feet onto the trampled ground. Maybe zhey were thinking?

Then, the dragon approached—slowly, as if trying not to scare Xelle. E wondered if it was frustrating that Xelle could communicate so easily, but Thunder couldn't tell Xelle what zhey wanted. Thunder stopped, leaning zheir snout forward, a happy tilt to zheir mouth.

Oh, right. Well, sure you can come over here. I trust you. And if the obsidian isn't appropriate to take, just give me the no sign and I'll go.

Xelle swung eir bag back on, yet Thunder continued toward em one step after another, finally reaching out zheir claws. Unsure, Xelle walked between them, wondering if dragons hugged?

And e really wished that dragons knew how to say 'ready' or some such thing because e was totally unprepared to be grabbed by a pair of huge, yet surprisingly gentle claws and pulled up into the air, quickly above the treetops, and with the view of the mountains stretching as far as e could see. Though incredibly startled, e was not nearly as afraid as e could have been. Should have been. Thunder's grip around em felt secure, and even eir expected feelings of vertigo could not quite manifest as they rose.

Wow, e couldn't help but mouth, eir shock immediately superseded by the sweeping view, green trees and sparkling white: more stunning and more *alive* than even the most skilled artist's visualization. E quickly covered eir ears to mute the percussive flapping of Thunder's wings as they flew up this particular slope.

Up and down they bobbed together, until Thunder descended again, weaving skillfully through breaks in the trees until landing softly in a patch of old leaves, protected from the snow by the canopy overhead. Only after landing zhemself did zhey slowly lower Xelle toward the ground, waiting until eir feet were just barely dangling over a smooth rock. Relieved, e hopped down.

"You know, I'm afraid of heights," e said, brushing off eir pants out of mostly nervousness and a feeling of control. "But I felt secure in your hands. Uh, claws." Xelle's legs did shake a bit now and—

Thunder tapped the ground, still quiet, and Xelle realized maybe zhey were signaling em not to be so loud. *Sorry,* she thought, trying to keep the thoughts quiet also. *What's going on?*

Zhey nosed toward a clearing in the trees.

Xelle gasped, immediately clasping eir hands over eir mouth.

Through the clearing walked, stretched, and rested at least a dozen dragons, of those e could see from here. Through their footsteps or their breath, the ground was bare of snow or phyta. E thought e even saw something glowing, back near a wall of stone. The large beings moved with both purpose and grace, down to the placement of their claws. Many shone with the sleek blackness of Thunder's skin, but they varied in other coloring. Some were brighter, some with color in patches. They were all larger.

Then Xelle realized that Thunder had heard that thought earlier about not getting a teenage dragon in trouble. They exchanged a tentative look.

Though e could have watched the huge pers milling about all day, ash, all week, Thunder had started sneaking—as much as a still quite large dragon could sneak over a ground covered in leaves and sticks— in a direction away from the others.

Zhey hopped down over a ledge. Xelle had the impression zhey were avoiding flapping zheir wings, but e wasn't quite sure how the, well, thunderous landing sound of a dragon was much better. That said, e knew almost nothing about dragon culture. Maybe their entire sense of hearing was different. Maybe they didn't hear the same way at all. Either way, e accepted Thunder's offered claws, as zhey lifted em down to a long ledge in what looked like a quite dangerous series of ledges.

No longer in zheir secure grip, eir fear of heights set in and e spun around, looking for something solid.

E saw obsidian.

She saw herself.

There was Xelle's face, fractured in the ridges of the otherwise smooth, black surface. Her new cap looked snug and keen. Her warm cape, draped over her backpack, billowed at the sides in the breeze aside the mountain, surrounded by powdery snow blowing from the trees above. And her face, only her gray eyes showing a slight reaction of surprise—she tried to smile but . . .

Thunder's shape emerged in the reflection, and she couldn't help but smile, as she gazed at the absolutely elegant and buoyant dragon behind her, at least the one, blinking eye that fit into the reflection behind Xelle's own features.

Again, she tried to think quietly. *Is it really fine to take some? I'm using it— Well, maybe I shouldn't— Would I put zhem at risk of trouble by telling them about my gar— Don't think, think about— Clouds, clouds. Oh, ash.*

Realizing quickly that keeping secrets from a dragon would be a tiresome endeavor even if she was doing it for zheir own protection, Xelle apologized. *I have a garden hidden in To'Arc, where I am trying to grow inkblooms, which I am not currently perhaps allowed to grow. I want to learn their magic. I don't have a specific plan, but I've always been fascinated by inkblooms and if they really work the way it's said that they do.*

Thunder hesitated, and Xelle turned to face zhem. Xelle truly felt like there was something else zhey wanted to know. She lived in To'Arc. She had a secret room. She wasn't a Mage. She had refused to pledge. She thought she was pretty ok at magic.

Just then Thunder tapped the ground, looking worried.

Magic? Being ok at it? No, ok. Where I learned it? Why I got into it?

By zheir eager nod, that was clearly it. Something like that, anyway.

Oh, I want to learn magic to help pers. Also, I enjoy it. The idea comforted me as a child, when I felt lost, and . . . I want to share that.

Thunder sat back, a curve of relief to zheir pointed face.

It's ok to take a couple of rocks? The obsidian?

Zhey definitely nodded. But there was still a nervous twitch to Thunder's shoulders that hadn't been there before they'd flown. And so Xelle got out her bag. After the first couple, Thunder pushed more her way. Feeling a sense of urgency and knowing the others still waited nearby, rather than argue, she continued to fill the bag.

Mostly she tried to take small sections, as there were plenty which had been chipped down onto the ground, either by weather or shifts in the hillside. The bag was getting heavy now yet Thunder was watching her so intensely—and so with hesitation she took one final piece; a large enough section that it could be a small wall mirror. This one she wrapped in a bandage-sized clothie before sealing the whole bag together.

Holy moons, how was she going to travel with all this weight? No more walking; that was for certain. But what, now she was going to put it back?

A poof of smoke flew by her face, and she waved it away.

Testing its weight, she considered that Arc Mages would cast lightness or air in the context of travel, but even the idea of casting for utility in the mountains chilled her. Slightly chastising herself for even considering it and perhaps making Thunder nervous, she quickly corrected her thoughts to note she would just have to try and not walk much.

Thank you, Thunder, I promise I will do my best to put this to good use. And if it doesn't work, I'll figure out how to bring it back.

Thunder had acknowledged the comments but was glancing back in the direction of the other dragons.

Xelle secured the smaller bag into her pack, trying not to think of the extra weight on her shoulders. *I should get on my way. I don't want to get you in any trouble.*

Thunder stepped forward, and tapped zheir claws together twice, after extending them. Xelle watched, confused, and then realized this time zhey were asking her if she was ready. Beaming, and in addition to whatever her thoughts were revealing, she tapped her own hands together twice.

When Thunder set out, it was downward from the ledge they were on. Then zhey swung around, only rising at the last minute as another hill grew in front of them. Of course. Zhey were avoiding being seen by the others. Or perhaps, having zheir own thoughts read.

Hoping her thoughts were safe to focus now but still trying to keep them low, she realized she'd be much better off being dropped off not where she'd been, but where she needed to go.

I'm going to Vattam, she thought, as the dragon would be unlikely to hear her voice over the air rushing past. Then, worried her background thoughts might confuse, she directed her thoughts as if speaking clearly. *I'll be going to To'Breath after that, but I need to be seen traveling there, even if you could carry me. So it would be best if you could drop me off a little on the way to Vattam. I don't know if you know what that is; it's the hu city that way.* Nervously, she pointed in the direction of where she thought Vattam was and concentrated on the image and location of the large city. *But again, if you could just get me going in that direction, oh, and on the hu road* (necessary to catch a ride) *I would be grateful.*

If Thunder was nervous in the mountains, zhey felt much more nervous outside of them—just the way zheir muscles tensed and the cadence of zheir breathing—something Xelle understood. She kept reassuring zhem that anywhere on the road would be fine, but zhey continued to press forward.

Another issue. To try and reduce the odds of being seen, zhey decided to fly high up. Like, really high up. And while, truly, nothing Xelle had ever experienced felt more secure than Thunder's grasp, no one was infallible, with or without magic. And so Xelle did not want to think about that and put all her energy into looking for landmarks, so she'd have some idea where she was when they landed.

One thing about To'Arc: they were into maps. Like, really into maps. And so Xelle did have a good sense of the layout of the world, including the parts where she had not yet been.

Finally, Thunder lowered in a spiral behind a grove of trees that were near to the road, as Xelle had seen as they'd approached. Zhey let her down, so gently, and Xelle stepped back to look at the dragon.

Then it hit her.

She'd grown so comfortable with Thunder, just over this day, that she hadn't thought through that she'd likely never see zhem again. It hit her all at once that she'd squandered the opportunity. She should have offered hugs, or told stories, or learned about dragons, or built snow bunnies, or asked more than only for help. She should have done anything.

Like Ay'tea. She understood the place he'd made for her now, but she hadn't appreciated it enough. He'd always been there, yet all they'd done was work. When she returned, she resolved to correct that.

But what could she do here? And why was Thunder's head tilted?

"Meeting you has been an absolute—" she almost said 'honor' and it was, but this dragon exuded joy and spirit even through zheir troubles (she could tell zhey had troubles) and how could she tell zhem something that felt so hu? "I am filled with joy that we met. I will remember you always."

With a long, smoky, sigh, if dragons sighed, Thunder turned away to launch back into the sky.

I wish we could meet again.

Zhey turned back.

Was that too forward? If you would wish it. I would like to see you again, but only if you wish it. And if it's safe for you.

Now she sounded like a traveler meeting a complicated wish spirit in a story. She stopped, and just sent the dragon her joy and gratitude for zheir help, like a colorful light emanating from all sides of her yet channeled toward this beautiful, kind per.

And as her . . . friend, she wanted to say, took off and flapped quickly out of view, Xelle breathed through the twinge on her forehead and the tears bristling in her eyes.

She did, after all, have a mission to conduct.

A mission. She chuckled.

Also, that was a dragon.

06 – *Four hours from Vattam*

One issue with being dropped off after specifically ensuring that no one was in sight was that Xelle knew she couldn't catch a moveroom for a while. From another view, she also knew that she was about four-ish hours from Vattam at standard moveroom speed, so as long as she could find a ride in the next couple of hours, she should be able to get in before nightfall.

And specifically, since there would be vrooms traveling with the purpose of getting incity by that time, she should be fine. She clambered up a low hill (oh, those stones were heavy, why hadn't she considered that more), got out a snack and a flask she'd filled earlier with snow, and watched down the road in the direction that she'd traveled from, albeit indirectly.

She was less worried now. In fact, she'd gained back much of her lost time, and arriving in Vattam tonight could be accounted for if she'd stopped at a village along the way, or spent the night with a friend. Perhaps it was a bit much to even think about the idea that Mages were tracking her arrival, let alone her progress. And she didn't think they were. But nothing about that strange meeting with the Arc Spire had been right. So if she could keep them thinking she'd placed full priority on their mission and keep her own secret projects secret a bit longer, all the best.

Xelle did not *know* that her secret room or even growing the inkblooms was against any serious rules. But as she'd not directly asked permission for the space, no Mage had ever discussed inkblooms with her, and the seeds had been decidedly difficult to get, she felt safer keeping the project to herself rather than giving someone the chance to whisk it away in the name of nothing. One thing Xelle had learned in her extended years as a Study was that she worked in the name of good more often than generalized restrictions did. And so, while she certainly didn't ignore rules (she knew what sort of abuses had caused them!), she let her own sense of justice be her primary guide.

What Xelle had not anticipated, but should have because that's how the depths of winter worked, was a new curtain of snow draping the road. Yes, she should be down from the high rim here, but so was Mytil and its winter had been a cold and snowy one, so it would probably stay this way maybe even through Vattam. Here, anyway, the chilly flakes poked cold against her face, and she couldn't quite pull the cape's hood around because the wind kept at it, and she still needed to see.

This was when she decided she would take the first ride she could get. Taxi or not.

Xelle still hadn't processed what she'd seen today. *Dragons.* Not just one dragon, but a group of dragons, a whole village maybe. And an outgoing teenage dragon, who'd actively helped her at least twice. She pictured Thunder's sleek turns, zheir keen pink eyes. Xelle tapped her own leg, as if to cement that it had really happened, in case she started to doubt it later.

Could she ever see them again? Would that be appropriate? Seems if dragons kept to themselves so much that hu never saw them, maybe there was good reason. But then, why had *she* seen them? Honestly, Thunder seemed excited. Maybe Xelle would never know. Yet she couldn't keep thoughts of the striking, winged pers out of her mind.

Finally, a vroom came walking down the road, its feet turning laboriously, but steadily, over the fresh snow. The boxy coach was quite small, but a toasty glow emanated from its interior, through front and side windows. Shaking herself alert, Xelle hopped down toward it. She regretted this, as she could barely feel her cold legs under her and worried how they might land. Fortunately (?), she also forgot about the weight of her bag, and she slipped down, landing inelegantly on her butt, with the snow a welcome but freezing cushion for her fall. She scrambled to her feet, waving out toward the road on wobbling legs as the vroom approached. "Hello!" she called, her voice shivering. "Are you willing to offer a ride to Vattam?"

"I'd love the company" was both the answer she most and least wanted to hear, as the moveroom pulled to a stop, revealing only the conn inside, xyr gloved hand steadied over the tiller. And it could be concerning that xe'd not asked for a specific fee. But, Xelle reminded herself, she'd stopped xem, not the other way around.

Now up close, the vroom may have been the smallest that she'd ever seen. It was a movecloset at best, if there were such a thing. (Now she was thinking if there would be a use for moveclosets! Moveboxes? Modular attachments? She'd talk to Ay'tea about that when she got back.) But thank Fira, the small vroom was as warm as it'd looked, and so she stepped in through the single back door, and latched it behind her.

Somehow, within the diminutive space, the vroom's interior managed to be intensely and uniquely decorated. Shelves rose over the low windows, carrying various trinkets she presumed were from the per's travels, as there were items from a variety of Regions, some she recognized and others she didn't. A tiny magipuck banner (she still didn't know the colors of each team) with a monogram embroidered on it swayed from a hook in the middle. One shelf had mementos likely from xyr homevillage: a little trophy spike with a small amount of gilding, darkfestival dangles with a design she did not recognize, and small framed drawings of what looked like children.

Beyond that, each shelf was painted the brightest colors imaginable. And nothing had shifted on them, so the trinkets must have been secured in some way.

On the floor, instead of purposeful floor mats, were a bit of a mess of blankets, nothing Xelle was worried to sit on, but not any that looked to have been cleaned in a while.

While Xelle tried to scoot backward toward the door, her legs still reached up near the tiller. The conn could reach over and tickle her toes, as close as they were, but she'd rather keep her legs out and let them dry than tuck them into a cross-seat. As such, she did her best to settle in, already feeling discomfort from their proximity. Nothing about this conn in particular, but sitting close to most pers caused her moderate but constant distress. In To'Arc, she had to watch where she sat around everyone. Except Helia, she supposed. And Ay'tea. She never felt uncomfortable around Ay'tea. She scooched back, making sure the doorlatch was secure.

"I'm grateful for the ride," she said. "Was getting cold out there. Name's Xeleanor Du'Tam, she or e."

"Ah, Tam. In the forest. I haven't been there specifically but I hear that it's lovely. You're a long way from home."

"Yes," Xelle said, suddenly turning to the window. Missing her homevillage was something she didn't like to talk about. But, as her parents said, a vast world makes one choose.

"You can call me Dor. I'm glad to meet a fellow traveler."

They started off, and though compact, the little vroom ran well. The undercoach was designed for smoothness, minimizing any forward rocking from the fuelstones, and whatever grease Dor used kept the noise soft. Other than the physical necessity of nearly touching both the clanking fuelstones under the floor and the traveling hu above it, the ride itself was fine.

Xelle found providing Dor company even more difficult than enduring the closeness. This was certainly not any fault of Dor's; the ride had been kindly offered. But Xelle had just interacted with a dragon and kind of wanted to parse that out in her mind, before her energy was taken in whatever was going on in To'Breath, and on top of other personal thoughts still bouncing forward for attention. Meanwhile the conn, who was very nice, chattered constantly about trivial matters, repeating how "times are changing," and then if Xelle didn't respond at the right points, the hu would glance over to see if she was ok.

"Haven't lost you?" Dor asked again.

"No, it's all really interesting. My mind gets overloaded sometimes," she tried to explain. Her mind was complicated, and explaining it moreso. She wasn't embarrassed by who she was, but it also felt invasive to always have to explain it to each new hu, to explain why her conversations weren't lively enough or her responses resonating enough for someone else's ease. Normally, she regulated her mind's state by finding reasons to step away, but packed in a moveroom so small that the mechanics rumbled against her rear, there wasn't anywhere else to go.

At least she wasn't asked any questions about herself. In fact, she had a pretty solid belief that the per hadn't considered her as a caster. Xelle supposed they weren't usually waiting on a rock, far from a village, freezing in place.

Or maybe it was more than that. Growing up outside the magesphere, she knew that most pers' lives did not revolve around magic. For a lot of reasons. First, that it just wasn't part of their lives. Practicing magic required a tremendous amount of time and risk, and they had lives to live. Second, they weren't going to spend the resources they had seeking out a Mage or trying to book one's time unless there was a need. Third, some actively disliked the rungs of power and access, and preferred to live a life without their stress or drama. And fourth, some were just plain against it.

Then, still a teenager (and now she realized more than ten years since . . . !), she'd first moved into To'Ever, where she'd met pers whose only thoughts, from sunrise to moonsrise, were of what magic could do, or how they could gain more access to it. Then she'd started working with the local governments, and understanding how the populace power structure interacted in a tenuous dance with the magical—each keeping the independence it could while drawing from the other. More ladders, this time to amagical resources and powers.

It was always fascinating to remember that some pers lived entirely outside of any of it. Xelle, in her case she justified her involvement because she was going to do good with it. But she—

"Haven't lost you?"

Xelle snapped around. "Pardon, I saw an interesting bird fly past and I can be easily distracted. Please, go on."

"Ah! That was a carrier. They glide for long distances, looking for specific grasses or buds; finicky eaters! Then they carry them back to the other birds in their flock." Dor turned away from the road to give her a smile. "It's like me. I'm a finder."

Thankfully, Dor returned to watching ahead. Xelle wasn't used to a front window view herself, not being a conn. Not that there was much for a conn to do (except definitely facing forward) on the run from To'Arc to Vattam. The wide road was kept in good state by the Tower, and despite a distant view of the mountains to the right rear, it mostly coasted over flat land, staying smooth and level through the few rolling hills. Many villages dotted the peaceful area, but none within sight of the road, so the view through the low windows was scruffy, flat, and with a spattering of trees.

"I don't prefer the cities, myself," Dor was continuing. "When I must, I prefer Wehj. Vattam is fine, if you like gadgets and change. I've had enough change for now. But you can't stop it, you know. Times are changing.

"Wehj can be a flame-torn place, I know it. And that's why I must be the only one who likes it best. I suppose not the only one, not with all the pers who live there!" Dor laughed at the joke. "But maybe we're all more flame-torn that we admit; and Wehj is the only one to admit it. There, a worker's a worker, and a boss is a boss. But there are more of the first type than the second, every time they remember it. Vattam, well this Lerf business is a fine example of it. The days are built on balance, and I'm not so sure about that. *Just not sure.*"

Ashes, Dor finally got her.

"Dor, what's Lerf?" She had no idea if this was a per, or a place. She hadn't heard of it. It sounded like it had to do with Vattam, and since they were at least halfway there, she'd probably better ask.

"I suppose it depends if you've been this way for a roll. If you have, you know about LerfSpecs. Same deal, just expanded."

"I do not," Xelle answered, tentatively. "Lerf . . . specs? As in glasses for eyes?"

"Yes! You'll see them everywhere in Vattam. They are 'special spectacles' that have the glass fired in such a way that hu see yellows and greens everywhere. It's said to make them happier than they were. Enhance their mood. Mind science." The last part was drawn out, as Dor reached up a hand to tap a temple.

So, happy was good. But if these glasses were making pers happy, why was Dor worried about them? "So what's the catch?" she managed to ask.

"The more Lerf makes glasses, the more he expands. New gadgets. New designs. Now there is a town named Lerf. Did you know, you can name a town?"

Xelle was still parsing out what a Lerf was, except Dor had just referred to him as a hu, so there was a per? Naming things after himself? "So Lerf is the hu who invented the glasses?"

"Yes, I'm just so used to hearing of him lately, I forgot to explain. Bon Lerf Du'Lerf."

Having named one's self after a town one created (?) already gave Xelle a strong impression of the per, especially given his (self?) titling of Bon. It wasn't that a Bon couldn't be so financially successful, many were, but Bon was a title of cultural value given not presumed, and it didn't match the profile Xelle was getting from Dor's tone. Anyway. Whoever he was, his influence had not reached Vi'Arc, or even Mytil. "Have you been to . . . Lerf?"

Xelle was always respectful of names but having a hu and a town named the same thing was confusing enough if she were not already questioning his motives.

"Not myself, no. But as much as I hear pers talk about it, curiosity may yet win me over!"

Not sure how much more she wanted to hear about Lerf for the moment, Xelle changed the subject back to birds. It turned out to be a good choice, as Dor went on quite a while about types of birds, favorite birds, birds with interesting Regional preferences.

Xelle enjoyed watching birds outside of the Tower windows but had not considered that there was this much thought to be given to their differences. Little Worlds, she called them. Entire universes of life and culture that others may not have even heard of.

For example, she'd had a friend back in Tam who was into tall ladders. Not just long ladders, but this entire culture of pers designing long, wood ladders, sometimes connected in a chain, and then climbing high into trees, sometimes to reach old platforms and sit and enjoy a cup of tea.

Pers would gather for this, there were festivals, even famous ladders with famous names, their own buildings made to shelter them. A whole culture, that perhaps no one in Vattam or even Mytil had heard of. She'd even asked around at To'Arc once, a Tower built around magic of travel, and after about five very strange looks, she'd stopped asking.

Dor was now listing birds that hid in trees. "Not babies, I'm saying. They look like babies, but they are grown birds. Don't startle one or you'll get a shriek in your ear like you couldn't imagine!"

She couldn't help but think that Dor would probably enjoy hearing about dragons. Yet Xelle felt sure her encounter should not be shared. At least not without the chance to ask Thunder. Xelle wondered if that could ever happen. If it even should.

The light began to dim, and finally Dor quieted a bit. "If you don't mind, Xeleanor, I could use some concentration. I meant to set out earlier today, on account of the light but you know how things can change. My eyes don't conn so well in the moonslight."

Xelle had made a full handful of comments the whole ride, but she graciously agreed to keep it down. Still, the small moveroom rattled more than she liked and there was no sign of Vattam in the distance. She tried to consider the ride as a complimentary leg massage even with its own heat vent, but any comfort from the thin blankets and greased joints had waned, and so the absurdity just made her feel more restless. Sometimes, her distractions decidedly failed.

Pulling off her gloves and reaching into her pack, she poked around for Helia's gift. She'd said to wait until Xelle was down, and maybe this didn't strictly meet the definition, but she could definitely use a boost. Besides the cramped ride and her weariness of jostling, however smoothish, the pressure of being so close to Dor for quite a time now was getting to her. Other things, too. About Thunder. Ay'tea. Actually, she was feeling down. Well, good. Not good. But anyway, gift time.

One thing about a gift from the wealthy was that sometimes the wrapping was as precious as the contents. Xelle wasn't particularly fancy—her black pants and pull-on shirt were generally her standard fare—but she did appreciate a fine trinket. Especially when there were memories attached.

In this case, the wrapping was a deep, shiny red threaded intermittently with gold. She took it, along with the ribbon, and folded them carefully into a small pocket of the bag. They'd surely come in handy at some point.

And so she turned to the item in her hand, a little weighty for the size, and cool in her fingers, and pulled it from its soft bag. It was a mirror.

There was a saying in her Region: *Beware the gifts of a well-intentioned Mage.* Yet as fun as it would be (maybe) to have a mirror that showed her the way ahead, or whispered secrets, this mirror appeared totally ordinary.

No, not ordinary. Just amagic. She wasn't sure of the exact metal of the handle and frame; it was darker than silver and with a tinge of, well, not yellow or gold but a sheen that added a rich complexity. The metal was turned around with ivy vines, clearly made with To'Arc in mind, which made sense if Helia had bought it on short notice. Its silvery face was exquisite: perfectly flat and even with four tiny embellishments on the top, bottom, and sides. Interestingly, the mirror wasn't circular, square, or even oval. It was more of a natural shape, perhaps like a leaf, or just the shape of a viscous pooling on a slightly curved surface. The forest green bag it had been nestled into was extraordinarily soft, meant to protect the perfect glass surface.

There was something on her face.

Yes, eyes and nose and such, but no, something new. On her forehead, but under the edge of her cap.

In the dimming light, she couldn't quite make it out and so she moved the mirror closer.

"You look fine!" Dor offered.

Xelle smiled, but still tried to make out what the mark was. Sure, she'd been climbing all over the mountains, it could be any smudge. But it didn't look like a smudge. It had lines and details like, well, a tattoo.

She'd actually been thinking of being tattooed, and had delayed the idea because she'd spent her coins on things like a secret room and other magic pursuits. But when she did pursue some skin art, she hadn't planned a tiny cryptic mark on her forehead.

Instincts taking over, she licked her thumb and rubbed it over the spot.

With a yelp, she jerked her hand away. It stung. The mark, not her hand. Noting Dor's concern, she decided this wasn't something she was going to figure out here in the cramped moveroom.

She did side-glance the mirror itself as she slid it into the soft carrying bag. Helia wouldn't have given her magic without consent. She certainly wouldn't have given her something that stung. She thought of her time with Thunder—she hadn't stopped thinking of it—but Thunder hadn't touched her face.

Again, it was a mystery for when Dor was not staring back at her.

"I get them too," the conn said in a low, kindly tone. "Too much oil in your food. Or too many sweets. My parent had us eat a lot of greens, but I can't say I can always keep up these years."

Xelle loved greens, especially with smoky nubs and a good oil, but if she hadn't been overloaded after a day with a dragon, she certainly was now. Of course, none of this was Dor's fault, so she thanked the hu for the (unsolicited, but maybe the rules got weird after spending several hours in a shelfbox) advice.

By the time the outer buildings of Vattam rose into view, Xelle wasn't sure she could do much talking anyway. Her mind had slowed with all the interactions and worry and closeness; what was left of it rattled in exhaustion and a vagueness of fear. It seemed, though, that Dor was now a little worn out as well—perhaps not many shared the moveroom—and so much more conversation seemed unlikely.

The vroom stopped sooner than she expected it to. Peering out, they seemed to be on the outer loop, the road travelers took if they wanted to avoid the city.

"I'll be going on for a bit," the conn said.

Dor hadn't specifically indicated stopping in Vattam; she'd just assumed it. Though, the per had also noted an aversion to running in the dark. Wait, why was she managing this? Dor had managed many decades without her, and would be fine now.

Xelle's heart froze. Payment always caused her great distress. She didn't want to underpay someone, but she didn't want to be taken advantage of, and then there was the third scenario where she knew it was an overpayment and she had to say no. And then there were pers that if you asked them, they'd say "whatever you think is fair" or some other awful concept that was like throwing someone like Xelle into a tub of ice.

"Did you have a payment in mind?" she eked out, her voice shaking.

Dor froze, staring at Xelle as if she'd disrespected the hu's parent. "Do you think I helped you . . . for coin. That I'm a selfish hu?"

Xelle was tired. Really tired. She scrambled to interrupt. "I thought you transported me for kindness. But it's my culture to ensure that a payment is not desired. Dor, I sincerely want to thank you for your deed today. It means a tremendous amount to me and mine."

That was actually all she had in her. She was starting to slump. Quickly, she gathered her bag and gloves. Frantically scanning the floor for anything she'd left or dropped, she reached for the doorlatch and stepped out, her bag plopping to the ground.

About as soon as she had, Dor was pulling the tiller and turning off, down the road that rounded Vattam.

"What the ash-storm was that?" she ranted into a swirl of snow-flakes. As a frigid wind hit her, she pulled her hood back over her cap and slid on her gloves. Impossible. That was a new one. Normally, you don't pay someone enough, or you ask the wrong way. Now a per's insulted because she disrespected uncommunicated benevolence? As if pers making a fair wage weren't benevolent?

She fitted the bag back on, groaning at its weight, and trudged toward the line of buildings ahead.

Apparently the inns by the outer loop were not of the same charm as those she'd remembered from a short visit years ago, or maybe Xelle had a sense of neighborhoods, as she tended to visit ones where art and community were prevalent. Either way, with the weight of the obsidian again on her back, she did not take terribly long to search out a place to stay.

The first place she found that had an open area was apparently offered to pers of all species, who seemed to be roaming the first floor quite freely, but the odor was not one she could endure. The second place had a very unpleasant clerk and a film of candle smoke, or something, over everything, but the rate was cheap and she didn't need to climb the stairs, so without drawing attention, she headed back through a narrow hall to her room.

The state of the washroom did not lend itself to wanting to use it to wash, but she did light a candle (she'd heard of hu suspicious of lamps, and apparently she'd found one) and give that mark on her face a closer look.

First, it was definitely there. Second, it was an intricate design— one she didn't recognize but was absolutely not natural. She pulled a clothie from Essie to wipe the rest of her face, avoiding the strange mark for now. Still staring at her reflection, she hung the clothie over a metal loop on her bag (she'd been proud of this idea) to dry by the morning.

The moons glowed in from outside, and the curtain didn't quite close. Xelle heaved her bag as carefully as she could against the end of the small bed, and hoped that she'd find a way to sleep quickly in all this light and chaos. And be soon on her way.

It wasn't until she made an attempt to try and calm the storm in her mind that an unwelcome thought drifted over. It *would* have been better to search for the obsidian after her trip, fretting or not. Even a few rocks would have been heavy. But then, another thread piped in—but then she might not have met Thunder.

If "meeting you was worth the weight I carry for it" wasn't printed on a greeting card yet, perhaps it should be. Maybe greeting card design would be next, if the inkbloom thing didn't work out. Xelle smiled, amidst the streams of moonslight.

07 - City of Progress

Vattam was the largest city in Alyssia. A rather weighty thought for a Study who had chosen to lug a bag of rare, potentially forbidden, obsidian around it without knowing the routes. She muttered something about building character, and set out to find her way through.

It'd been a while since she'd visited the City of Progress, as the signs over the entering roads, and the gift shops, and painted brick side walls proclaimed it to be. Quite a while since she'd navigated the lines of moverooms making their way between huge buildings that were part of everyday life here.

One would think that a city full of everyone in all directions would cause a hu to feel small, at least the humbling sort. But instead, it made Xelle feel like she was in the one place that mattered. The one place where everyone else knew to be. The pull was undeniable.

Having grown up in a forest village, cities never ceased to feel comprehensively mystical to Xelle, as much, even, as the opulence and discovery of the Seven Towers, as much as the wide open areas where fewer hu dwelled, and certainly the endlessly rising mountains. All caught her heart in different ways.

Some Mages traveled between all such places—a house in the forest, a flat in the city, a home in the Tower. They grumbled about their schedules and their constraints even as they turned the world in their hands.

Even if Xelle had that kind of money—even if she spent it in such a way—Xelle wouldn't know how to feel, not knowing where was home. Which place was hers.

Shaking these thoughts away, she tried to focus on her day ahead. Given her detour through the mountains, she'd assumed she'd need to hurry through Vattam, but having arrived in reasonable enough time—well, why? It seemed a shame to pass through such a place without a little excursion, so her revised plan was to find something nice to do, have an interesting dinner, then set out fresh in the morning. The idea had her feeling buoyant.

That still countered by the weight of her bag, she set out to find a vroom. This time, with a cheery sunny morning and plenty of options, she waited for a taxi to take her to the central city.

The first taxi was spacious, and the two other hu sitting against the other side made no gesture to talk. The interior had been painted a sunny yellow, and a delicate border had been painted in by someone who had a lot of love for the effort, but otherwise the vroom was totally empty—not even a seating cushion except what looked like a custom one used by the conn.

The lack of seating almost turned the walls for her. She couldn't help think of it as forced cheer, without comfort, or an overthrow of someone who had tried. Yet, she focused on the yellow and tried not to worry about the rest. She could decline the ride and wait for the next taxi, but she was excited to go. Besides, it was chilly. And since she couldn't hear the sound of a secondary heater as the fuelstones idled, these hu were probably eager to be on their way.

"Where you headed?" the conn asked Xelle as she wriggled off her bag, distracted by her quick decision. She'd already told xem 'central city' when xe'd stopped, but xe must figure she had a specific destination in mind. As most travelers would.

"By the Post," she answered. She could just say 'anywhere works', but she was feeling worn down from the last few days and didn't have the energy to invite more.

The conn chuckled. "New incity?" The pair on the other side exchanged an almost subtle glance.

What had she said? Oh, the Post. It was practically a default drop-off or meet-up in most places. Well, this was Vattam; there must be dozens of Posts here, maybe even in central. She'd spent a lot of time in

Mytil but had never been assigned to a Post there. She needed to think more before she spoke, especially if she was supposed to find insights at To'Breath.

"Sorry, I was just trying to make it easier. Anywhere works, as long as it's somewhere pleasant I can relax and spend the night."

"That's easier!" xe said with a lilt to it.

Ugh. Xelle never loved that—when pers said something rude with a cheery tone. Seemed like a way to trouble without consequence. As in, 'Well you can't be sour at me, look how cheerful I am.' Accountability dodgers were the worst. She glanced up at the yellow wall.

Xe did tell her what the fee was, and Xelle murmured to herself, calculating what a standard tip would be. As she began to count the coins out, she saw one of the pers abstractly watching her. Maybe not on purpose, but figuring out payments had her uneasy enough.

Reminding herself she would never see these pers again and she was the only one likely flustered, she muttered a thanks and tried to take a comfortable cross-seat, facing inward, as she pushed the exact amount of coins into a pocket for later. She'd rather look out the window on her side, but she didn't know if it would offend to turn away from the pers, when they were facing inward. Either way, she could think about the dragons again.

Or, that mark.

She almost reached up to touch the mark on her face, but didn't want to bring attention to it when she didn't know what it was. No one seemed to notice it, or at least care. This morning, it had been the first thing she checked; presuming it was a magic mark, maybe it faded with time. And maybe it still would, but the tiny design was solidly still in place this morning, though no longer sore.

And yes, she was concerned. This was not a normal thing! An unidentified magic mark in the midst of everything else she'd recently learned was alarming at best. But without knowing more, and still feeling herself, she wasn't eager to run to a Mage about it either. She would see whether it was still, well, on her, at To'Breath. Go from there.

Realizing she was staring ahead and the hu might think *at* them, she shifted her gaze to the floor. It was painted a dark rusty color. And glossy.

This was silly. If she wanted to look out her window, she should do so. Awkwardly, she used her arms to shift around the other way. Awkwardly, because she almost forgot her bag was right there and so mid-turn she had to lean onto her other arm and shuffle the rest of the way around. Happily, now she could see no one's reactions, nor imagine what they were all thinking about her when they were literally just sitting there.

Settling herself while rattled was difficult, but fortunately Vattam offered streets upon streets crowded with new sights, so she peered out into the snowy morning with interest.

Perhaps if she had a word to describe Vattam, it might be energy. The various enterprises were always working on the next advancement, the next design. And in return, they received a corresponding flow of Alyssia's resources, creating pockets of tremendous wealth.

The people here celebrated a spirit of competition, which seemed reflected in the number of magipuck banners in windows and stripes sewn into coats, as well as in the rather pointed advertisements painted on sidewalls, and even on the vrooms. She understood that that spirit generated good things that helped pers' lives, but it also made Xelle uneasy, in a way she hadn't quite sorted. Xelle worked as hard as she could and she'd love to be rewarded for it, but she liked working with everyone else, not having to work against them. Something like that?

She thought that's why she preferred Mytil. Not to say there wasn't competition in Mytil—it was actually rather fierce—but it felt more focused on the accomplishment. More goals to reach for together, and to cheer the ones who reached it. Wins to reach, not winners and losers to distribute.

Anyway. She probably romanticized Mytil a bit. Growing up in Tam, it had been the big city, the place of sparkle and wonder and curious shops and new foods. She'd missed it tremendously when she'd rushed off across the world to To'Frond. And then, at To'Arc, she was closer than she'd ever been to the gleaming city, alive with art and culture. She could go for the evening, even.

Probably not the best idea to get distracted dreaming of near-home Mytil when she was riding across far-away Vattam. Giving herself a few taps to the side of her legs, she almost started to hum, then remembered that three pers were sitting behind her, two faced right at her back. She almost chuckled, which would definitely have made it weirder. And she was not turning around now!

The edge area of the city where they'd started out had ended with a series of signs that couldn't be read from this side, and now a maze of multi-story buildings blocked her view from anything beyond, forcing her to look exactly where she was, the way a city could do. Many rose from plain molded bricks, often painted with slogans, or the credentials of a local politician, in addition to standard advertisements. Very few carried art for art's sake, though many of the branded designs were shrewdly artistic.

As they passed crossing ways, her view would open, and for a few seconds, she could see down a street, road, even a boulevard where smaller homes and buildings fit like puzzle pieces into the spaces available around the large blocky structures—or sometimes the other way around.

Signs at many intersections reminded the traveler they were in the City of Progress, just as shops aimed at visitors often blasted the motif. Xelle supposed having a theme was nice; most towns and villages had a focus of local pride—in Tam it was a small waterfall—but perhaps simply going for 'progress', as if something so universal could be claimed, poked at her for the same reasons she'd just been considering.

Yet the view was fascinating. Xelle enjoyed the accenting of the buildings. She wasn't sure what else to call the aesthetic of the design. Large, clear windows flared out diagonally from front walls, trees were strategically placed around the snow-covered streets and office gardens, and there was acute priority in architectural drama: both usable elements like high floors, skyways, and balconies, and those simply meant to draw the eye, like shiny metal beams, protruding structures, or double-height entryways. Stark elements. Bright. Solid. Not like the integrated richness of a Tower, or the domed art district of Mytil.

An eclipse passed over, but the conn continued forward, to her surprise. The conn on the way here hadn't stopped either but with one younger hu not wearing symbology of belief or status, it seemed safer. With a larger taxi, she'd figured the conn might be worried to offend. But then, clearly the vrooms ahead of them weren't stopping either. Now that she realized it, the groups of hu walking down the roadsides were mostly continuing on their way. It was a long-ish eclipse, and she only saw maybe a couple people drawn back by the building walls.

She wondered how much of this was cultural—pers simply not superstitious about eclipses—and how much was practical, as in with crowded streets of people, having half the people stop would cause a lot of bumping. Then, maybe those were related.

Just as the full sun returned, the morning light slid up the side of a huge, windowed building, illuminating a brightly-painted sign.

Lerf Makes You Laugh

Under it was an abstract painting of some kind of fictional per. Like a wobbly bubble? With a smiley face? And huge eyes? Xelle wasn't laughing; she was rather alarmed. And makes you laugh? Like, forcefully? She enjoyed entertainment and would proudly admi when warranted, but she got to decide what she liked. This seemed totally reasonable.

As the building passed by (yes, she knew that the moveroom was passing, but perspective) she could see a crowd of pers through the huge glass windows. Before she could crane around, the building was out of view.

By the time they'd reached the central city, she'd seen at least four more references to Lerf. And this wasn't even Lerfville. Or wait, that's right. Lerf. She let a small chortle. Helia called it a snortle, because she'd said it was somewhere between a snort and a laugh and she claimed Xelle did it often.

Like one time when they'd been walking was *often*.

"Solo, out here," the conn said, as they abruptly pulled to a stop. The pair was still seated across the moveroom, and Xelle nodded them a curt goodbye as she leaned up, paid the conn along with her pre-staged tip, then stepped out into a full gust of frigid wind.

The last thing she was going to do at this point was question where xe'd dropped her off, so as the moveroom pulled past, she was delighted to see that she stood aside a small river, with birds sailing overhead, a stunning view of the hill across, and facing down what looked to be a charming row of shops, drops of water dripping peacefully from tiny icicles in the morning sun and large empty patios where goods were brought out in warmer weather. From what she could tell, at least what she knew from Vi'Arc and Mytil, these looked like the rare confluence of shops that were used by both the city's residents and by visitors, one of those districts where parting with one's coins was a pleasant experience.

Much less charmed, as she hefted her loaded bag onto her back, audibly apologizing to the bag itself for overloading it. At least she'd made sure Essie was safe on top, not getting squished by rocks. The thought did cross her mind that, now out of the mountains, a pledged Mage would surely, with discretion, cast to carry the bag along, but then she realized it was loaded with an unfamiliar reagent, and she had no idea what might happen. She cringed at her own potential oversight, her heart pounding a bit.

Reminding herself she'd not done it, and barely even considered it, Xelle walked into the closest shop, shuffling her boots on the coarse mat. Finding a shopkeep straightening an intricate fabric over a huge roll, she tried not to flinch at the hu's exposed crownhair. It wasn't unheard of, she'd just spent a lot of time in the Tower recently where no one did it. At first, she tried not to look, because crownhair was such a personal thing. Then, she remembered it wasn't strictly personal if the hu was freely exposing it. As was xyr right. Then, she thought, well either way I shouldn't stare. The image of the hu's spiky, mostly mahogany hair flashed by, overtop xyr ears and across the back of xyr head, and only fading to a lighter shade on the top where it had been left a little longer. The mahogany, she couldn't help but think, often reflected satisfaction, or deep family connections. Which had improved since the longer hair had first grown. Was that pride, or more? She had to stop thinking about it.

Her eyes flicked around. She was sure she looked odd already, glancing around like she was confused. As always, she did her best and tried not to let her voice shake too much.

"Hello. Would you know a place where I could store my bag for the day? I'll be staying incity for the night and I've packed it too heavy."

Xe shrugged without totally turning around. "I'd take it here, but if you're staying riverfront, one of the best inns incity is just across that bridge. More efficient to reserve a room then come back this way. Stepladder. That's the name," xe clarified.

For a moment, Xelle considered it unexpected that the shopkeep didn't make even a soft pitch for these absolutely gorgeous fabrics, but then if Xelle were in the market for expensive drapes she probably wouldn't be stomping around the city carrying her own heavy bag.

She began to fret whether offering a coin would be polite; surely in a place like this a chip or two wouldn't mean much, but when the shopkeep rushed to greet a customer without giving Xelle a second glance, Xelle decided she was safe to be on her way.

With an attempted thank you wave that no one saw, she hefted the bag and started across the bridge.

The inn was easy to spot and find, rising with solid elegance from the hill. Xelle realized, with worry, it must be expensive, and the Tower had only given her a budget to cover an approximately two-day trip, there and back, plus a little cushion. Her own money had been absorbed into her garden room for quite some time.

She was right; the beautiful inn was very expensive. Well worth it, she was sure. Even the view of the gathering area, of lofty wide beams from cushiony chairs, looked like somewhere Xelle could agree to live in right that moment. The fact that most pers could not even stay the night in such a place was not a thought healthy for Xelle to dwell on. When she started to apologize for taking xyr time, the clerk interrupted.

"Could give you a summer room," xe said, followed with a scrunch to one side of xyr face that seemed to indicate xe was unsure.

Without knowing if she was reading that right, Xelle stumbled over her words; she'd never heard of a summer room, and so she started to ask what one was.

"Up the hill a bit; cozy, nice view and privacy, with a roomy outdoor shower and a toilet out back. Cold as a buttocks on marble with all this weather, but for one night and with good blankets, it could do."

Xelle didn't know how to tell xem that this would surely be warmer than sleeping in one thinnish blanket in the mountains, and that she wanted nothing more than to put her bag down and so her standards were inappropriately low. (Even with three nights not showering, she tried not to think. At least she wasn't sweating.)

"I'd be grateful," she said instead. "I will use those good blankets, however."

The clerk grinned broadly at this. And when she tried to offer xem a payment, xe waved her off. "Nah, I'm not even supposed to sell them now. But you looked tired and my perk of working here is being cute. If you don't mind, though, keeping it tidy? Fold back the blankets, and drop the sheets when you leave." Xe tilted xyr head toward a large cart in the room behind xem.

"Of course." Xelle nodded, and took the offered key and roll of fresh sheets. "Thank you so much."

While one more trek—this time up a hill—was wearing, she found a lovely little room, cozy and elegant, with lace curtains and enough tassels that she was sure one of the innkeepers had a side business selling tassels. She flicked one against her fingers, delighted by the softness.

Groaning, she scooted her bag into a corner, out of view of the huge window. (She decided not to draw the curtain as not to draw attention to her occupancy. So much for that privacy.)

It did occur to her, that though theft was uncommon, perhaps leaving a bag of a substance of unknown value (and power) unattended in an unfamiliar city wasn't the wisest move. But the fact was, no one knew she had it, and someone picking her plain, scuffed bag to loot, and then understanding the nature of what might look, in the dark room, like a bag of rocks or even broken glass, would be quite a sequence of events. She stopped and stared at it. If one did know, xe'd probably think xe was messing with a Mage and run. She couldn't help a grin at that.

Xelle relished the spring in her step as she crossed the bridge for the second time, and set to exploring the fashionable neighborhood, almost as sweet as gingercookie houses in a sugar frost, looking equally unreal.

In fact, and she hadn't considered this before, for all the bold, impressive architecture she'd passed through on the way here, central Vattam had a much older look; not quite Arc Region, but maybe what she'd heard of Grand on the Arc Side. She supposed that made sense, with the buildings being older. She did smile, as the archway over the bridge had been recently painted with a stylized City of Progress motif. Though, progress didn't mean everything was new, she mused.

If progress meant to move forward, she thought, and forward meant toward something better, and sometimes moving wasn't better, then maybe the entire concept of progress was oversimplified.

Either way, if the simplification was trying to say *Do Better*, that's one she could endorse.

08 – Excursion

The chill in the winter wind calmed as the morning light warmed it, and without a bag weighing her steps, the stroll through the line of shops was an absolute treat. She sampled tints of vinegar in one, and bought herself a soft pair of socks woven with rose blossoms in another. (She didn't really have money to shop for herself, but she knew they'd bring her joy, and she hadn't had to pay for the room.) Beyond the first shopkeep, others were showing their crownhair, mostly in the inside spaces, as those walking outside wore caps for warmth.

Though she was almost getting used to the sight, Xelle would never show her own crownhair. She liked keeping it long, as it grew through her times of joy, uncertainty, and leadenness alike. So much would be revealed by exposing it, and so much lost by cutting it. She patted her new, warm cap protectively.

The area grew busier as the sun peaked overhead, though she imagined not as busy as it could be. This didn't bother her, the way close spaces could. She enjoyed the mix of people here; it was fun to see pers from all over Alyssia smiling and bustling along, even better to join it. A few wore what she realized might be LerfSpecs, though by no means was she going to stop them and ask. As she grew accustomed to the unique flow of the main and cross streets, she relaxed further, and basked in the energy of the lovely winter day.

Seeing a shop entirely dedicated to toys, she thought how nice it would be to get her niblings a gift. Hall's oldest: bright, funny Vallie, had already turned 4, and even little Loren was now a year old.

The broad front window boasted a multi-layer display of color and motion, and thinking it might take a little focus to parse through all that, she decided to sit down first for an early afternoon snack. Xelle doubled back to a small side road, where she'd just passed an unimposing café that had almost drawn her in the first time.

As she finished up her crackers and spreads, she flicked through her coin pouch to check how much she had. For this, she'd dip into the second pocket, the one held for extras. There wasn't very much, but she hoped she could find something nice. Didn't need to be fancy, just something they'd enjoy. Attempting to hide a parting swipe of her finger against the plate and into her mouth before slipping her gloves back on, Xelle plunked an extra coin into the jar at the exit and headed out again.

The toy shop proved to be an unexpected challenge, and she wandered through its neatly-kept aisles much longer than she'd wanted to. The shelves were stocked with all sorts of lovely playthings, but many of the traditional toys were not so different than those they could get closer to home. Other items were too large to be carried, and many of the amusing gadgets were either much more than she could afford or had the look they might not survive being in a house with a stomping toddler. (Or being carried in a bag full of rocks.)

Nervously offering a thanks to the shopkeep because she knew she'd been inside a long time, she stepped back onto the street, and found herself facing a painted window boasting good luck charms.

Now, Xelle didn't believe in good luck. ... Ok, Xelle absolutely believed in good luck, she just—well, it was complicated and there was nothing wrong with the gesture, whatever its effect. As she entered the shop, she saw another person with xyr crownhair exposed, but this time it was banded into a knot over xyr head, striped by its colors and textures. Xelle noticed how small the shop actually was; the painted window and the door comprised the width of it, and a blue-painted wall sectioned off whatever else was behind that. The shopkeep clasped xyr arms. As xe stopped, the strips of loose fabric comprising xyr skirt swayed, one way and then the other.

"Hello. This is a shop for the curious and believers." Implicit in that, Xelle supposed, was a lack of welcome for those looking to argue.

Xelle warmed to this hu immediately. She knew the idea and knew the feeling.

Xelle knew that, despite that many (in the Towers) would say that Alyssia revolved around magic, there were pers who'd never seen it, never wanted it—and those who either doubted it or believed it must draw from foul sources. This didn't bother her. Magic offered power and risk and the presence of mitigating voices seemed wise. What bothered Xelle was when pers demanded she explain her craft, justify it. When she hadn't asked them, nor offered the debate. In her first years, having herself grown up away from magic, she'd not known how to respond. She'd argued, and even demonstrated, just to be laughed away no matter the strength of her response.

It had taken being in Vi'Ever with a class, and seeing a teacher of hers approached this way, to help her understand that she didn't have to engage with pers who weren't really interested in her answers. And while a Mage would never get away with a firm greeting such as this shopkeep offered, she appreciated it. She wished that she could.

"I understand," she said. The hu's stretch of the face made Xelle think that hadn't been the right answer either, and so she stumbled to address why she was here. "I'm incity just for the day. It's lovely; everyone has been so nice." The shopkeep did smile politely at that. "I have two young niblings," Xelle continued. "Nothing in the toy shop seemed right, and I don't know what clothes they might need. Perhaps, well I don't know if you have a nice gift here. I don't have much money," she offered, feeling the comment was rude as soon as she'd said it.

However, the note seemed to amuse the shopkeep, or some such thing. Xelle never knew; once things started slipping, it got like watching her own actions through a lens.

The shopkeep pulled out a few small items from around the room and set them on a high table, centered with a square of velvet. One immediately caught her eye. It was like—a metal vine. Perhaps a paperweight or small shelf embellishment. Why would a metal vine be recommended for a young child?

Xe must have seen Xelle's eyes direct to the item, as xe quickly swept the others away. "Individually cast, each mold unique. Go on," xe said. "Won't hurt to touch. The luck is in the way it's held; each per has to find that for oneself."

Xelle picked it up. The metal had a satisfying weight, and she imagined it would be pleasantly cool if her fingers weren't covered. Smooth, too. "Vallie," she said.

The object was plucked from her hand and wrapped in tissue, as if Xelle had decided. Not that she was upset; she could see Vallie enjoying such a thing. "The other is younger," she said. "Loren." Xelle thought of her cooing little nib, just an infant when Xelle had last been there. When she looked up, the shopkeep was just opening xyr eyes, as if they'd been closed.

"Such winter," xe murmured. Xe left behind a curtain for only a moment, and returned with a closed fist. Opening it, a smooth oval settled onto the velvet square.

Beautiful. A stone of some sort, with a rich opalescent sheen. If someone had asked Xelle to identify its color, even approximately, she could not. Even a palette like soft rainbow, or dawnslight on water, would oversimplify.

There was no way she could afford this stone.

"The stone is a gift. If you agree to take it to Loren, then I request you not argue. The vine is four ixa." Xe tapped xyr other hand then stepped back, as if waiting for Xelle to produce the coins.

Four ixa, or the amount as she understood it in the Vattam dialect, was a lot of coin. More than she'd meant to pay for both. But with the one item free and not wanting the stress of saying no—besides, she felt good about both items, she thought?—Xelle held the coins out, not sure whether to put them on the velvet or the hard surface. The shopkeep held out a hand, wrapping xyr fingers tightly around them before slowly lowering xyr arm, as if the coins had been absorbed into xyr skin.

Xe was certainly still holding them; it just had that look.

With a quick thanks, Xelle hurried back out to the snowy street. Normally, this was when she'd react when she'd bought something so quickly. Her mind would spin, and she'd worry—had she been taken advantage of? Should she have thought more? Were these the right items? But strangely, she felt thrilled. The trinkets were so interesting, so right.

Only after she was walking away, Xelle realized the opposite had also occurred: she'd just been checked out, with no offer to buy anything else or even look at the other wares. Maybe she should have bought a luck charm for herself; she could certainly use it. Or a gift for Helia—Helia had no shortage of coin, but she did love unique and pretty items. Well, she wasn't going back in.

Xelle still had a little coin, and there were a few more shops down a side road where she could browse. But she was feeling a bit tired from all the interaction and uncertainty, and she remembered that she could always stop through on her return trip. So she tried to sweep away all the questions and worries (or at least ignore them) and just walk down the last road, looking at the shops from outside but not going in.

This turned out to be fine, as these shops were more for home wares. And some pers here must have some very nice homes! She did stop in at one little spice shop, and rather than spin on endless possibilities and what she could afford, she asked for a recommendation. The hu sold her an efficient little sampler, and told her if she was traveling, to save it for home to enjoy the tastes of Old Vattam. The way he pronounced Vattam was a little softer. She loved language and thought to ask, but just then another hu walked in with several jars to refill, so she gave the tin a little hug where the shopkeep could see, and turned back onto the side street, winding her way back up toward the river.

She took a deep breath, now enjoying the chill, which felt warm amidst her joy, and gently worked the tin into her large pant pocket, now at its limit with the wrapped luck charms as well. (The socks occupied the other side.) Letting her mind settle, she walked, peacefully, down the street, drifting amidst the dots of purposeful shoppers.

And, finally, as the sun set and many of the shops closed for the day, she stopped at a beautifully decorated alcove bar she'd spotted earlier, with rich colors of paint, draped fabric in dark purples and burgundies with metallic threading, a warm hearth, and a variety of eclectic art on the walls: paintings, flower sketches, and even a detailed mosaic in baby greens with tints of teal and slate.

The storybook nature of the cozy space offered the chance to spend an hour in another, more perfect, world, and so she hoped it wasn't reserved, or that a drink wouldn't cost too much. The seating nooks were empty, though she supposed it was still relatively early and the frosty weather must have muted the crowds throughout the day. She could imagine what the curved benches would be like in the golden summer light, with the front flaps open and a warm breeze from the river.

Lives for other pers. She could only glimpse them.

"Welcome, friend." A hu walked out from behind a tall curtain. "I am Mara, any, and we serve herbal drinks."

Xelle didn't want to offend if that was an elaborate way to say tea, but she was at the point of the day with cold toes and a buzzing mind where she was hoping for a drink. A drink drink.

"We have teas," she continued. "Hot, cool, or sparkling, and a variety of spirits, all served with herbs for season and mood."

Xelle responded casually, as though she'd been considering the tea. "Spirits with herbs? That sounds interesting? What do you recommend?"

Mara looked her over as if she was deciding fabric for a drape. Whatever she needed to assess didn't take long. "An unusual winter. I have an Ever Region Arc side peakward, clear spirit, infused with lavender that I would gently warm and serve in a small glass bowl with a finger dish of dried forest blueberries."

Like Xelle was going to argue that.

Soon she was seated at the warm countertop, her cape draped over an artistically forged, wide hook, and a warm cup set down on a dyed piece of lace. "Thank you," she said, pulling off her gloves and setting them to the side, after realizing her pockets were full.

Taking a nod, Mara picked them up and draped them atop the hook. "You're welcome. I hope you enjoy. It's a cold night to be out." The hu apprized Xelle's cloak while stepping back. "A fine weave. It's simply impossible to best the weaves of Arc Region, especially mid."

The glass rolled a moment against the soft lace as Xelle steadied it. The hu could tell where she'd bought her cloak!

Mara smiled. "Didn't mean to startle you. But I see pers from all around here and they usually like to say where they're from, where they've been, where they found their finery. One gets a sense of it. Good thing for one to know. There are pers who keep an eye to such things, for a variety of reasons.

"What else can you tell? If I may ask?"

"Ah." Mara's lips pulled back as if he wasn't going to give away all his secrets. "You're a Study. I wouldn't have been certain which Tower but then you jumped at Arc, so it's likely there. Don't ask me to explain the first part, but you haven't the affect of a Mage nor the shades to draw any other way. But you're definitely in the study; your hand has the specific bump of someone who uses their long, impractical pens, and there are other tells too." Mara hurried on quickly as if avoiding discussing something. "Your wristwarmers are standard Tower issue; gold thread to connect you to your cloud city or the like."

Just as Xelle was about to ask Mara about that last, a couple walked in, draped in matching magipuck colors, a deep blue and gold marked with the sign of Vattam (it seemed there were multiple Vattam teams).

It was then Xelle noticed the absence of magipuck banners in the bar, probably more to maintain the aesthetic than any concerns about clientele preference. Magipuck was not popular in the forest, and it was generally avoided in Mage circles. Xelle had nothing against people's fun, but within the magesphere, the idea that the puck was 'magical' seemed an intentional offense. No casts were involved; the puck, sticks, and protective gear were inset with fragments of fuelstones, naturally repelling each other when close.

Realizing she appeared to be watching the couple, she turned her eyes back.

Mara gave her a wink and went to offer his herbed libations to the pair. They seemed frequent customers, and ones with a fair amount of coin, as Mara was fairly well absorbed into ensuring their entertainment.

Xelle settled back into the drink. She wasn't usually one for lavender, but the mixture and all its components had been made with such expert subtlety that she thoroughly enjoyed every drop. A treat that she would remember for a while, she thought. All of it.

Mara did give a warm and friendly farewell when Xelle paid for the drink (hoping she got the tip right) and bundled up to go.

"Thanks, I think I'll remember this a long time."

Mara put a hand to his heart. "My best compliment."

Thus Xelle was not completely frozen when she wandered back to the inn, content and grateful to have experienced such a lovely and satisfying day, and gazing out at the moonslit snow, as though it were a dusting of crystal glitter. It could have jarred her to remember she'd agreed to sleep in a small, thin-walled room, where she presumed the lamps had been taken in for the season, but instead she took it as reason to prolong her glorious day a little longer, settling into the warm main hall—grabbing a large, squishy chair around a roaring fire, crackling within a big, all-sides chimney.

She let the warmth sink in.

Leaning back, she mostly stared at the flames and relaxed, trying not to think through what the next few days would bring, reaching To'Breath and having no actual idea what she was meant to do there.

More aware now that she had signatures that revealed her as a Study, Xelle was less surprised when someone asked if she was visiting from a Tower. "Yes, from To'Arc," she said, feeling no reason to conceal the fact. Yet there wasn't quite the reaction to that she expected, and she considered that on all of her previous Tower travels, she'd always been with a Mage. Never on her own.

There was a bit of sting that she would be treated differently if she simply claimed a status that was hers for the claiming. *Why do you make things difficult?* she tsked to herself. It cut both ways, she knew. Something else she'd consider later. For now, she should probably get to that bed, with the warm covers the nice hu at the front desk had offered. Yes, a little more cold to endure, but soon she'd be to the Tower, where of all her issues, heat would not be one. Xelle stretched, and reached for her gloves.

"Not staying for stories?"

"Sorry?" Xelle offered a look to indicate she wasn't sure what that meant here.

"Oh, you're in for a treat!" A stout hu clapped, almost knocking over xyr thinner companion.

"Watch it," the other said. "My knees!"

"Your knees were just fine kicking me a whole minute ago!" Xe turned to Xelle. "On the schedule, once a week. The best storyteller in Vattam tells a fantasy." Glancing at Xelle's hand halfway into her glove, xe added, "It's open to all," with a reassuring nod. "Even this one." The last with a tilt of xyr head to the side.

"Best storyteller in Alyssia," xyr companion declared, mood undented. "They'll be serving huge mugs of beer: grain or root, and you can settle in and listen. It goes long enough but not too long."

"Just enough to finish the beer!"

Another hu had joined. "Is xe new? Here, the beer's on me. If you'll have it? Welcome to Stepladder Inn. Grain?"

Xelle nodded, with thanks, and soon a small but sturdy side stand was holding a large mug of beer, and Xelle was watching how quickly the hall began to fill up. Maybe she shouldn't take one of the best seats, but what was she going to do, carry the table and the beer? No one seemed upset; more like getting there early for a good seat was common.

Soon a hu walked in, and set up in a large chair positioned not in front of the fire but on a raised platform in a plainish chair, far enough from the chimney that anyone had a view or could scoot into one. Xe ran a hand over xyr smoothly-shaved head, then with a fast back and forth rub, lowered it.

"Hello," xe started, now giving a flick of xyr hands—one that Xelle thought was meant to be cheerful, because it almost looked like the flame. "Who's with us tonight? I see familiar faces, I see new ones." Xe smiled at Xelle, but kindly and without pressure.

Understanding now, that she was about to hear a master storyteller, she settled back, pulling her legs up into the chair and taking a sip of the beer, which was smooth and delicious, just the right amount of flavor without feeling that it was arguing with ya, as Na'Foose would say when e'd take her incity as a child. Smiling, she set the mug back down onto a wide, woven coaster.

And right when Xelle thought her day could not have been more amazing, the storyteller began. His name was Bard Jimmi Du'Ard, he, and he spent the first whole section chatting about his week. This turned out to be delightful. Even though she didn't know the hu, he made his weekly trials and triumphs sound like a check-in with an old friend. She wished her old friends would talk to her that way, not always about matters that were big.

Then he started with a story that he'd even written. Xelle hadn't quite been sure what a fantasy was, and had to admit, she was eager to find out. There were several ways it could have gone, and the way it did go was both surprising and wonderful. It seemed a fantasy was a story about imagined magic—not real magic, but magic invented to weave the tale of the storyteller.

In Jimmi's tale, magic did not involve phyta, but a resonance of metal. She thought of the metal vine in her pocket, but since it was for Vallie and there seemed something personal in that, she didn't reach for it.

Each character, from a group of castle-dwelling nobility in some imaginary place, was read with a distinct and often humorous voice. One had the accent of Ever Region seaward, and while it was a bit exaggerated, it was how pers spoke there. This got Xelle thinking about her own speech. Did she sound like someone from Ever Region mid? Like the bartender had mentioned earlier, how much of her essence was apparent to others? And To'Arc . . . Had her time at To'Arc changed her speech? She couldn't think of it then, as the story continued on.

Then, right when she was plenty entranced, dragons entered his tale. She half-drank, half-breathed some beer and coughed awkwardly into her arm, realizing she didn't have Essie or his handy clothie. The storyteller glanced to see if she was alright, and she thought he paused on her face. No, her forehead. She'd almost forgotten about the mark. Then, she still had it. He'd looked back across the crowd. Pers were always hesitant to even joke about dragons, but Jimmi jumped in, describing them talking and flying and breathing plumes of fire. Whatever he could imagine, these dragons could do.

She couldn't be sure he'd noted her mark; he'd moved to telling a whole sequence about a villain who'd accidentally bared his embellished buttcheek to a laughing crowd of enablers, and hadn't again looked her way.

The story grew serious, and the villain, a wicked Count, became not funny at all, expelling the dragons with magic and enacting terrible sadness on the castle-dwelling pers. Then someone sarcastically called the village baker a hero, and ze became so fed up that ze enacted a scheme where the Count was outnumbered and ran out into the night, never allowed to return.

"Remember," he concluded, reading in the main character's higher pitched voice, "sometimes the hero is simply the one who tries." And he shut the book.

Whatever the other per had said, it ended all too quickly. Perhaps because she'd never heard such stories. She wanted to tell the storyteller how much she'd enjoyed it, but by the time she'd collected her thoughts, the chair and platform was empty and the room mostly as well. The hu who'd bought her a beer—she couldn't thank xem either. Even the just-emptied beer and stand had been taken away by one of the staff, already gone.

Not bothering to stifle a yawn, she stood, not realizing how stiff her legs had grown after walking all day, and then holding still while Xelle stayed transfixed by the event.

She stared at the empty chair. If a made-up story could be so fascinating, she wondered if we could make up better twists for our own.

09 – Cold Awakening

She awoke not entirely uncomfortable in the warm roll of soft blankets, glad she'd fallen back asleep, as she remembered staring out the open window at the snow falling through the moonslight and worrying, because she knew she needed rest. It wasn't too long to tidy the small room, which she'd mostly used for bag storage and probably snoring, and, not seeing the hu from the morning before, she tried to drop the sheets off discreetly just in case it could be an issue for xem.

The clerk at the desk said there was a circle not far from where she'd been dropped off where moverooms loaded and unloaded passengers for outcity trips. And while the weight of her bag had grown to be momentous in her mind, it was actually manageable for a brief morning walk, if not a brisk one. Her mind circling back on this quickly, the straps started to pull intolerably just as she saw the arc of moverooms ahead.

None of the vrooms were going to To'Breath. One large vroom was about to leave for To'Grand. A few were headed back toward To'Arc, an idea which did tempt her. And most were on the way to Wehj, a few commissioned toward towns in the area. One was waiting uncommissioned, but Xelle couldn't pay that kind of rate, even if she could justify it. Certainly the pers of Vi' and To'Breath liked traveling to this charming district for a day of fun? Though, she supposed, they'd likely not be adding passengers at the circle on their way back.

"The'll be one soon," a conn assured her, xyr loud words turning into even bigger clouds of steam. "Always someone going to Breath, if you just give it a few."

"Breath?" another conn called out. "We're just leaving and can take you if you're one." Xe pointed to a moveroom that was much smaller than the others. Not as small as the one she'd endured the other day, but still by xyr addition of 'we' it seemed she'd have to be in talking distance yet again. She started to tell xem no, and seeing her expression, xe began to walk away.

Xelle was cold. Even with money for inns, she'd now slept outside twice, once essentially. It was nearly as cold in Vattam as it'd been in Arc. Even the benches were covered with a snow that had started overnight, and she wasn't eager to get snow on her bag or her pants, nor stand here and get snowed on indefinitely.

She was also tired all over. Interacting made her tired. She hadn't been able to sleep well; the storm had been active in her mind. The alcove, the storyteller, the shopkeeps, all swirling in doubt and hoping she hadn't done anything wrong, or too much wrong. Yes, she might have to share the little vroom, but she could also just not participate in any discussions. Some fuelstones started up beside her, making her jump.

"Hey," she called, her voice shaking. The conn turned around. "Going to the Tower itself, or the Region?"

"To the Tower." Xe signaled a cost for the ride. More than she'd expect, but nothing unreasonable. She walked over, turned for one last look at the snow falling on the long, straight patch of river and the surrounding roofs, and the tall inn up on the hill. She could see the line of 'summer rooms', and she smiled.

Xe opened the door, and started to take her bag.

"I've got it; it's a bit heavy." She stepped up into the interior, which was small, but with enough room to stand. Unlike the taxis she'd used before, where the arrangement was: find a place to sit, there was a line painted down the floor. The passenger was seated against one wall, casually eating an apple, and on the other side, a small number "3" was marked across the floorboards in the same white paint. Xelle wasn't sure what that meant. Each side had a stack of cushions, so just, to keep pers from sitting in the middle?

"You're section three," the conn said. "I'll have my screen pulled in a moment; you're welcome to pull yours as well; there's the handle." Xe gestured. "I'm Julla, any, if you need anything. Call or tap on my screen. I won't stop until we're outcity."

Xelle still did not fully know what was happening, until Julla sat on the forward-facing bench and pulled a smaller level beside the tiller, causing a screen (that's what ze'd called it) to slide noisily between zem and the two passengers.

Then, the tiller must have been pulled, as the fuelstones started up and the moveroom chugged away. Grabbing onto the wall, Xelle quickly lowered herself to a seat, while positioning her backpack beside her.

"So what's our future?" the passenger on the other side of the line said.

Xelle couldn't help but smile; the expression brought her back. When she'd studied at To'Frond, she'd learned that a lot of pers from that area had rather formal ways of addressing simple subjects. Formal to her, anyway. But it made everything sound more interesting, a thought she'd kept to herself. This passenger's accent wasn't Frond Region, she didn't think, but perhaps it could be Charmside. She thought of the herb bartender from last night, and thought maybe she'd never see pers the same way again.

This one was tall, with legs much longer than the floor space was designed to hold. Xe held them a bit inelegantly, with one bent up and the other sort of flopping to the side. Unlike Xelle, the hu (whose thick coat was stuffed into a storage nook) was dressed in a more formal but still comfortable style, with a sleek, long, mauve tunic corded with warm blue. Xyr crownhair was pulled into a soft-looking sewn turban, the sort that looked elegant but could be easily taken on and off. Tiny chains wound over xyr ears, and it looked like xe had a few small tattoos along the side of xyr face—

Xe raised xyr eyebrows, and Xelle glanced away. And, now, seeing the lines on the floor, she could see there was a second shade she could draw so that they wouldn't see each other on the ride to To'Breath. What would have been a big relief just a minute ago now felt awkward.

Would they look at each other while drawing the shade? Who would do it? Should they both agree? Or just one? Would xyr legs be too cramped? Why not look out both windows? Her breath hastened as she tried to answer the questions.

"Xelle, she or e" she got out. "I mean, Xeleanor Du'Tam, she or e. I mean you can call me either. Either name. I don't know . . . about the wall."

The passenger nodded solemnly, but Xelle felt xe was teasing, inside. Or something. This annoyed her. Well, they'd pull the wall then.

"Rayn Du'Sharre, she. Happy to pull the screen but if you need a tie-breaker, we probably haven't talked to a lot of Studies from other Towers and it could provide interest." She bit what was left of the apple with a loud *crunch*.

Oh. As intense as her last day in the Tower had been, the whole incident in the mountains had really thrown her out of that spin, which had honestly been welcome. Then, she'd thought that, during her travels, she needed to appear like a populace traveler, and so she'd let the Tower business drop in her mind. Not *drop*, but only poke a few times as a strictly future event. It had been refreshing. But now she was on a ride that would end at To'Breath, the place where, she now remembered quite clearly, the Arc Spire had sent her to be some sort of covert agent.

Thinking of it fresh, the entire concept was outrageous. And meeting a dragon on top of that. She wasn't going to say all this to the stranger across the vroom.

"I study at To'Arc." For some reason, she had the urge to explain why she wasn't a Mage. But then, this Rayn looked about her age and wasn't either. Not sure why she was making it a competition.

"I thought you might," Rayn said, after she finished chewing. Almost. "I could hear the Ever Region in your voice. But you've picked up the Arc mannerisms. Like your eyes. They look ahead a step like it could be an endless journey."

Xelle squinted a little.

"Sorry, I can be direct. Spend half my time trying to wrap it in a robe." Rayn glanced off at the ceiling before continuing. "I'm at To'Ever. Had spent several years in another occupation, but couldn't get past the thrill I had thinking of magic."

Xelle understood that. "I studied at To'Ever myself, sounds like well before you were there. Growing up in Tam, it felt like part of my home. Anyway, I left, and spent a short time at To'Frond. That *really* wasn't for me, and it was just so far away, and anyway I've been at To'Arc a while. I like it. It's a magic that can be so light, like an oil wash over bread, or it can be so deep, like if the universe went on a thousand times past what we could see." She stopped, not meaning to go on. Rayn was watching her pensively.

"I'm glad you've been to To'Ever," she said.

Xelle knew exactly what she meant. Practitioners of Ever Magic were particularly secretive about it. Part of the reason was cultural and beyond Xelle's full understanding, but she thought another aspect was that Ever Magic required objects to create enchantments, including ones that could be extraordinarily powerful and potentially used by others. While the use of magic was strictly regulated across Alyssia, revealing which objects were most needed as well as what could be done with them could tip old greed and old imbalances.

"I did like it," she said. "It was just where I'd always been and something felt missing."

Rayn only nodded, at least on that subject. "I actually went through Tam once; we needed a piece made, and the Tower carpenters were backed up. Someone recommended a hu in the area, but he'd left years before. Tower sources aren't always caught up." She laughed.

Xelle did not laugh. "Obnoxious."

Rayn raised her eyebrows and waited.

"Rod. He's from a couple walks over. Everyone kissed his cheeks because influential people would go seek out his carpentry after he became some sort of self-fashioned *thing*. Then they'd be shocked I didn't do the same. Not an admi." Her face scrunched. "Used to dance with a lot of the teenagers at festivals. Not sexual, exactly—more enjoying the night. Still, it was all control. The teenagers tended to be more likely to agree, despite not wanting to, but thinking it was innocent enough. Luckily I had parents that told me about following guts and saying no. My sib even worked for him a while, and finally got the sniff and quit. Anyway, apparently old Rod moved out to the wealthy part of Wehj, so hopefully I won't have to deal with him again."

"Sore spot," Rayn said, slightly chewy as she'd appeared to finish up the apple. Yet something in her tone didn't bother Xelle. "Your family sounds nice."

"They are," Xelle said, relieved to rid her mind of thoughts of Rod. Or at least start to. "I have one sibling, Hall, who has two curas. He's absorbed into parenting these days, and he also spends a lot of time helping people in the village, with a whole lot of things. He lives there, in Tam, still, and I suspect he'll stay. My parents live there also, in the house Hall and I grew up in. Vuia, Lleyx, and Foose—I use Na for all three." She smiled; she couldn't help it sometimes thinking of her parents. When she looked up, Rayn was smiling too.

"As I mentioned, I'm from Sharre." She looked over, as if trying to gauge if Xelle knew about her hometown.

Xelle shook her head. "I believe it's Charm Region, but I don't know much else."

"Charm-ish." She paused, shifting her seat. "People from Sharre don't really talk about it; I guess I got it in the threads. Visit sometime and you'll understand why."

She found that a bit ominous, but wasn't going to push the per if she didn't want to talk.

"Except a few ex-romfriends; they'll all be thrilled to chat." Rayn rolled her eyes. She looked at Xelle like there was more to say. Xelle tilted her head in response. "Apparently dating the Mayor's cura will get your actions viewed with more scrutiny especially when you tell her she's a tool and it gets overheard by her ren, the Mayor, and half of the city government. 'Oh, hey time to go study magic across the world.'"

Rayn began to laugh and Xelle couldn't help laugh along with her. Strange that she'd called her town a city, but that could be local dialect too. Xelle learned more about the nuances of language every day, it felt like.

"What do you think of Vattam?" Rayn was clearly changing the subject when she hadn't really said anything about her own family—she'd feel bad, but Rayn had brought it up. Anyway, Vattam.

"I didn't get to see much, just spent most of the day in that old village area near where we left from. That was nice, though; I'd like to go back someday. I had a really nice evening, especially for just popping incity. Good luck, or something.

"I've spent a lot more time in Mytil—if you're at Ever you probably have too—and not a lot here. In fact—" She hadn't really been watching out of the windows as she really should be and wasn't even sure if they were out of the massive city— "I don't think I've ever been *right here* before. Kind of exciting. Hello, new place on Alyssia.

"What I did see—" she went ahead and continued as Rayn seemed to be processing something "—was impressive. Here, I mean. The city." She pointed a thumb over her left shoulder. "Building after building constructed with simple elements, like windows and beams, that somehow caught the eye almost as if it was all elaborate architecture. Pers who seemed to follow their own paths—" She paused, not sure she wanted to get into eclipses and crownhair and other sensitive subjects when she had just met this per.

Rayn didn't seem worried, though, she slashed out a small lightning with her fingers in concurrence of Xelle's observations. Right as she thought maybe she could get into some of it, she remembered something else.

"Just learned about this Lerf town, though." Again, she hesitated. Not knowing Rayn, she didn't want to offend. Well, she hadn't called herself Rayn Du'Lerf at least.

"Lerf! Stop!"

Xelle stopped, not sure what that meant.

"Come on, what did you think? No, never mind." Rayn waved, though seemingly at herself. "I think this whole Lerf thing sounds way 'too'. Maybe I'm wrong. But my gut says one starts naming places larger than like, a room, after oneself, someone's guardclip fell off."

Xelle relaxed. "Yes, I thought the same thing. What the ash?"

As Rayn began to chuckle, Xelle added, "I felt pretty alerf about the whole thing."

They both broke into laughter, enough that Xelle worried the conn would think something was wrong and stop the vroom. But ze did not.

It appeared that they were still incity, in some form, as buildings lined the road they were on, with rows of homes sprawling behind. Sometimes these things were hard for Xelle to process. How she could grow up in a town where she knew or could figure out where almost anyone lived in a few blinks, and then there could be a place like this, where it felt like the whole world existed together, happily without her. And then there were all the Mage Towers, in themselves places of wonder, every moment known, and tracked, floors and floors of pers, some who barely left. The cities. The forests. The mountains. There was just so much.

"Everything ok?" Rayn asked, from where she'd casually leaned back against the wall.

Hmm? "I was, I'm looking out the window. Yes, I'm fine." Xelle didn't know what she'd done to cause the other hu's worry, which began to worry her more. "I worry a lot," she spouted out, immediately feeling embarrassed. "I mean, more than other people. Sometimes I worry when there's nothing to worry about. And sometimes it's hard for me to talk to pers."

"Oh, I'm sorry." Rayn's face fell. "I didn't mean to push you into anything. Here, we can pull the slider."

"No." Xelle was only making it worse. "No, I mean, only if you want to. I don't want people to close doors, I just want them to understand."

What? It was at this point that Xelle reached through her own fog and grabbed herself with a firm metaphorical hand. She'd had enough awkward interactions over the past days, she was not going to make things worse for this per, who actually seemed really nice and had some things in common with her.

But Rayn was already talking. "I'm guessing you haven't had enough of that. I'm sorry. Even in a life of magic, we tend to operate off of what we can see."

Perhaps inappropriately, this made Xelle think of her older nibling. Vallie had little eyesight; she hadn't since birth. There wasn't a context to share this, so she kept the thought to herself. "Thanks," she managed to say. "I have issues with sleep too." Sleep? Why was she pouring everything out on a taxi? At least she could get whatever this was out of her system before they reached the Tower.

"If you'd like to talk about it, I would be interested. No pressure at all."

No pressure. Finally, for she had difficulty with this, she looked in the per's eyes. There was a kindness there, back behind several layers. Harder layers. And maybe it was a justification, but it suddenly felt nice to be able to talk to someone she wouldn't see again anyway. A stranger on a taxi. There wasn't much there to mess up. She took a breath.

"I have names for some of these things. There's the storm. It's in my mind all the time. Even when I don't think about it, it's there. Just shaking around, like a can of dried cornmeal. No. Like the cornmeal was simultaneously being thrown in all directions in my mind." She tapped a temple, on the other side of the mark. "And then there's the night ivy. Pretty names, right?" She shrugged. They helped her feel less lost. "My mind never rests. It's always thinking and reaching out, growing a thought, then moving to the next. I've learned that I can't stop it, so instead I try to grow with it, drift within its waves. Try to avoid loops or distressing nightpaths. But it's hard. And this is the sleep part. In the day, there's much more. I say the wrong thing. I get flustered. I can't look at pers, or sit near them."

Suddenly she didn't want to say anything else. Not about her reactions, or the way they discredited her, the way pers— "Thanks for listening. If you have something you'd like to say, I'd like to hear it." See, that sounded odd too. Xelle focused out of the window, at the passing homes, which only now started to show breaks, as if the city were a huge pat of soap, releasing side bubbles to become towns and then villages.

"Xeleanor." She snapped to see Rayn's expression, then looked away. "I hope that you'll learn to accept who you are. If you do, then you'll find friends that appreciate you. The rest aren't worth it."

Ay'tea likes who I am. The thought jarred her, and feeling a rush in her chest, she turned away. She felt conflicted. Conflicted by this unknown mission, how long she'd be away, and whether she could put things back to normal with Ay'tea when she returned. What, even, normal meant.

Rayn became quiet, the conversation drifting off. But she did not draw the shade. Instead, she watched out of the windows a while, only breaking to toss the apple core outside, once the roadside was empty. Lulled by the rhythm of the fuelstones and the vroom's feet against the road, it seemed to surprise them both when those rhythms slowed, and the vroom pulled to a halt.

"Toilet here. Good souvenirs." Julla didn't even look back, but walked off in the direction of a low, long building.

Xelle'd had plenty of shopping the day before, and with an unknown time at the Tower ahead, wanted to limit spending until she was back. They did get up, stretching, and headed for the toilet, awkwardly silent as they walked.

Sitting back into the moveroom, Xelle shuffled Essie out of her bag. Her legs were sore and she'd love to pace around longer, but with her bag too heavy to carry and having visions of the moveroom (and her obsidian and spices and good luck charms and fancy mirror) taking off with her doing toe stretches in the greenfloor, she just felt safer getting back inside.

Rayn soon joined her, making a curious face at the substance Xelle was rubbing into her hands. It did have a strong smell. It comforted her.

"Handrub," she explained. "Just congealed alcohol with a little oil. Makes me feel better about using public spaces, especially toilets."

"They did have a sink?" Rayn didn't say it unkindly.

"Makes me feel better," Xelle said with a shrug. "I always keep some in my bag, Essie." She patted the little block-printed bag as she tucked the tin back inside. "He's always here for me."

Rayn's eyebrows rose, but she didn't say anything.

Maybe Xelle was being a bit open with someone who could report back through Mage channels that To'Arc had a Study who might need looking into. "I know, I gendered my bag. I don't mean any disrespect by it, it's just that he's, it's been a friend to me and I like . . . him feeling real. And I don't think it disrespects him since, you know, he's a bag." She grimaced, not sure how the per would take it.

"Gender is complicated anyway," Rayn answered. Xelle was surprised to hear the personal comment from the hu. "I go with dawn gender, and, sure, but— Anyway, it's complicated." Rayn adjusted her turban, and then smiled forward, as if resetting.

Yet this was a subject that got on Xelle's mind, and there was rarely a chance to discuss it. "I think I know what you mean," she said, cautiously. "I relate to dawn genders too, but if you aren't enthusiastic about it, pers say well you must be a cloud gender, or a spark gender, and I think—well, I don't know. What if I'm a dawn gender with elements of a cloud or a spark gender, and then they say oh then you must be a rainbow gender. But it doesn't change, so that's not right. What if it's the whole concept that I can't grasp and I just want to be me? What if I'm just not into it?" She looked up, and exhaled with shaking breath. "It's pretty funny to have hundreds of genders and not one term I can see that fits, huh?"

Rayn was watching her contemplatively and Xelle realized she'd let the taxi talk get a little intense. "But the bag, he's a dusk gender," she said, fumbling for something to bring it back. "I feel sure on that."

They laughed again, this time more quietly but also less awkwardly. Still, the conversation felt heavier now and so when the vroom started up again, they sat quietly for a while, watching the landscape change through the windows as the buildings became smaller and open spaces more frequent.

When the conn had said ze didn't stop while in the city, ze hadn't also added that ze would stop *constantly* once out of it. Sometimes, ze'd pitch some roadside shop or amenity. Xelle wondered if the per had a contract with these places; it would have seemed clear, but ze also stopped to gaze at beautiful rock formations or views, all with a muted enthusiasm that was hard to discern.

Still, the journey passed quickly. Each stop, while still chilly, felt a little less cold than it had before. Xelle enjoyed discussing theories of magic with Rayn, and she seemed to enjoy it as well. Even the idea of Tower secrets—not secrets, more like guarded ideas—was a smidge blurred as Xelle had studied at To'Ever and was from the Region.

They were almost there before the subject of *why* they were traveling to To'Breath even arose. Xelle didn't want to avoid the truth; not to anyone but especially this per, and so she squirmed in place, thinking what to say.

"Well, you know To'Ever," Rayn said. "The Mages don't travel as much, so when there's a task of any sort, they send a Study they trust. Even when it's a short task and they could use magic to speed their travel."

Xelle laughed, nervously. "Obviously To'Arc is all about travel; it's sort of our thing." Not to mention its ties to inkblooms, hence her secret project. "So our Mages are happy to go for most things." Her breath caught, realizing she'd put herself in a corner. If the Mages were happy to travel, then why was she on a task for them? But telling Rayn she was here on exchange felt . . . incorrect. She glanced around, trying to be clever enough to dig the right tunnel.

"If I make my way to To'Arc, I'd be most curious to see the gardens." Rayn turned on her floor cushion.

Did she know about Xelle's gardens? Her mind was starting to fog.

"The other Towers," Rayn continued, "have gardens of color, of grandeur, each striking and unbelievable. Yet I never hear much about the gardens of To'Arc. Vines, of course. Trellises, I imagine? Something makes me feel that without the need to brag about themselves, they might be the most striking of all."

Xelle took calming breaths. Trying not to make those breaths too obvious. "They are, I think. I mean, I agree. They are simple, calm, straightforward, yet with transfixing elegance. They provide a path ahead, yet always a bend to change it. Walking through them . . . gives me peace."

Rayn's eyes looked like she was trying to imagine it.

"And a place to stop, to rest, or to innovate. Frames to hold phyta, or segments of glass to shield the sun. Small, outdoor rooms, really, even usable in the rain or snow because of the vines covering them. Each Mage has a favorite one; at To'Arc favorite garden rooms are more of a culture than favorite moons!" Seeing Rayn's smile, Xelle relaxed some.

They talked about the high-beamed gardens of To'Ever a while, until the moveroom crept to a stop. They looked at each other, stifling a laugh. As they were clearly not at a Tower.

Julla's voice called out. "Last stop. Sunset over the gorge. Toilet isn't the best if you can last another bit."

They both buried their laugher into their respective shirts, until Rayn called back. "Wonderful. Thank you!"

The sun was indeed setting over a sizable gorge, and Xelle, tired now, just sat and watched it and tried not to worry about what it was she should be doing. Quickly, though, she blinked, when Rayn couldn't see. While she knew it wasn't possible, ever since she was a kid she'd had the notion that blinking intentionally could capture an image into one's mind forever. Maybe even into a drawer, where someday one's grandcuras or grandniblings could look through them.

She wished it were so simple. And though it was ridiculous and she'd never tell anyone about it, she blinked. One image of the setting sun as the moons shimmered to life in the sky, and the deep gorge, and the really nice passenger who happened upon the same bizarre ride that she did.

Sometimes, life was just so beautiful. No, she knew, all the time, but sometimes there were those moments. That were . . . sublime.

This time, she waited a little longer, because she could see Julla sitting. And when Julla rose, Xelle did as well, hearing Rayn standing beside her.

Quietly, they got back into the moveroom and settled into place. Julla entered through the front door, the wall still pulled, and shuffled into place. They heard some shuffling, and crunching, as though from a snack, before the fuelstones started up and the vroom pulled off.

Rayn's mouth twitched, and she looked like she was hesitating to say something. She leaned forward and spoke in a low tone, "What's eir legend?" The words drew out.

Xelle didn't know the phrase, but it seemed pretty clear she was asking about Julla's behavior. Or perhaps the question of why ze operated a rather small, yet fully customized taxi then acted rather annoyed by it. "I have no idea." Feeling a welcome release of everything that had built and circled over this trip, she began to laugh. If Julla had an odd taxi, then surely ze had odder passengers. Xelle couldn't help but grin.

As Rayn's smile broadened, she began to sing.

> *Taxi, taxi, I've got a place to go*
> *Taxi, taxi, take me all the way to snow*
> *The moons are gone, the sun is out*
> *Please say your feet can run this route*
> *I've got to know what it's about*
> *Taxi, taxi, fare*

Rayn's voice, while simple by singer standards, was really beautiful, and moved Xelle, as did the melody of the piece, which masqueraded as almost a child's song, but rang with a layer of melancholy.

Though her parents, especially Na Foose, sang a lot, Xelle was not familiar with the tune. She was getting the idea, and maybe even ready to try and join in with a harmony, when Rayn suddenly cut off.

"Look," she whispered, pointing across in the distance. She hesitated, as if wanting a better view but not wanting to move into Xelle's space.

Xelle gestured her over, and they scootched over toward the windows, staring out as the Tower drew into view.

It turned out to be much different to see a Tower for the first time in the moonslight. She wondered, thinking of it, if when the Arc Mages had sent her, whether they knew she'd never been to To'Breath. She'd met visitors from the Tower, and she'd been to Vattam briefly, but she'd never been to To'Breath.

The Tower was partially obscured by rows and rows of rolling hills, arranged with shape and flow and brushed over in a pearlescent glow by the moonslight, as though the world had painted its own art. And rising from it was a single column, reflecting an ethereal shade of white. Xelle had heard that every window in To'Breath was covered in veils, but she could not see them from this distance, only the elegant rise of the Tower gazing over the hills.

Xelle was still staring as they stopped at a wide front circle, which led to a large metal-framed entry building beyond which surely the Breath Atrium awaited. The moveroom slowed again, and Rayn took her bag and hopped down. Xelle expected to follow, but as she considered it, she wasn't sure about making introductions to the night shift. Also, she could use some time to collect herself. About to ask if she could speak briefly to Rayn, she saw that the per was already walking up the path.

She could wait until morning. She could check in then, when she was fresher in mind, and she was sure she would run into Rayn while they were both there. She started to doubt the info they'd shared; maybe Xelle should have had the goals more in mind. Seen if she was willing to share info on To'Breath. On what they knew. Like Rayn had said up front. Here she was, sent on this important mission, and all they'd talked about was stuff.

This was on top of the usual doubts; the raps on doors of her mind after meeting someone, worrying that she'd said too much, not said the right things, or come across strangely. That she should rewind time and try again, this time getting it right. They'd talked about some rather personal topics; she hoped she hadn't gone too far. Or done it wrong. Or—

"This your place," Julla said, pulling open the wall and gesturing forward.

"Yes, but if you're going to the village, I'll take off there?"

Julla nodded, but did not pull the wall as ze curved away down the hill, toward Vi'Breath.

10 – To'Breath

Fortunately, it seemed some cultural elements were common between Tower villages, including lower-cost Nook & Bunks on the Tower side, for those visiting the Tower but without an invitation to sleep within it. The desk clerk warned her that the rooms were cool in the unusual weather, and Xelle smiled politely. Even without getting into her various accommodations during her trip, the cool air and light dusting of snow here in the milder climate of Vi'Breath seemed practically balmy compared to what she'd traveled through. The small space was perfectly fine (and finally, a shower!), though she was ready for the relative luxury of a Tower room and the chance to settle there a bit.

She slept well, a little shocked by how high the sun was when she took back out to the street. Given that she'd be able to rest her bag soon, and her mind would be clearer without the pressure of finding another vroom, she decided to walk the distance between the village and the Tower itself.

The trip to the Tower was uphill, something she should have considered more carefully in this decision, and so her back and knees were aching well before the circle pass drew into view. Fortunately, the road did not rise and fall with the surrounding hills, and more fortunately, the cool, breezy morning prevented her from getting sweaty after her shower. The small things.

It was a very pretty walk. The road wove in between the small, rolling hills, where Xelle could see paths leading to seating areas, white with a thin layer of snow. These were not covered like at To'Arc, but she could imagine sitting in one with the color of spring or the warm sun of summer. Seeing a group of benches, she was tempted to stop, but the idea of finally setting her bag down kept her moving.

To'Breath looked a lot different in the sunlight than it did in the night. What had appeared a smooth, elegant Tower shape in the moonslight actually had a great amount of detail amidst its sleekly shaped exterior. An uneven pattern of little extensions and nubs protruded from the alabaster Tower at all levels. And by the roads taking off from the main circle, Xelle guessed that a complex of smaller buildings rose behind the Tower, cleverly blocked from view.

As she approached the main entrance, worry prickled her all over, to the extent of a feeling of physical sickness. She'd planned on strategizing on the way here from Vattam, but she'd enjoyed the conversation. Then she'd fallen asleep like a wet, dropped towel, mostly spending the walk willing herself to heft her load of mountain obsidian. Xelle realized . . . she had no plan. And she was at the entrance.

"Hi, I was sent here by the Arc Spire to see if you're discrediting one of their Mages, but on the way here I met a dragon, shopped, and made a nice friend," didn't seem an effective way to advance her magical career.

Pers were watching her now—were there specific protocols about walking up to Breath Tower?—and so she didn't have much choice but to proceed in. Worrying her even more was how to look like her bag wasn't weighing on her every bone, which would lead to questions she didn't want to answer.

And so she tried to ignore her own awkward swagger as she walked to the check-in desk, and swung down her bag onto a wide-tiled floor. Again, she had no idea what to say. She put on her best serious face. Confidence. Pure confidence.

"Pleasant winter morning. I am Xeleanor Du'Tam, she or e, a Study at Arc Tower who was sent here on exchange." Remembering, she fumbled for the officially marked paper in a side pocket, alarmed at how it had been pushed into by something in the bag. ("Something," the narrator voice said in her head, "which was probably a giant load of rocks.") Acting as though it were flat as Helia's mirror, she smoothed the crinkled card onto the table, and tried to look aloof.

Or alerf, she joked to herself. That had been a good joke. She stifled a grin.

Perhaps the idea that Xelle was there for suspicious reasons hadn't crossed the mind of the desk clerk, as xe looked completely unconcerned, and reached through several drawers, sliding a few items into a small linen bag embroidered with tiny white flowers, and passing it over with a hefty little book that looked like it'd been read by only a thousand pers.

"Here's information on Tower, structure, regulations, and such. Do you have any questions for me now?"

Xelle forced a polite smile. Yes, how about everything? Or what's the deal with Ascension? "For now, just directions to my room." She hoped she got a separate room and didn't want to think anything else for the moment. Bag so heavy.

"Any accommodations?"

She didn't think she could quite count the extremely heavy bag as a reason to need the first floor, besides she liked high floors anyway. As for her disorders, an inability to summarize her needs into something neat often prevented accommodation in new places. If she lived somewhere, she could explain what she needed, or explain why staying with others would be too much, or explain why certain door handles hurt her arms, or why some lights were too bright, or drafts too unsettling. But in a new place, going through a list always seemed to minimize.

"No," she answered.

"Then fourth floor, thirty-fifth cee. Door locks from the inside. Please keep the window shut unless you're there. Quiet times are listed in the book. Check-in at the Study library desk once you're set. Welcome to To'Breath, Study Xeleanor."

She pretended to be putting something in her bag, then waited until the per turned away to heft it up again. A slight grunt escaped her, and she put a hand over her mouth as if burping. "Yes, thank you."

And Xelle hurried on through the following corridor and looked around to find any lifts, ramps, or staircases.

The Atrium.

There were seven Mage Towers in Alyssia (and of course the fabled City of Halina) and Xelle had been fortunate enough to see three of their Atriums. Suddenly remembering what an honor it was to see another one for the first time, she stopped, shuffling out of the path and sliding her bag to her feet.

The huge space was unusually open, without columns or arches to provide weight and depth. Instead, the primary element was the gorgeous alabaster background itself, reaching out nearly as if to embrace. Yet, not that it was plain. Not at all. Small cosmetic walls protruded at geometric angles, protruding and then ending without apology, each decorated in tiny patterns: lines and irregular shapes that evoked the idea of leaves, flowers, and stems. Platforms rose from the main floor, so well designed that they could function for seating, speaking, lounging, even for the idea of the art itself. Even more entrancing, the room was adorned with colors of white, blue, lavender, some even with breathtaking shimmer or sparkle. Only small patches of life dotted the space, crawling masses of green that looked like they were peeking through a cover of snow. It was decorated for winter, she thought. It must be. It was extraordinary in its design and care.

"Such subtlety," she said aloud, but to herself.

But that was Breath, wasn't it? Subtlety. Reach held close. Suddenly excited about the prospect of exploring this new place, she had one goal in mind.

Smooth drawers, soft lamps, and polished, white trim to frame a lofty, sky blue ceiling: the room was nicer than hers at To'Arc. Though that wasn't entirely on To'Arc since she'd moved most of her possessions into a muddy space under a vroom ramp. That said, if she had a room like this at To'Arc—

Xelle started to feel overwhelmed. There was no place she ever knew if she belonged, or whether that place was somewhere she'd over-looked, or left, and she was so many years in now. She had to stop thinking about it. Not here, anyway.

She set down her bag.

Seven. Spires.

Perhaps, finally unburdened, she should burst onto the tiny balcony—*she had a tiny balcony*—and sing a song of her arrival. At least the idea made her laugh. She did walk out to it for a long moment, the view mostly a few rolling hills and the side of a well-tended service building, not alabaster, but a pretty gray stone.

With relief, she unpacked the items she'd be using while here, and hefted what was left from her bag and pockets: stones (!) and mirror and shopping items from Vattam, as well as her cold weather clothes including the new cape and cap and small cooking items, into a tall drawer and slid it shut, wincing as the drawer glid over effortless tracks and closed with a *thump.*

"Oops, sorry," she said, to the drawer.

Yet the noise had echoed the slamming of her own mind against realizing, balcony solo or not, she was . . . here. To see if someone was undermining Spire Mage Pelir for a confusing and unknown reason.

This felt absurd.

Yet what would she do now, unload the drawers and return back? Fail in the only task the Spire had ever given her? Was it . . . some sort of test, even? For her Petition?

No, the discomfiture on their faces had been sincere, and she had not been at the center of their concern. Or even in it. Deep unease had pulled on the air; she could feel it still. Then, she would do what she could for her Tower. As Na'Vuia had always told her, doubt is a healthy passenger, but never let it conn. This was a new place, a good experience, and—maybe she could find something out.

And not standing here.

First. She wouldn't attempt magic until she better understood the regulations. Besides, Arc Magic would waft through these corridors like cooking with her Na's smoke salt. For now, she was a simple Study on an exchange and she needed to watch her steps. She did, however, closing it carefully this time, use her Na's (another Na's) old trick and position a scrap of paper that would fall if the large drawer were opened.

Normally, she'd have no reason for suspicion, but the unprecedented Mage insurgence concept did have her a little on edge.

She moved toward a framed, oval mirror. Another night had passed, and maybe her magic mark had finally passed like an angry pimple, best unremembered.

It was there.

Finally in good light and with an unbouncing mirror, she leaned in. Delicate lines, almost too precise for the trendiest micropainter, formed an unfamiliar design, in the outline of a square, yet perfectly curved to the arc of her forehead. She hovered her finger over top, and—touched it. Nothing. No pain lingered; her skin was soft.

Perhaps it was an old cast, something left in the mountains, drained of power except to whisper this last stamp. There was nothing she could think to do about it now. Then, to the library. She adjusted her undercap, put her old cap back on, and headed out.

Again lifted by the idea this was a whole new Tower to explore, she felt distinctly bouncy hopping down a wide spiral staircase. It seemed empty, and she got distracted, running her hands on an elaborate enamel of tiny green leaves outlined in gold that wound around the banister top.

"Watch it!" a voice called, and Xelle tripped over herself. In a moment of updraft she gasped, spun back, and the idea of falling onto the hard marble steps flashed in front of her. Briefly, she imagined her last moments. A thin pair of arms caught her, pushing her upward.

She looked around, the lamps of the staircase seeming to flash in her eyes.

"I'm sorry, you just about ran into me!" The hu was lanky, tallish but not tall, and wearing a beautiful gold robe, buttoned down the front. Yet xe was not a Mage. She'd seen Breath Mages before and they followed the same pattern of making sure everyone knew they were Mages. The hu looked irritated.

"I'm sorry." Xelle threw her hands over her mouth, wobbling to stand up. "Totally my fault; I'm really sorry."

"You're well?"

At first Xelle worried at xyr intent, then realized xe was asking for concern. She did just bounce down the stairs, almost knock this hu over, then almost plummet to her demise. Excellent first impression, like always.

"I put down a heavy bag, and . . ." She stopped. *Xelle, what are you doing!* She took a breath. "I'm fine. I just got here, and you know how it is to see a new place. I'm very sorry I knocked you over. I mean, that I almost did. That you caught me. You're good at it." Xelle paused. "Can we start over?" Her hands shook.

"I think I'd prefer it," the hu said, kindly but still with irritation in xyr voice. Strangely, Xelle was relieved at the irritation.

"I'm Xeleanor Du'Tam, she or e, and I'm on exchange from To'Arc. I just got here, like right now, and I really need to do a better job."

The hu kept glancing up the stairs, and she felt bad for detaining xem. She opened her mouth to tell xem to please go ahead.

"I'm Kwillen Du'Satta, e. A Study here. If I can help you get somewhere, I'd like to, but I'm late delivering serums to the low floors, so otherwise maybe we'll run into each other later?"

Xelle caught on eir words. Then she saw eir smile. "Ok, you earned that one. No, I'll be fine. I just . . . I didn't read the book yet."

"Ha! I've been here two years and I refuse to read that flame-charred book. They can't make me. I haven't even returned my copy." Eir grin was slightly sinister. Then e stopped, tossing eir head in the direction of the next floor. "They can wait. What if I get you to the Study Hall? You'll have pers to talk to there, and ask them about going to Morale Night tonight."

"It's really called Morale Night?" Xelle blurted out. She had to stop doing that, and her chest constricted again.

"No. I'm a bit of an ash-kicker. They call it Yellow Room, because." E lifted a hand.

That was apparently the real name. "Will I start to be able to tell when you're serious?"

"Probably not," e answered. "A curse of my life. Also, if that's a quest you've donned, then Kwill. It's fine to call me Kwill."

"Xelle," she replied, not sure what to make of the harried Study. Other than eir saving her life, and all. Maybe she would have rolled to the side or something. Still, that ceiling flashing into her view was not something she thought she'd forget.

She always remembered the most unfortunate things. "I'm supposed to go to the Library table?"

"Library table?"

Xelle searched her mind, but she was rattled again. "I forget what they called it. I need credentials for my research exchange, I think? For the library."

E glanced at her as if not sure whether to reveal that as a visiting Study, her credentials would be limited. Then e probably realized she knew that, and relaxed. "Also through the Study Hall. Come on, though, I do need to go." Kwill turned and started down the stairs, not looking to see if she followed. Which she did.

The Study Hall was familiar. As many ways as there were to arrange tables and resources, all the ones she'd seen looked basically like this, only varying in their décor. It was clear To'Breath liked the texture of small patterns. This room featured them also, and felt unconstrained to switch from one to the other, even switching the soft colors of the walls and furniture with such ease the eye caught the nature of the change rather than what had caused it. (Until further inspection, which Xelle loved to do.)

Like the Atrium, even the phyta appeared seasonal; subdued winter cover peeked up from small beds and livewalls. Xelle imagined that when spring arrived, there might be fresh green, and tiny flowers—the phyta around with Breath Magic centered.

Hopefully she wouldn't be here in the spring.

Realizing that she'd been drifting, she drew her attention ahead. Running into Kwill (as in, literally) after all this would be terrible, not to mention its impact on her efforts not to draw undue attention.

E stopped in the middle of the space. Xelle stopped a good measure back. She thought she saw em chuckle.

"Behold! A whole room without Mages. Pers are pretty easy here, and should be willing to help. If you're interested in Morale Night, just ask anyone to show you the space, as long as they don't look too absorbed. Sorry." E shook eir head. "I'm sure you know how pers work. I'm just not used to this stuff. My Ma hid me in the towel stack whenever we had guests." Glancing at Xelle, e sighed. "Not literally. My physical tending was fine. Now, I really do have to go . . . let's see, research credentials?"

Again, Xelle had made no effort to practice her story about whatever exchange she was conducting. She didn't even quite remember what was on the paper . . . the one now being held at the check-in desk. With a glance to Kwill, she remembered, she just had to get to the table. The desk. Whatever it was. Which was wonderful, because Xelle would have felt awful not telling the truth. She nodded.

"Here, follow me." Off they went again, until they passed under a stunning geometric—not an arch, it wasn't curved—well, overhead thing, constructed with a spinning structure that made it look almost not physically possible. She'd have to come back and study it later.

"Over there. Good luck."

Kwill was almost back out the door when Xelle remembered to thank em. "Hey, thank you. For everything. Perhaps I'll see you."

E waved back over eir shoulder, and was soon out of sight.

And the librarian, well, this was a Mage, was watching her. She supposed she did look out of place. There were reasons Studies could be older, but Xelle still dressed like she was carving wood in a tent on the water side of Tam. She remembered the shopkeep in Vi'Arc, who had told her to be herself. She hoped that was good advice.

And, she definitely appreciated that Kwill had not dropped her off right at the desk, giving her at least a few moments to collect herself. She walked up. "I'm here on research exchange from To'Arc. The Front Desk has the card." She smiled, politely and hopefully boringly.

"Subject of research?"

Fira.

Crown of Helina, what had she thought they were going to ask her? She was too used to running around To'Arc doing her thing. Ok, subject. Not hard to pick a subject. She was not here to learn Breath Magic. Frankly, she was just getting at a point of really understanding Arc Magic, and it wasn't the right time to cloud it, so saying a magic thing could go poorly. But she was a Study. Which meant magic. But magic had many facets and inputs.

Think, think, think.

Ok. She was here to see what people were saying, or doing. Maybe there was, like, a talking thing. What did that even mean, and—she was at the desk and the hu was starting to look irritated—

"History," she said. *History?* Oh, it was printed on a class ledger on the wall behind. She'd seen it and just, what, said it? Well, she couldn't change it now.

"Yes, hello. I'm here on exchange to study Alyssian history. Xeleanor Du'Tam, Study at To'Arc. You . . . you have the best history here. Wonderful records. On history." She fumbled in place, sure she had just ruined everything. "I get nervous," she added. *I get nervous?*

The hu . . . beamed. What else had she done? Trying to recover, Xelle gave a little flourish, and made the sign of the Arc. Then, realizing that might not be preferred, the sign of the Crown. Was that too much?

"The other Towers don't respect us enough, you know," the hu opined. "So it takes my notice when one has a keenness of our assets, even if they only value them for a Study."

Xelle forced a smile.

"We have the most in-depth historical records of the whole Crown," xe bragged, raising a hand to xyr chest. "Your access will be limited, but not so much as in a topic of casts."

"Of course," Xelle said, politely. And she took note of, after the Mage had written her some sort of pass card, the hand signal that xe flashed. It reminded Xelle of a puff of air, made by the fingers. Hoping it would not be too much, Xelle flashed it back. *A Breath,* she reminded herself. The Mage smiled.

Now she knew four signs. Which, really, was pretty sweet.

Way too tired and distracted to do too much more, Xelle pocketed the card, and went back out into the Study Hall. Finding a group that looked friendly enough, she asked, not remembering the name of Kwill's Morale Night, if there were any social activities. She did have to act delighted hearing there was one tonight, and a stout, gruff Study gave her a full account of how to get there.

Then, hoping it wouldn't reflect too poorly on her (hopefully no one was like, watching anyway), she went back to her room and pulled a chair onto the balcony for a while, staring out the window from afar. The snow was falling again, lightly, but swirling in a chaotic fashion that she thought both To'Arc and To'Breath would appreciate, for different reasons. Not To'Frond. But they never had snow.

She took a breath. Was Ay'tea at home, watching that snow now? It was a romantic notion, the idea of watching the same snow, and she should not be thinking romantic notions of her lab partner. Or should she? It was so confusing, and again, she remembered she could not make decisions now.

Helia wouldn't be watching the snow. Helia didn't need to; with her money, she could hire a hu to dress as snow and dance on her giant balcony. But, that was unfair. Helia was kind; she'd always been kind to Xelle. Not just kind. Xelle liked being around her. Suddenly the image of them kissing came to life, and Xelle felt awkward. What had happened to her these last days? Maybe no more lavender drinks.

She sighed.

Opting for the soup mix she'd brought with her over the room's tiny stove, she didn't go out for dinner. She was spinning already with all the pers she'd met. All the pers she'd left. How she'd done nothing right with any of them. How not long ago, she'd felt confident in her work, her abilities, and suddenly she'd landed on a different road, trying to see through this whirlwind.

That was fine. She'd get back to it. She always had, and always would.

The social event was in a windowless room off a pretty mezzanine, and it went like all the social events where she didn't know anyone going in, and like most of them where she did. She milled around the room, sat at empty tables that no one joined, stood again, and finally resorted to examining the Breath-style art across the bright yellow walls.

She realized, she hadn't really even asked if Kwill would be here; perhaps e'd mentioned it for her benefit alone. And Rayn—she'd really enjoyed meeting the To'Ever Study, even sitting back awkwardly against the sides of a frequently-stopping moveroom. She pictured the tall hu, shifting her legs around the low cushion, trying to get comfortable. Would she know of this?

No one resembled Rayn, or even wore the style of dress that Xelle presumed to be from Sharre. Thinking of it, she couldn't recall that style in To'Arc, and even when she was down in To'Frond, she had no specific memories of it. Maybe it was simply Rayn's own look.

The event didn't seem as forced as Kwill had implied. Pers joked, laughed, even sang. A few sat around puzzles or games. Pers were so young here, she realized. Did Xelle look this old at To'Arc, as well? Ay'tea, he was older—maybe she hadn't looked in the mirror.

She stopped. Certainly Helia's gift wasn't some sort of prompting. She didn't think she'd do that.

Kwill.

So glad to see a familiar face, Xelle rushed across the room, slowing down when she saw the hu watching with an eyebrow raised.

"Hi. If I may? I'm just . . . bad at parties."

E leaned over, whispering as several more pers approached. "I am too, but new Studies always want to get to know me when they learn about my family."

"Well, I nearly knocked you over then made you late," she said.

"I noticed," e said with a laugh.

"And I'm here now because I've had an overwhelming few days, I keep meeting pers—some . . . extraordinary—and all I ever do is say goodbye."

Xelle realized she'd been far too personal, as the hu's eyes blinked and e turned momentarily away. Spinning back, e gestured to a pair of Studies who had just arrived at their side.

"Hello. This is my friend Xeleanor. She's here on exchange."

"I'm studying history," she added, raising her hand to offer the Breath.

By the impressed tilt to Kwill's eyes, she was glad to see she'd done it right.

11 – Nothing to See Here

A week had passed since Xelle's first day in To'Breath, and she thought she was going to have to head back to Tam for as little as she'd found for the Arc Spire Mages. She pictured them in long robes and shaped caps, perpetually waiting around their glossy table as in a cartoon, arguing that they'd sent the wrong per. She tried to tell herself it didn't matter, but they'd trusted her, and she didn't like to let people down. And Pelir . . . something serious was going on and even if Xelle was just one vine of investigation, what would it mean to return empty-handed? What if there was some key here, some little hint, and all she had to do was notice it?

It was hard to notice anything. One difficulty with having picked history as her purported exchange subject was that everyone expected she'd spend her time poring through the history section of the open library, absorbed in old books for hours.

Xelle did love old books—communicating over time exceeded the abilities of magic—but there were practical matters involved. In her mind she'd imagined sacred, almost glowing pages with intricate gold illuminations clearly highlighting topics to browse. Well, none were clear at all. Some were very pretty; that was true. They were also worn, sometimes stained. Sometimes weirdly stained, as if no one had informed a previous Study that they were sipping soup over a future revered artifact. And most of them poofed up a cloud of dust with every new page that got right into her nose just as many times.

Enough so, that a Mage was called in to offer her a small inhalant. She didn't know what was in it, but as it kept her from sneezing over every book in their library, she decided not to ask.

There were newer books, of course, summarizing history, analyzing it, and contextualizing it with modern perspectives. And if she were a Mage, surely she'd go to that row, and seek what she needed. But she was a Study! And she was here to study! And so, she decided, she was better off meeting their expectations for a bit and using the time to decide how she could try and learn what the Arc Spire had thought she could learn. The more she came up blank, the more she couldn't understand why she'd been sent at all.

The upside of her time in the library was that, while most of the books were no more than dusty propaganda or obligatory research, a few were rather fascinating. Accounts of events she'd never heard of before, told in intense tones that indicated an urgency that no longer existed—not in the corridors of any Tower she'd visited. Most interesting of these were the allusions to conflict. She had learned in first classes that Alyssia had not always been so peaceful, but it sounded like the shift of a mountain into place, not a real and scattered fear caused by pers with names and clashing objectives.

While the books sometimes alluded to these conflicts, they never detailed them. Maybe those accounts were restricted to Breath Studies, or even Mages. It made no sense they did not exist.

For the first few days, Xelle kept an eye open in the Study areas for Rayn, figuring she'd walk through at some point and Xelle could say hi. By the time she considered maybe she was working in another section of the Tower or whether it would be appropriate to ask after her, Xelle remembered she had said she was only planning to be here a day or two, so she was likely all the way back to To'Ever by now. Disappointed, she put her brief traveling companion in the bin of fun memories from the trip, but otherwise out of her mind.

She started to contemplate whether it would be wise to tease out a few detection casts. Detection was a middling cast, but one Xelle had worked a lot on in her early years at Arc. She supposed back then it made her feel powerful, in the way pers wanted magic to make them feel, but without casting something so loud or distinct it would draw the attention of the Mages.

And she felt absolutely poofed when she realized that detecting Breath Magic, and certainly worrying about it for the last while was entirely pointless. The whole Tower was full of Breath Magic. Was she going to bust open every door in the Tower and declare, "Ha! It's you!" That was somehow doing magic . . . right here where it was supposed to be done?

There were other magics, of deception or such, but again, the Breath Magic had been detected at To'Arc. So she couldn't think of any of her skills in magic that would help, even if she wasn't worried about going around spraying Arc Magic without knowing whether that was even within the rules.

She tried to ignore her feelings of dismissal that they didn't need to send a caster in the first place, and instead, she tried to talk to pers. At meals, in the corridors, in the library. In the more casual conversations, no one indicated anything suspicious or Arc-related at all. As for a more directed strategy, it became quickly clear that while she could try to learn specific things from specific pers, walking around the Tower irritating Studies when she couldn't ask the one question that she had was simply not a plan.

And, yes, only Studies. She'd barely been invited around any Mages at all (mostly the sneeze-alleviator, as the library Mages were too harried to chat), and given that she'd presumably been sent here to study some books then go home, what was it that she'd even ask?

She was taking too long, and worse, she had no idea what to do better. No way to figure out anything. It seemed pretty . . . normal here. At least in the Study Hall and library. No big conspiracy; just a lot of Studies hanging around and being rather serious about their work. Her body sunk at the weight of it. Nowhere to go. No path.

On top of that, she'd been added to the list of pers eligible for Study errands. At first, she didn't mind, thinking it got her out of the library. But the errands were annoying, and it was quickly clear after her third one that she was being tagged much more frequently than the Breath Studies, who never got them days in a row. Not such a subtle message for a Tower known for subtlety, she grumbled.

Xelle let a rather vocal sigh as she slid a book onto an old, carved bookcase, and turned to apologize to the Mage who was walking over, down the long skinny row. The Mage was young, not much older than Xelle perhaps, and kept xyr dress simple, with a modest sash and only three indistinct tokens. Xyr expression was flat, made somehow more prominent by the tight-fitting cap that xe wore.

"I'm sorry," Xelle said. "I'll try to be more careful." She knew how to stand up for herself when needed, but angering library Mages over loud sighs wasn't on her list.

"You're the Study from Arc?" The Mage twisted a little, as if distracted.

Xelle had a distinct impression the Mage knew the answer to that was yes, but took the point to start an exchange. So, then, it wasn't about the sigh. Probably about why the flames she was here. She should absolutely be on her way. Except . . . she'd been trying to talk to a Mage. Maybe she should play this out. As long as she kept her slate blank, she'd be fine. She pushed herself to focus.

"I am," Xelle answered politely. "Xeleanor Du'Tam, she or e. I'm studying history."

She expected the Mage to probe further, as in which aspect of history: the obvious question. But it was as if xe knew Xelle was just randomly reading books and wanted to spare them both the embarrassment.

Perhaps she was inventing all this. But it was her impression, and of all of Xelle's difficulties in the world, she'd learned to trust her impressions.

"The Mages are concerned here," xe said, rather blandly.

Xelle hesitated. No one was obligated to introduce, but the lack of introduction set a tone, if intentional.

Xyr neck twitched. "Thyra, e."

Rather simple for someone who could have at least added 'Du'Breath'. Xelle nodded. "Breath Mages? Concerned. About what?" she asked, giving the book a final pat before turning around.

"The Ascension. Your Crown Mage is retiring. We've heard . . . disturbing things about Arc Mage Pelir. You must be concerned also." Eir eyes darted to the side.

At that moment, when Xelle looked at Thyra, she understood a few things. First, Thyra struggled to communicate. Xelle knew a version of this feeling, and so knew that the Mage was serious about whatever e was doing, to toll emself this way. And, yes, Thyra was a Mage. To walk around so boldly impersonating one, even taking library duty, would require higher stakes than talking to a Study, who could be invited to a score of other places. On top of that, e was a Breath Mage. Skilled in the study of subtlety magic; there were many ways e could hide and listen and learn, without turning the magic. Yet, e'd chosen to approach her directly, cornering her in the stacks like a distracted friend.

Which meant, she thought, whatever e was trying to find out, it wasn't on behalf of To'Breath, who could pull her into a room and speak in private as normal business. So, then, for whom did Mage Thyra work?

She considered just asking. Seriously, like, we both seem aware here, what's going on? Yet there were so many unknowns, so many risks. So, she kept her slate clean until she could think more, simply answering the question.

"Yes, I am concerned. Especially hearing what they are saying about Spire Mage Pelir, who everyone says is just. Pelir's integrity is not my concern."

As soon as she said it, she flinched. Xelle didn't actually know the truth of Pelir, she just presumed it from what she'd seen and heard. Suddenly it struck her: what would a world be like without trust? "My concern is why someone would say it," she added. Should she ask who? Was that too direct?

Thyra glanced away. "I wonder if there is enough concern at To'Breath."

"To'Arc," Xelle offered, and Thyra nodded. "Seems clear there would be." She wanted to ask what the per knew. It seemed too obvious a question. She struggled, thinking what to say or ask, when the Mage again spoke.

"If Pelir does not ascend, then who will ascend?"

Well, that was a good question. One she wanted to turn away from for now. "What do you know of Arc Spire? Of its Mages?"

Thyra's eyes narrowed. "Not much. I don't live there. You must know a lot about them."

No, this wasn't how it worked. Xelle had indicated her faith in Pelir, showing which side she was on of whatever this was. Thyra didn't need to toss the pitcher, but e could do better than a non-answer. Condescending, too. She didn't care if e was a Mage; they had to be close to the same age, and they could probably help each other out. She just needed to ask em. "You must know a lot about To'Breath. I'm not familiar with the ranking Mages here; your insight would be valuable to help me navigate this exchange. And maybe other things."

"I'm far from ranking." Eir hand moved in a rhythm. "Not connected to power. Your exchange, let's—"

"You know what's going on and said there was concern. It might help me if—"

"I shouldn't discuss this with a Study."

Xelle stood silently, her heart pounding. And by the twitch in Thyra's face, e regretted the jab, the attempt to solicit a shift. She at least took satisfaction in that. "Yes, I do agree." She turned around to leave. She'd been going to lunch. She'd go to lunch. And think. She walked away.

"Xeleanor."

Irritated, she did not turn around.

"Xelle."

Stopping, she turned, just shy of the end of the row.

"Sorry," e said. "I'm sorry. This . . . will make me think."

Without a response, Xelle turned and left the library, off to enjoy a spicy seitan stew, served with the decision that whatever she was going to do here at To'Breath, she needed to do it.

Nothing had come to her the rest of that day nor the day after her strange encounter in the stacks, and at some point she really did have to figure something out or just go back. Running Breath errands instead of practicing her casts or working on her garden, or—

Frustrated, she'd taken a trick that had helped her before, and set down a piece of paper, writing down every idea that she had. It was an unimpressive list.

Read more history books until you have an idea (no!)

Hang out in Study Hall and get bolder on topics

Poke around this huge Tower like a weirdo for . . . something?

Storm into Breath Spire and demand satisfaction

~~Helia's mirror is enchanted and we can talk~~ (just glassssss)

Find Thyra again and be like here's the deal – *JUST ASK*

Tell Kwill everything; e's clever

Just go home – deal with consequences

~~Why did they pick me for this~~

~~I made a whole (place) but can't do this~~

She'd been in her room too long already today, staring at this nothingness, and she finally dragged out into the corridor determined to reach new ears, no matter how hard it was for her or what they thought of her for it. The Atrium. The corridors. She was not going to spend another day staring at those books. Her conversation, as it were, with Thyra had elevated the urgency in her mind. That this was bigger than Arc Spire, that there was the possibility of outside influence. But who? Who would want to hurt Pelir or even To'Arc? More needed to be done, even if she had no idea how to do it. She turned to close the door. Clipped to it was a Tower card, covered in neat handwriting.

"Ugh," she groaned aloud, figuring her neighbors were growing used to her at this point. Receiving another errand when she'd already done several was an injustice she didn't think she could protest. After all, she was the guest.

At least this errand sounded easy. No finding random people and trying to figure out the protocols. This was just gathering ingredients and having them mixed, for use in potions.

The supply rooms were huge here, as she could imagine for a magic based heavily on physical reagents. But they were well-organized, and Xelle made her way through. She double-checked and triple-counted each one, then proceeded to the checkout to show her list. After a minute of writing things on ledgers, they told her where the mixing station was. A hu tapped the countertop. "Be nice," xe said.

Be nice? What did xe think she'd do?

She felt less nice when she saw the tremendous line at the mixing station.

Everyone in line was a Study, as far as she could tell. That figured. The Mages probably mixed in their own labs or somewhere else. She thought of her and Ay'tea, running their own lab, really, as senior Studies. She was getting the impression that would never happen here.

At the thought of Ay'tea, a funny pang hit her again, and she pictured his face, his tight smile. In a lot of ways, this whole trip felt like another world; like she'd left her own for a while, pushed it back, just at a point when she had decisions to start considering. Did the world work that way? Was there a divine being of pause? If so, convincing the Arc Spire to send her on an apparently pointless mission was a dramatic way of accomplishing it. Away from Ay'tea, and Helia, and away from her inkblooms. She couldn't even feel the thread she'd tied to the little phyta anymore—it was meant to be quiet, so she thought she'd know if it had broken or resonated distress. Just another situation she wasn't tending while she wandered around here doing nothing. And then there was Thunder.

Oddly, Thunder wandered in and out of her thoughts like zhey lived behind a curtain. Sometimes Xelle replayed the key moments, from the feel of zhem landing to the shock of seeing all the other dragons. And other times, Xelle could only hear the memories at a distance, as if they were too overwhelming to put forward.

Thinking about Ay'tea could be like that too. Except she would not have to confront how she felt because she would never make it to the front of this line. On top of that, and the long wait in line accompanied by an iced coffee, Xelle needed to use the washroom. Kinda bad.

Just as she was thinking of asking if her spot could be held, she made it to the counter, and hefted up the carrying tray she'd checked out from the supply rooms. "Hi," she said with a forced smile, as she was now also hoping she hadn't pulled anything in her back. "Need to get these mixed."

"I'm Nenn, he. New here?"

Xelle nodded. "I'm on exchange. I think I've got the instructions, but please let me know if anything's off." She pointed to the card.

He smiled, leaning slightly over the counter. "The mixing of base reagents becomes critical when you get to making the potion."

"It sounds interesting," Xelle said, not wanting to linger when the line was long behind her, even if she didn't really have to *go*. He was looking right at her so her eyes moved back and forth a bit. "Do I wait over there?" She pointed off to the side.

Nenn shrugged and started to reach for the tray.

"Would it be fine if I stepped away? For a—"

The hu picked up the tray and started to turn around, but then halted in place. He turned back to Xelle. "Oh, no, I'm sorry. These weren't in here evenly and they've fallen over. I can't mix them like this, not without their labels. Once you can set them up, please get back in line and I'll do my best to help you."

He pushed the tray back over the counter. Someone behind her made a noise like a waterball falling, and bewildered, she stepped aside, her view of Nenn blocked as she stared confused at the tray. Realizing she was losing time, she set it on a bench next to a statue of something or other, and rushed to put the liquid vials upright, ignoring the sprigs and other items for now. At least one had spilled, and not understanding what she was doing, she had no idea if there was enough, or if it—

She had to pee bad.

Well, she wasn't going to get in the line again and waste all that time, and she wasn't going to let him see her eyes tear up from his flame-scorched window. Collecting herself, she tried to think about anything else.

But all the other things that came to mind were far away too. Ay'tea. Helia. Her teachers. Thunder. Her parents. She was here by herself.

She was not by herself.

"Yes, we've told them," Kwill said, setting a hot cup of tea in front of her. "He's a master ash-hole, third class. Does it with enough variation that no one can prove it. And you don't want to be the one to raise the issue. Not if you're a Study. Not if you want access to the precision mixers."

"That's terrible!" Xelle had seen that several times—there were abusers that were dealt with, and then others who carried selective invisibility, until enough of their victims pointed the same way. But in a position of such relative power, it was especially rankling. "I feel like everyone knowing it is quite enough proof?"

"I agree. But he's used by Studies and only infrequently lower floor Mages, and the next layer up doesn't need the drama. Or they're all scared of him too; who knows."

"We need a revolution." As soon as she said it, Xelle remembered this wasn't her Tower.

Kwill grinned. "Word is, he resents Studies because he 'dropped out' himself, but he works in the Tower because he can't lose the influence of it. And worse, everyone has just learned to accommodate him."

Xelle noted that Kwill didn't address her point.

"Besides, revolutions need leaders," e added.

They fell into silence. She would have asked why Kwill didn't do it, but e had an uneasy look in eir eyes.

"So how do you get your ingredients not thwacked?" she asked instead.

"You butter his biscuit," e answered. "Not any oil blend either, but the good stuff, like Frond Region avocado charmnut butter."

Perhaps this was getting too literal.

"Oh, Nenn," e continued, not really in mockery but with genuinely tangible irritation, "you're so great, oh Nenn, you look so good today, oh Nenn, I'm so grateful for your help."

"Does he at least mix them well?" Not the point, but she couldn't help be curious.

"Well enough." E set down the teacup. "Xelle. I know pers. This was supposed to be a quick errand—they don't care who does it. I'll take it to someone I trust and turn it in for you. If you don't mind, let me go alone; she's trying to keep it in the basement that she's got a whole secret lab."

Xelle coughed wildly, wrenching to the side and reaching quickly for her clothie.

Kwill, politely, continued. "I trust you, but she doesn't know you, so I'd rather not put her in that position. That works for you?"

Grateful, Xelle pushed the tray over to indicate her consent. Then rubbed a little alcohol on her hands and slid the tin back into her pocket.

"That smells good," e said.

She was about to say what blend she used, but e'd glanced at the list. "Great. Easy stuff. I'll do this later. I promise; it'll get in."

"You don't have to promise me anything," Xelle said, grinning. "I trust you."

Kwill stared at the card a little longer, then looked up. "What's Arc Magic like? If you don't mind?"

Xelle perked up at this; the opportunity to discuss something familiar to her. Except, could she? "The thing about Arc Magic, and I've studied two other prongs so I have that perspective, is that it's the hardest to describe. I am sure that Breath Magic is equally complex, but it's quite simple to tell someone that you make potions and they do things." She snapped up. "Was that offensive?"

"No, makes sense. Give it a spin?"

She took a breath, staring at the wall and trying to concentrate. "As you know, the phyta who guide us at Arc are wanderers. Vines and rootthreads and certain covers and such. And like their magic, what they do is . . . grow. Grow and move and find and change. It's like a gem so big and so complex that one could spend one's whole life studying communication magic, only seeing through that facet, and think they are seeing everything. But then, for example, travel magic, is a second facet. And on and on, getting into bonds and pulls, and I still, honestly, truly think, that the gem is wedged into the rock and we're only seeing the start of it."

Falling back against the seat, Xelle laughed. "All that and I've told you nothing. I'm sorry; there's no reason to withhold a description. It's just *complicated.*"

Kwill stared at her, not rudely but as if e was thinking about a topic that Xelle couldn't even see.

"You love Magic," e said, quietly.

Did she? Yeah, she really did. Xelle nodded.

"I was forced to go here. Everyone goes here. Family honor."

She could have told em, 'Do what's right for you.' Or, 'They don't control you.' But e hadn't asked. And e knew that, anyway. E'd probably been told that again and again. Frankly, it annoyed her when pers told her the same thing. They were solving an equation when they didn't know the inputs, the outputs, or the formula. Xelle thought a moment, if it would be appropriate to say anything. She did. "I can't judge your situation. But as an official Arc Study, I can tell you, there are nearly always more paths than those that first appear. And if you ever need to talk, let me know."

E sat, looking rather small. Xelle felt awkward. "Am I allowed to cast?" she finally asked. "Arc Magic, to be clear."

"Not really." Kwill smiled, brightening a little. "But you're in my room and if you keep it easy no one will get huffed about it."

Xelle nodded. This would be more difficult than normal. Surrounded by unfamiliar objects, none of the right phyta, and agitated from her attempt to mix reagents, it would be harder to connect with the arcs of being. Yet they'd told her, the Spire Mages, that she was ready to be a Mage. She could do this.

But, what to do? Much of Arc Magic wasn't visible, would require extensive time, or certainly consent. Something simple then. Movement. Connection. She remembered her and Ay'tea's first days in the lab, introducing simple casts to amuse each other, and she pulled a tiny piece of light from Kwillen's center lamp, with an expensive pod that gave off warm yellow tones. Letting her eyes close, she sensed a Tower-issue lamp in the outside corridor, and brought in a little blue light from that, drawing it in.

Startled, something changed through her closed eyelids, and opening them, she realized Kwill had cast something also, something released from a small instrument. The room had dimmed, letting the yellow and blue dots of light glow brightly, like in a glowplant marsh. Smiling and rushing into it like the waterfall on a warm day, she threaded the lights together until they turned two shades of green, then moved them, pulling their essence, and creating a large vine floating across the room.

Xelle hadn't cast for so long that her material was forcefully free, and so she leaned into it, drawing and feathering, like the most beautiful doodle. Then, letting it go, they sat silently as it faded away.

Joy coursed through her. Excitement. Why would she run around To'Breath without a plan when she could make a plan? She felt excited to do something, anything. She needed to do something.

Kwill tapped on a metal tube, and squinted eir face, and the room drew back to its normal lighting. "What did it do?" e asked, a little breathless.

Suddenly Xelle was confused. "You could see it?" She didn't know of any limitations to Kwillen's eyesight but—

"I could see it. Beautiful! I'm saying what did the cast achieve? What was the magic?"

She air-snorted a little, then covered it up like she was trying to answer. "It was just supposed to be pretty. And show you some Arc Magic. And maybe make you smile."

E burst into a big grin. "With skill like that, you should be a Mage!" The mistake was realized immediately. Xelle was years older than the Breath Study, about seven from what she'd learned. By normal accounts, she *should* be a Mage.

Why wasn't she a Mage? Perhaps it was the same answer as why e wasn't telling eir parents that e wouldn't be a Study. The answer: Not everyone's business.

It felt like they'd communicated the thought together, and now they both smiled.

Xelle leaned forward. "So—Should Be Mage Xelle's searches aren't going well and I'm not sitting in that library one more day. I need to talk to some of the Breath Mages. Ideas?"

Kwill didn't seem challenged by the question. "Sure, if it doesn't matter which Mages, just request interviews. See who pops up."

12 – Pop Up Mages

One might have thought that Mage interviews would be fascinating, no matter the subject. But Xelle, in order to have some documentation of why an unknown Arc Study was requesting the valuable time of Mages, had to link it to her exchange topic. Which was, generically, 'history'. Which basically gave interested Mages license to discuss . . . anything that had happened. Before now.

And so she spent the next several days meeting with the strangest assortment of Mages the Tower had to offer. At least, she hoped.

Meaning—on the scale of good strange to bad strange, well she wasn't going to call most of it good strange.

First, there were the history buffs. They were so excited that Xelle wanted to learn from them, that rather than asking her interests for the exchange, they gushed on for hours about what they felt most interesting. Xelle learned a lot—like, a lot a lot, but she found nothing having to do with why someone might be using Breath Magic to influence the Arc Tower Ascension, and she thought her face might crack from how long she had to hold it in expressions of interest—often amidst torrents of unfollowable detail.

Then, there were the . . . well, she didn't have a better way to phrase it . . . old pers. They had lived history, so they wanted to tell her? Half the time, Xelle felt like an outlet for the fact that no one wanted to hear their stories anymore. Sure, she wanted to be kind, but it's one thing to be kind for a conversation, or two, or three, and another thing to hear someone drone on with no variation in tone for four hours, making all sorts of rather natural sounds on top of that. And then going down side paths about their own families and contacts as if there was no question Xelle would want to hear any of it.

Again and again, she attempted to lean the conversation toward any topics of relevance. Tension between Arc and Breath. Stories about Ascension. Mage scandals. Even, very carefully leaned into, internal rebellions. But nothing. Absolutely nothing. She could suggest that maybe the Mages were straying from the topics for sensitivity but she just didn't get that. They wanted to talk about what they wanted to talk about.

Yes, she was grateful for their time and effort. But her time and effort was relevant too, and each day was another after which she might pack up and go back with absolutely nothing. She reminded herself, these were the pers who offered to do this. This was not a random data sample. While she was not going to question Kwill's judgment—e did get her with a lot of Mages—she was questioning . . .

Ashes, she was questioning everything.

She walked into a small discussion room, glancing at her sheet of paper before she sat down. An art piece made of metal circles and lacquered twigs hung on the wall. She'd been in this room at least twice, but here she was, sitting again with nothing to do, and she would stare at the art again.

A per walked in.

"Hello!" Xelle stood and offered the Breath, which no longer even felt new in her fingers, as many times as she'd done it.

He (info in the notes) returned it, and then sat, just where she'd been sitting.

So that was fine. She picked up her papers and moved to the other side of the table. "As you know, I'm a Study from To'Arc, and I'm on an exchange related to history. However—" (Again, she tried to frame it to prevent a general rambling of history but it appeared he was going to interrupt.)

"I love history. Was glad for the opportunity to meet."

So that was fine. "Yes, as I am. While I'm here studying history, I'm looking for opportunities to better understand links between Towers.

And have they changed over time or always been as strong as they are today." She smiled politely.

"Oh, yes! Have you heard about Rebuses on the Lake?"

This sounded different. Except usually 'the Lake' referred to Heart Lake, in the center of Alyssia.

"ROTL?" he offered, not waiting for her response, and pronouncing it like 'rowtl'.

"I'm not familiar?" she said, trying to get a sense where this was going and whether she should nip it in the bud.

"Oh, you're in for a treat." He scooted forward and Xelle was certain her eyes opened wider.

"ROTL is a group of Mages from different Towers, who get together at a new location around the Lake—it changes every year—and we enact a scenario. Depending on who put it together, it can be a scripted intro, or we just put on sigils, interact and see where it goes."

"Wow," Xelle said. "So is it related to real historical scenarios, or—"

"It is completely fiction. That's what's great! Our lives are so controlled, and scheduled, and based on what the Tower wants us to do, right? And for a couple of weeks we can really get out and be ourselves. It's exactly what you're talking about."

"That's really nice. I'd love to hear more sometime—"

"Well I can tell you about last year. A Charm Mage was running it, and I admit even with what people think about To'Breath, we weren't sure that a Charm Mage would be able to rub in the grit that . . ."

"I'm fed up! Fed! Up!" She circled around Kwill's room. E preferred talking in eir private room, alluding to magic keeping pers from listening in.

"We won't start rumors, either, I'm aro."

She'd glanced at em in some irritation at this, then been unable to hold it at eir amused, nearly sparkling, grin.

"Fed up?" e answered now, barely reacting to her rant. "With the interviews? It's only been a few days." She'd admitted to Kwill she was looking for something specific, but had tried to protect em from the details.

"I swear, Mages are entirely awful. How do they outrank us?" She didn't mean it, of course, and that was a lovely thing about Kwill—e'd let her get things out without feeling obligated to hush on every unfair, private word, uttered in exasperation. E trusted her.

"This last per refused to talk about *anything* other than his ROTL." With a glance to Kwill, she could see e wasn't familiar. "It's larping. Cross-Tower Mage larping. They do it at Heart Lake."

Kwill's eyebrows took an interested tilt. "I didn't know that was a thing. For Mages, I mean. That sounds really cool."

Xelle's arms waggled around as if she were turning into a balloon puppet, but she just was out of . . . *everything*! "I know! I'm sure it's awesome! But I've been here, out of my element, everyone is new, and mixing potions, going somehow from no rank to less rank, and all the while the whole scorched Ascension could be in danger. Maybe he likes sledding too—or crochet! Crochet is lovely! Or tall ladders! This isn't the time." Kwill's mouth was open, but she kept going. "In fact, I tried at least five times to turn the subject back to Tower relationships. When I finally gave up, I thought maybe he'll tell me in the larp. Like the larp will explain which character is sus. What a plot twist! Honestly, someone should write that story. If xe knew more about larp. But *I* know about being sent away, right when some serious stuff was happening in my Tower, and I can't do anything about it. I. Am. Totally. Useless." Her mind was completely spinning, now, and—

Kwill raised an arm, and Xelle knew immediately she'd spent all her tickets on spouting questionable but well intended stuff. Except, maybe that last bit hadn't been so well intended. She sighed, ready for the speech.

"I'm not here to lecture you, Xelle. But that last crap gets flushed." Irritated, she scrunched her face.

"And I'm not sure if you realized that you just spilled out that the Arc? Ascension is in jeopardy and you're looking for, like, a suspect? So if you're ready to talk, I'm ready to listen. Unless you want me to find more Mages for a chat. I know a hu who is extremely into harp manufacturing, tuning, and ensembles, and I could get you two—"

Xelle made a huge fart noise with her mouth, which both told Kwill what she thought of eir comments and hopefully served to reset the whole conversation, after, well, she didn't realize she'd said all that, but sure. Time for it. Kwill looked slightly horrified and so she continued.

"I'm seven years older, remember? A lifetime of wisdom. And practice in rude noises. Ok! I was sent here because someone is using Breath Magic to discredit Spire Mage Pelir, who is the likely candidate to ascend to the Crown when Crown Mage Jehanne retires." She waved a hand. "It sounds pretty unsubtle when I say it like that, but anyway that's essentially what they told me." She hadn't mentioned it was the Arc Spire who'd *sent* her but e could figure that out if e wanted. "Except I have nothing to work off of and the more I consider the exchange the more asinine it sounds. I've seen nothing suspicious. Why would I? It makes no sense." Her voice rose a bit in frustration. "I'm a *Study*, not an *operative*."

Kwill let an extremely long sigh, then went to eir cabinet, from which e brought back a long, tall bottle, and then a short vial. E lifted the bottle. "This is the good stuff. I may have forgotten to tell you I'm rich." E lifted the other arm. "This is a headache potion. The stuff will still knock us on our asses if we aren't careful, but this will at least prevent any unpleasant effects we don't otherwise cause."

Bringing out two glasses, they first split the potion, then e poured them both a glass of what turned out to be somewhere between wine, fine vinegar, and an herbal syrup. And that was probably not a good enough way to describe it, but it was delicious, and lent itself to sipping, which Xelle did, remembering Kwill's caution.

"So, yes," e said, "Mages are entirely weird. The whole lot. I can say this as I grew up around them. Even my sarents were Mages, my great-sarents. Totally unhealthy, I assure you. Try getting through midschool surrounded by velvet-robed adults who think if they don't turn simple statements about lunch into legendary banter they'll lose their pledge."

"You clearly have issues," Xelle commented, noting whatever was in the glass was already settling her nerves, at least the top cloak of them.

"Loads," e answered, bracing eir slippered feet right up against the elegant tabletop. "But back to yours, it's quite funny that you mention you are not an operative. I'd laugh if I didn't like you. I mean, you've got the feel of the place by now? Right? That's what we do. Operative Tower, basically." Seeing her expression, e paused. "To'Breath is dedicated to stealth, subtlety, and the tiniest elements of nature. So, yes, that they sent an Arc Study to Breath as if you'd thwart someone that powerful at Breath? You're right. It's asinine." E took a little sip and raised the glass. "That's no frost on you."

Xelle would have normally said 'then why' but it was clear Kwill was not done.

"First, if you've studied at three other Towers, you've surely noticed that Breath is the one often looked down on." E paused as if e was omitting the next sentence. "Which could be why they sent a Study; I don't know. But back to operatives and how they work, I don't need training here to understand that. The wealthy—Vattam, Wehj, everywhere—are worse than the Breath Mages! Sneaking around, undermining faith. See. You said your parents aren't Mages. I'm not sure how many Mages you know. Most of their ongoing training isn't designed to advance the craft: they do that on their own. It's meant to keep them alert, their senses sharp, remind them that the world isn't as perfect as they say they've made it—protect them from external influence. They just *say* they're here studying new planes of existence."

E stopped, taking a while to drink from a glass of water, and then a sip of the drink, after an extended moment of breathing it in. "You want my opinion? Someone sent you to stall."

Leaning back, Kwill seemed to be letting that sink in. What Xelle was thinking, though, is that by this point, e could have asked why she hadn't told em earlier. She was glad e didn't. It wasn't trust, really more the—

"Stall how?" e went on. "I have no idea, knowing nothing about this. But I wonder who's using your absence as a reason why no further action should be taken. Or even just waiting out the silence." Kwill paused. "If there's discord emanating from Arc, the problem is in Arc. Wherever it originated."

She shifted. See, this was the sort of thing Xelle didn't like to hear, and it hit harder than anything she'd told herself. Things always felt simpler when one wasn't in the middle of them, she tried to think.

"Or," e continued, "someone wanted you off of the trail, and Breath Magic was an easy explanation. It's possible—likely, I'd say—Breath isn't involved at all."

Ugh. Xelle ran her palm across her forehead. It could be true. It *felt* true. And what then? She wasn't even on any trail, now or before. How had she gone from a bland Study with a productive yet mostly non-magic project to a player in some . . . *intrigue.* (She thought the term sarcastically.) And now, what, she was supposed to figure out if she'd unknowingly stepped in someone's . . . thing? Or she was a flatcap on the cross-Tower diamondboard? Suddenly she wished this was some inventive larp. And she could applaud it then go home.

But it was more than that. Even the edge to Kwill's nonchalant expression chilled her. It was one thing to be on a serious errand. But if she couldn't even believe her own Spire, if the issues were that bad . . . this could be some dangerous ash. Danger? Really? Fira, Xelle, look around. Bad actors at To'Arc? Sneaking? Discrediting? It all sounded dangerous. And maybe that was the problem. She wasn't taking this seriously enough. Thyra had seemed serious about it; thinking back, e absolutely had, but then the conversation had gone oddly and then fully off the table, and since, all Xelle had done was meet with the Ramble Squad.

"Do you know Mage Thyra?" she asked.

Kwill shrugged. "No." E reached for another sip of the syrup-drink. "Since we're opening up, I really like your tattoo. On your forehead. It's elegant. I'd steal the artist if you'd ever tell me. How far away is Arc? Can't be far, right?"

As absorbed as Arc Mages were with maps, it was strange to hear a Study not know how far away a Tower was. More than that, her strange mark had jumped out in the mirror day after day, but the fact that no one here had noticed it had lulled her into a place of comfort. She'd even considered it was invisible to others.

Xelle wasn't going to lie to her friend, but the story of meeting a dragon and having a strange mark in its wake was still too raw, too personal, too *unknown*, to share. With anyone. Except Ay'tea. She could probably tell him. Could she? Anyway.

"Thanks! You're welcome at Arc anytime. Or where I'm from, more Ever." It never escaped her that Kwill referred to cities and Towers as the extent of the world. "To your previous question— I wasn't on a trail. I wasn't doing anything. I mean, I hoped it was because they trusted me?" Sounded silly putting it like that, but when she'd met with the Arc Spire . . . they hadn't actually made her feel small, despite her insecurities about it. Not at all, really. They'd made her feel . . . relevant.

Whatever the ash that meant.

Kwill broke into a snort, steadying the shapely glass with deft skill. "That's a great point. If the actual *Arc Spire* trusts you, or even if it's my version and you'd done something cleverer than you realized, either way—you must be pretty special."

Xelle kept the third version to herself. That it was the opposite. She was a sad, old, Study, too late to the game and too unwilling to pledge, and now she was simply a flatcap, about to be knocked off the board without much cost.

But her friend wasn't done. "If they trust you, then what's your intuition?"

13 – Role Playing

Honestly? Her intuition was to get the flame out of this place. She'd found and seen nothing, and the Ascension wasn't going to wait some indefinite amount of time for her to figure it out. Jehanne could hold off from retiring, but she shouldn't have to. Besides, she didn't mean to think of it this way, but she was also . . . in her seventies? Eighties? Who knew what could happen. And what did any of this have to do with Xelle?

In fact, the more she thought of it, the more irritated she was that she hadn't questioned this whole situation more. Right from the start. Go somewhere and seek something? And, to here, because they'd detected Breath Magic? Even if they had, that didn't mean anything, they'd probably detected something mundane, the things they used here all the time—adjustments to light and color, a puff to lighten mood, a quick cast to conceal a fart.

She'd been so set to stand by her independence, she'd limply followed their prompting across the world. Except, she was *glad* she hadn't pledged, because she wasn't going to be subjected to that sort of nonsense *again*. (That raised the issue of what she *would* do, for one could not be a Study *forever*, but she pushed that all from her mind.)

Looking back on her visit from strictly the point of why she was sent here, the only remotely interesting thing had been her brief interaction with Thyra, the Mage who'd approached her in the library, and who she'd not seen again. So when she sat down and made a list of the things she needed to do before she left, finding Mage Thyra was one of them.

Thyra would not be found. Kwill didn't learn anything asking around, nor did Xelle with the few casual contacts she'd made, including pers in the Study Hall and the Library. Starting to wonder if e really lived here, Xelle decided to try asking at the Front Desk, after all, e couldn't be too covert if e was walking around on library duty. The desk clerk wouldn't give out any information that would help locate em, but confirmed e was a Tower Mage and offered to leave a note.

Feeling silly, she wrote down, *I'd like to speak to you before I leave. - Xelle* and handed it over. And just in case, Xelle tried waiting around the library, even standing several times in the same row where e'd approached her. In case that was the secret sign. (She grumbled about this while she was standing there.)

In between all that, she thought more about what the Mage had said. There wasn't much, and it had gone by so quickly, but she did remember Thyra had continued to ask about Arc. Which matched what Kwillen suggested—something was going on at Arc.

She thought about their conversation more, about whether the Mages had trusted her and just been wrong about the source of their trouble, or whether they'd known and simply used her.

Trust. The word stuck in her mind. Like she'd heard it several times lately. Or read it. She drummed her fingers against the bookshelf. Discrediting the whole Ascension, no matter who took it . . . Making pers not trust To'Arc? Was that it?

No matter who took it— Thyra had asked her that. Who would take it? Fira, that seemed to be her best clue. What if it wasn't going on at Arc, but right in that room? Hadn't that been her first thought? *Ugh!* Well, what if she could actually go back and flip the mat on them? At least give it a try.

A new emotion lit in her, one she wasn't sure she had a name for. To'Arc was her home. Magic was her passion. Trust. Truth. These were the beams that kept the floor in place. She couldn't call herself a Mage, but she didn't need approval to be a good per. To try. To do what she could.

And so, she was going home and she was going to find out what the char was going on there. All she had to do was wrap up her ash-swept mission first.

During her times at the library, at least when she wasn't waiting in the row, she made a big show about seeming pleased at what she'd learned, and taking gratuitous notes, which if anyone had looked at them were mostly flower and vine doodles, with an occasional geometric pattern thrown in, because those really were a cool part of the aesthetic here.

And thus, when she arose excited, and let the Studies around her know she'd found what she was looking for, she hoped that word got to anyone who may have had an eye on her. A curse for that kind of concern, but that's where she was now, at least until she better knew what was going on.

Saying goodbye to Kwillen was not as hard as she'd thought it would be. Not that there was a specific reason, but they'd really become friends, and "hope to see you someday" is a heavy stone to toss. Whether e was the best at not thinking about such things or e'd thrown up a shield of eir own, e was perfectly cordial, offering her warm smiles and a firm press. And on her end, she was missing her home, and the thought of returning to it (as well as maybe doing good there) helped numb the thoughts of what she might be letting go.

"It sounds strange," e added as she was about out of the door. "Keep your senses tuned."

Not wanting to get into the stress that laid on her, she just nodded and turned into the corridor. E hadn't laid the stress, of course. E was absolutely right, and she'd been thinking of it frequently, as it were.

And if she would have been emotional standing in the Atrium one last time and taking in all the alabaster and blue and shimmer, she was much less so by the distraction of her still extremely heavy bag, which apparently had not walked itself to Arc Tower and unloaded during her stay. "Well, then," she said. "Other direction now."

She thought again of her secret room at the other end of her trip.

She'd continued to wonder, from time to time, if the magic she'd tied to her inkblooms had stayed intact, and when she sat totally quiet and immersed herself, she'd thought she could feel it, quietly resting in the background. That could also just be hope, and she was glad she'd not had reason for alarm. Hopefully the phyta were resting under the old ramp, undisturbed. Either way, she'd know soon.

Swaggering to the Front Desk, which again was her only way to not quite let on how heavy her bag was, she told the clerk she had emptied the room and was returning to To'Arc.

"Thank you for your hospitality. Your libraries are impressive, and I'll be sure to tell the Mages at To'Arc about all of them."

The clerk beamed. "I'm so glad to hear that. I'm glad we were able to provide service to To'Arc. May our hands always be extended."

"May our hands always be extended," she agreed, signaling the Breath to the clerk. Realizing xyr confusion as xe paused, she signaled the Arc instead, to which xe returned the Breath with visible relief.

Xe stamped some papers and asked a few questions, then offered her a Tower moveroom that would get her to Vattam. "No charge," the clerk bragged. Xelle waited, nervously, for a pair of Mages to request something then leave before she leaned in. "Is tipping standard?"

"They definitely appreciate it," xe said with an irritating nod.

She bit her tongue. Why couldn't they just pay what was deserved and leave Xelle out of it. "Is there a standard amount?" she asked instead. "That would help me."

Luckily, xe gave her a number that she thought was likely on the low side, but at least now she could count out an amount that she had with her (and go a little higher than that), put it in a pocket, and not stress about it the whole time.

"Should be here soon; you'll want to be out there. There are a few already going."

So not her own moveroom, then. Well, she couldn't expect that. Slowly, she moved toward the entrance, suddenly feeling her mind spin. Sad and heavy and unsure, and a lot more. Which was to say, she'd been preparing to leave for days, but at the direction that she must leave exactly now, all the things she hadn't done flooded her mind. Should she have done more interviews, with her new thoughts in mind? Talked to Kwill more? Worked harder to find Thyra? Even spent time in Vi'Breath! She'd been here all this time and not enjoyed the village.

She shoved through the cloud in her mind and walked out to the front circle, peering out over the rolling hills and to the village below. She turned around one more time to stare up at the huge alabaster Tower, both simple and complicated, so much subtlety in every detail that it almost challenged you not to notice it. Just to be taken by it. And appreciate—appreciate all of its form and nuance and a sense that you should appreciate things you couldn't see.

The higher she looked up, the more the veils layered, billowing in the windows and over open vistas, each sheer covering dyed such a light color that some might have considered them the same. Sometimes it felt she was starting to understand To'Breath, and maybe even a sliver of what it represented.

Xelle's sense of this Tower was met by the idea of how far away she was from her own, and the heaviness of retracing her path. This happened whenever she traveled any distance, but it remained an uncomfortable feeling, never dulling when it returned. Being somewhere far was exciting, but there was a specific moment that pulled her from going back—the idea that she was so far away, like that was an accomplishment in itself. Like she was someone interesting here, someone who could say, 'yes, I am from there'. And if she took one step in the other direction, it was no longer an adventure but a slog, where she became no longer away, but just . . . not home.

The moveroom pulled up, unaware of her musings and worries. The vroom was plain inside, just a few floor pillows, and walls painted in a soft blue. Four others, not Studies but non-casters, piled in.

Xelle worried about her closeness to them or whether they'd expect conversation when she was already feeling overwhelmed, but instead they were absorbed in talking about some sort of remodel; they used a host of terms Xelle didn't know and after a while she drifted back into the cloud of her thoughts.

14 – Every Step Closer

The lot from To'Breath talked the entire way to Vattam. Xelle missed the conn she'd had on the way here; at least ze'd stopped every two minutes. She could have used the breaks just to gasp at the silence.

To clarify . . . Xelle did not mind conversation, even without her own involvement. Often she enjoyed listening to it, the chatter a pleasant distraction from the specific and vague worries that haunted her. But there was a threshold of overlapping self-indulgence, unpredictable squawks and gasps, and punctuated prattle where it turned into a full-circle assault of noise and irritation, and all she wanted to do was go back to To'Breath, learn a silence cast, then return to the vroom just so she could cast it.

And thus it was with the design crew, until finally the vroom stopped and the conn announced they had reached their drop-off. The moment passed, she started to feel guilty for her escalating thoughts regarding her fellow passengers, but as they'd still not said a word to her, even as they noisily passed coins to the conn and piled out from the back door, she decided to try and put them from her mind.

It occurred to her that she might now be over-tipping the conn, since there were several pers in the vroom, and they'd all tipped as well. But she was in no place to second-guess it now, and so she handed over what she'd put into her pocket with a warm greeting, then lugged her bag away and down onto the cold afternoon ground.

The winter had eased during her month in To'Breath, and so it was a small surprise to see snow again in Vattam, though no longer the blanketing layers she'd tromped through on her first visit.

This time, she'd not been dropped off at the travel circle by the river, but more, from what she could tell, in the more literal center of the city. Convenient to being in the city, but less convenient if one was trying to get out of it. She gazed around, taking in the shadows on the frost-laced street.

An eclipse passed over and Xelle waited; she'd been trying to get a sense of the time. Once the light returned, she decided that while it was not too late in general, it was too late to make it back to To'Arc without also running into the night. There might be conns willing to make night runs, especially from the huge city, but rather than figure that out, she'd be better off stretching a bit, then catching one last vroom in the morning.

She wasn't eager for a long walk with her bag, but she could at least make it down the hill where she saw buildings of sizes that might include inns. As she'd already taken her excursion on the way in and her mind now held thoughts of getting home, she focused on more practical matters.

Some of the buildings stretched out in the style she'd seen before, wider rather than high in cases. Offices of invention, or small production facilities—specialty shops for both gadgets and their components. She walked toward larger crowds, hoping to see if there was something of interest around, and of course, where she could stay.

Nervously stopping a few pers to ask, she was intrigued to learn the wide buildings were massive stores. "They'll have anything you need," one hu bragged. Xelle wasn't sure about that. Still, with interest, she wandered in to what they'd called the utility store. To Xelle, that would mean some tools, some supplies, and a recommendation of which village to go to for the specialty gardening shop, or brickmaker. What could take up a whole—

This place had everything. Drawn toward the rows of larger devices, she laughed to herself—or probably it was out loud—as she slung her bag down in front of a wheeled cart, made of thin metal rods. A sign said Folding Carts but didn't have a price. Glancing around, she looked for a shopkeep. How did this work?

A per in a green apron hurried over. "They collapse," xe said, pointing to three more, apparently, by the wheels, leaning against the wall in what was otherwise just rows of thin metal rods. "See down here." Xe tapped a metal hook. "This secures it, for use or storage."

"Oh, that's nice," Xelle said. She wasn't sure why she was having a hard time talking to pers already. Then she remembered listening to the overlapping voices on the run here. *Ah. Right.*

"How do you know the price?" she asked, nervously. She hoped this wasn't a place where you argued about it. She'd heard of places like that and only dreamed she'd never find one. She heard some liked the control of it, but for Xelle it would be like moving to tipping land with only a handful of coins. Un. Bearable.

The . . . salesper (? shopkeep didn't quite fit) pointed to small hanging tags, each noting the price. Xelle sighed with relief. Then she saw the price.

She was sure it was a fair price. And probably one chunk of the obsidian in her bag would buy the whole aisle. That was totally made up, but something like that. But, secret stash aside, when she considered that she had to find a night's lodging, hire at least one more moveroom, and she'd checked out her last Basic in advance (though in fairness she'd been gone most of the month)—she wasn't sure she wanted to run her coins that low.

The salesper picked the cart off of the display and set it in front of her. Argh, that was unfair gameplay. Still, she pushed it a little. Big, coated wheels, felt solid. Strong metal, wouldn't give. Wouldn't work everywhere, but on any road or even path it would roll nicely. She could store it in her room, the secret one. Ah, adjustable handles! Her back would be saved!

"May I ask, are you," xe dropped to a whisper, "from To'Arc?"

Nothing to hide on that front. "Yes." She smiled, though not enough to suggest her slate was out for display. This time, she didn't even ask what the telltale sign was, but this was definitely a conversation she and Ay'tea would have when she got back.

The hu nodded, as if xe'd just guessed a jackpot question. "You walk like a travel Mage; I thought so. Even if you are looking at carts. Could be a gift. Now—I've got a set of old rollersweep frames. Got them for a steal! Not literally," xe added hastily. "Just need to fix them up with paint and brushes and I can finally add a second bath to the house. *For my spouse,*" xe emphasized. "The gears are all stuck together and I was going to take them out for acid, but if you're here—" Xe raised xyr eyebrows as if Xelle was supposed to understand. Xe snorted. "Ash, I'd take an ixa for the cart."

What? Oh, xe meant, like . . . a trade. She began to worry through the dynamics of this. Magic could be charged for, like any skill, though Mages would always perform core functions when they could. The per was offering her the cart as payment. (Almost!) And no, she wasn't a Mage or supposed to do this, but the salesper also wasn't asking for graduate casts. The magic it would take to unstick some rusted gears was minimal; it was first classes stuff. The thing a kid with a deep mind might do on accident, before understanding it.

She went back to a question her parent had always asked her: 'Who would this hurt?' Xelle glanced around the huge store, aisle after aisle of items, stacked higher than most buildings. She sensed no deceit. And fire-bomb, did her shoulders hurt.

Lesson for the future when acquiring heavy items you can't cast magic on.

"Where are the gears?"

This aspect was punishing, as they walked all the way to the back of the building and into a series of sheds. Xelle had a moment of relief; she should have asked where they were going. Could be an outlying village, the per's backyard two hours away, for all she knew.

She also regretted her purity in not asking to take the cart with them. The presumed order of operations seemed much less critical as she ached her way to the back of the place, and wound through a series of dark, dirty sheds.

Xelle was ready to unleash the proverbial Fira's throne of magic by the time she saw the things, arrayed against the side wall across from stacks of vroomfeet. And if there was supposed to be ceremony about it, she didn't bother, except to take the obsidian to sit outside, just in case. Breathing, quickly sliding into her abundant material, she felt around the rusted frames, feeling to see what might move. Easy.

There was a terrible clattering as the frames tumbled to the ground. Xelle jumped, apologizing, trying to see what she'd done. "I'm sorry!" she said. "I thought they were tied back." Trying to regain herself, Xelle went in less gently, sweeping her hurried touch over every surface, whispering free and smooth, with speed.

When she stepped back, the per was already over, inspecting the piled frames. Xyr hand reached out to spin a gear, which whizzed around in glee. "Fine, just fine. They turn like birdsong. We'll cover any damage. If you could just offer two ixa, I'll walk you out with that cart."

Two? Xelle wanted to knock xem over too. Again, totally harmlessly. Just an image in her head of the salesper bouncing over like a balloon for that nonsense.

She should have argued. The frames weren't secured. Or whatever xe was playing. Anyone could have bumped them! Nor were they damaged, not old, forged metal for a sideways tumble. But there were times the coin didn't feel worth the toll on her mind. Maybe she was enabling such things, but maybe pers whose mind didn't jump at every input could be the leaders in that charge.

By the time her backpack was loaded in the beautiful, sturdy cart (it was really nice!), she was out of the giant utility store, and her shoulders were buoyant with relief, she decided that if she ever giant-stored again, she'd go with a shrewder bargainer. If she could remember it. (She prompted the thought to stick.)

Closing time for many of the day shops was approaching, and Xelle still needed to find an inn, assuming there wasn't a Nook & Bunk handy. Yet, seeing her blurry reflection in the window of a bookstore, she slowed to a stop. Inn *next.* Wheeling the cart in and resting it near the door, she greeted a very friendly shopkeep, who boasted the best selection of factual volumes in Alyssia.

Xelle was all set reading factual volumes. For the moment. Yet it made good banter to drop that she'd met a few of the authors of featured historical titles (she had) and it provided her enough distraction that she could wander to the fantastical stories section in the back.

She settled on a short book, short by novel standards, but one that should last all the way back to To'Arc, no matter the companion. The book purported to be a fast-paced story, one about truth and lies.

Just a month ago, the concept wouldn't have connected with her, but now, knowing that someone was impacting the stability and trust of To'Arc, and not yet knowing why she'd been sent to find apparently nothing—both why she'd been sent, and why it'd been her—much came into question.

This loss of her own trust felt . . . like a death. No, not a death, like an illness. But not an illness. Like she was sitting in a cold room and two of the walls blew away, and the roof looked unstable, and she worried the snow would come in, and everyone else in the room acted like everything was fine and continued to pour the tea.

In another world, she would have lingered in this lovely store, but it was getting late and she was ready to be home.

"Xeleanor Du'Arc," she said, waving her way out of the store. "I hope to see you again." She raised the wrapped book into the air, nervous to tuck it into the backpack-laden cart.

When she'd lifted and turned the cart back onto the walkway of the shadowed street, she realized what she'd said. "Du'Tam," she said out loud, as if to the pers walking by. "Xeleanor Du'Tam." What did that mean? Was she ready to pledge? She hadn't been ready when she left. Had something changed?

This inn cost more than she'd intended, but not so much that she didn't pay it and enjoy the night's sleep. *Inside.* Cutting into her Basic now, she wondered if the Mages who'd set her trip allocation knew how much inns cost incity. Maybe they received discounts. Maybe they rested before the city. Either way, in the morning she was not dismayed to learn the best pickup point was a solid walk away; pushing her cart and watching the golden light bounce around the dramatic architecture and sculpted shadows of Vattam was a delight. Even more of a delight when she stopped partway for a coffee and cream in her travel cup, the cream a soft cashew laced with winter rose syrup.

Two other hu waited for a moveroom to To'Arc, so she was relieved to see that the one that arrived was spacious. While she couldn't hope for the sliding dividers of Janna's (?) moveroom—an invention she found more inspired all the time—it looked at least large enough where she could keep her space.

Then the door opened. This moveroom, rather than moveable cushions, had a series of affixed chairs. There were reasons taxis didn't do this; a luxury moveroom might feel like an entire furnished home or office space, but those were hard to clean, hard to maintain, and not well suited for varying groups of travelers and cargo. Utility moverooms tended to use cushions or at least benches, to provide flexibility. Well, whatever. Focused on getting home, she'd take it.

She was so tired by this point that she asked the conn to lower the ramp, so she could push the cart (bag included) inside without giving it a lift. Quickly assessing as the boards were retracted, Xelle moved into the seat closest to the back door, pulling the cart in front of her, as there was no room to the side.

And so she was shocked when one of the two pers sat next to her. The next seat over. With not much more than a glance, the other per sat across from xem.

"Excuse me," Xelle said, pushing the cart with great effort, and awkwardly scooting and rolling it in zig-zags to get past the pair. She moved up closer to the front, though not the seat next to where the conn would sit.

Fira, she was glad she had that book. The pair of passengers seemed to sour distinctly at her after that, as though she'd insulted them by moving. Beyond that, they were apparently enjoying a bragfest, each one-upping the other about their oldest curas. At first, they'd looked over at Xelle, as though she'd obviously want to hear it too. But after a few "Yes", "Oh, yes, he sounds wonderful", "Oh, that is an accomplishment", she had turned in the seat at as much of an angle as she comfortably could, and even held the book up at an uncomfortable height, just to signal *I am reading a book.*

Happily, she enjoyed the book. It was by an author she'd not heard of before, but the bit about truth and lies had caught her. The story was divided into two narratives, one by an older character, musing about the passage of time, and a younger character, acutely only aware of its passage in that moment. This pricked at Xelle, thinking of it, and she shifted in the chair. She wasn't young, not anymore. But she wasn't old. She turned the page. While across from her, one of the pers nearly shouted something out.

It was not lost on her that the one time she'd had a moveroom with a pullable screen, she'd had a delightful companion. "Oh, irony," she said through a sigh.

Apparently she'd said that aloud, by the look she got from the pair. Totally unaware of what aspect of their curas' accomplishments she'd just called ironic, she gave up and just kept reading the book.

The story's end was satisfying, and thinking that Helia might really enjoy it, she tucked it back into her large pant pocket where she hoped it wouldn't bend too much. As if remembering a companion silent beside her, she leaned forward and patted her bag, through the top of the cart. The pers beside her peered in distaste. She gave an extra pat.

It all felt surreal as they pulled down the road, and as the outer signs of Vi'Arc emerged in the waning light, the snow against the road piled even higher than when she'd left it.

All at once, her life rushed back, and tears clouded her eyes. She turned away, not knowing how these pers would react, or if she'd ever run across them again, given their destination.

She hadn't been gone so long, just weeks. Yet, she'd had to put it all away, somehow, to not think of what she'd left. Here, she was nearing them all. Helia, who would smile and be thrilled to see her. Clerks and stewards and labmates and hallmates and everyone who made this a life. The Arc Spire, who knows what they'd do but they were her Mages and she was ready to face them. And Ay'tea, her easy-going, funny lab partner. They would get back to work, and fix whatever weirdness had happened, and— She pictured, again, the professional hug she'd offer until she could consider the rest.

Her heart froze. She didn't know what would happen. But she was home and he'd be here. He was good at puzzles like this. She should have told him the whole story. Why hadn't she told him? But she'd tell him now.

And she'd never take him for granted again. She swore that to the inferno.

The others were dropped off at Vi'Arc, and she relaxed again, as the conn pulled up the road toward the Tower. Suddenly, she realized she'd forgotten to set apart the coins and the tip, and she scrambled into her pocket to count, counting again and again to make sure she had it right.

The conn stopped.

Excitement and longing and home all bounced in her mind, and all she could see was waiting out the window. She reached for the cart, but the conn had xyr hands on it and they lowered it to the ground together, and she pressed the coins into xyr glove and then rushed toward the Tower entrance about as fast as one per pushing a cart full of rocks could go.

She howled into the wind.

Thyra sat on the chaise, listening to tonight's musicians playing across the long hall. Just a little magic, enough to amplify the tunes past the rows of gathered pers. Eir eyes closed, and e imagined each note to be a droplet of peace, flowing through em. Steady.

E held the creased note in eir hands, then folded it again. E should have replied, sent another note. E preferred to talk by notes. But it felt wrong, felt confusing. The Arc Study appeared to know no more than any Study would. And at the same time, she knew everything. Saw right through Thyra, as if e were made of glass. Thyra was glass, but eir objectives were granite. They kept em strong.

It didn't make sense. Or maybe it would, but e had to sort it.

Increasingly, it seemed Xeleanor had been sent without much knowledge, not more than what Thyra had gleaned all the way from here.

Yet, if they meant to obscure, they'd picked the wrong hu. E felt sure of that. Xeleanor was a different type. Sharp, aware, keenly empathic, unimpressed by status. Traits her Spire Mages might not have understood.

The clouds of smoke had grown too heavy. Too heavy for Thyra, too heavy for eir people, too heavy for Alyssia. If they didn't know, then someone better learn soon.

Maybe. Maybe e needed to go to Arc directly. Maybe e needed to go there, away from eir small comforts. Alone in a sea.

If the stakes were as high as e thought they were, it would be worth it.

"Complacent!" e blurted out, shrinking back as some Mages turned in irritation. *Complacent,* e thought to emself. *To think everything must be well. To think nothing could ever change. To point to the platforms we built.*

To think we could never fall from them.

15 – Weight

Xelle tucked her bag into a washroom cubby, knowing if she'd been seen entering she couldn't afford to go right to her room (either of them). Nor could she afford the Front Desk or its questionnaire, and so she'd skirted around it, not even stopping to marvel at the Arc Atrium, but only to stash her bag (and stop to pee) before rushing upward to the highest floors where the Spire Mages presided.

Even out of session, as they turned out to be, there were five layers of stewards to get through. Xelle felt rather satisfied as one by one, she convinced them she'd just returned from a mission assigned by the Spire, and they must hear her report directly and immediately, and no, no, no Front Desk.

Mage We'le caught her popping around to see who might be in their chambers before the stewards decided otherwise. "Oh," she said, a light blue drape framing her face. "Xeleanor, I am glad to see you back and full of spirit." Her eyebrow raised, and Xelle wondered how often uninvited guests made it into the Spire of the Tower. "You have news?"

Xelle flashed the Arc, and, remembering who she was talking to, added a respectful bow. "Spire Mage We'le," she said. "I'd feel best addressing the convened Spire. I'm already here, if the Spire is available."

We'le, positive and encouraging from all Xelle had seen of her these last years, stared at her now without pretense. As if assessing something. She smiled, a tiny smile. "That would be in order." The Mage drew her hand to her chest, and Xelle felt a hint of passing magic, like a sensation on skin—a tiny chill, yet with a structure more complex than anything she'd studied or attempted. We'le's hand hovered a moment, over the smooth sky blue fabric of a tailored shirt, and then lowered. Xelle could feel it now, a call to meet. Calm, but nondelay.

The Mage gestured her down toward the meeting area, and Xelle noted how much more normal these Spire Mages looked making their way into the large room, as opposed to being seated already. Willing herself to her plan, she watched each carefully as they found their places. Tall Gloria in a tall gold cap, clutching a stack of papers and glancing over to see Xelle (We'le had already entered) with a bothered look on eir face. Nainol, short and round, seeming to be speaking to someone, though Xelle couldn't tell who. Awayna in a fuzzy brown robe and cap, her chair running for the moment on small clinking fuelstones, walked in, an aide trailing behind her carrying her things, leaving after setting them down. Next Kern, his bowed head making his pointed green cap look as though it led the way, reviewing a paper as he walked.

And she was glad to see Pelir, looking well, but, as xe often did, with energy turned inward, as if hiding behind the bright colors and sash. Pelir seemed a hard one to read; in that regard alone, Xelle could see how someone might fear Pelir's power on the Crown. And finally, the only one who walked as if her station were simply part of her being, neither elevated nor humble, but simply true—Crown Mage Jehanne, in silver and gray and with a black hat unmistakably shaped as a crown itself, who turned and gave Xelle an entirely direct look that she read as 'this better be good'.

Unfair. *Unfair,* Xelle thought. *It's not good, it's the only toss I have. And you're the one who put me in this spot, with nothing to go on. I'm sawing with a nail here, and you know it.*

She hoped the Crown Mage couldn't read thoughts. Certainly that would be turning the magic, she reminded herself. For a hu. She pushed thoughts of the dragons from her mind—she had to do this.

Xelle stayed back, trying to keep her face placid as the Mages settled in at their seats around the table, the different shapes of each headpiece reminding her of pieces on a diamondboard. She almost smiled, noting that they'd taken the same seats as before. With this, Xelle wholeheart-edly agreed. Less worry. Seating preferences addressed.

She took a breath. If she was really going to attempt this, then she needed to go. Really—she already had. She tried to stand with stately poise and will herself to overcome the pounding in her chest.

"Thank you, Spire Mages, for convening. I am honored." She bowed, then added the Arc. Only Awayna returned her version of the Arc, and then Nainol. The others sat still.

It was late in the day, and the light was waning in the window behind. Soft, beautifully colored lamps joined with it to create a perfectly balanced glow, painting swaths of azure and gold against the elegant columns while regally illuminating the distinctly shaped group of Mages. These were the same Mages. The same Mages, she reminded herself.

And Xelle, she was the same Study . . . In that thought, intended to calm, instead a spark ignited. She was not the same Study. A month away, a month to consider, a month that did not feel her own, no matter how much she tried to make it. She was here; she must do this; they were watching her. She struggled to grasp the points she'd repeated. She smacked her mind around them like runaway balloons.

Her heart still pounded.

"I agree that the rumors about Spire Mage Pelir put To'Arc in danger," she started. "I would now say grave danger. As Crown Mage Walja said before the fledging Councils of Reach, the access to magic for some and not others relies on trust—deep trust. It seems that whoever moves to discredit Spire Mage Pelir does so to disintegrate that trust, those efforts effective whether Spire Mage Pelir ascends or not. For, if someone else ascends, there would always be doubt behind xem for the way it was done. If not an obligation to whoever cleared that path."

She paused to look at each Mage, as quickly as she could. Some appeared fixated, others blank, Gloria openly agitated. It was Kern who caught her eye. Writing on his paper. Hadn't he just been reading?

He certainly wasn't writing her Walja quote. Before he could look up to see her watching, she continued.

"But, to my report. I did not find evidence at Breath Tower." She lifted her arms, and took a long breath, looking around the room to see their disappointment, their anger. Whatever it would be.

Jehanne and Pelir showed nothing. Awayna squinted, as if waiting for more. Nainol was squishing some sort of small ball, yet gazing directly her way. Gloria tapped eir pen, with a casual frown. We'le sat almost blankly, but Xelle thought she detected a spark in her eye. That was of note. And Kern was covering his paper into a folder and leaning back in his seat, eye toward her but not at her.

"Yet I do have a hypothesis, one that explains the lack of averments to it." She paused. *Here goes.* "I do not think that To'Breath, or even Breath Magic is involved." At least two Mages made small grunts or hmms, We'le's eyes widened, Kern sat forward, neither leaning nor upright, but held as if by tension. Distracted by watching the Mages, she almost added 'you underestimate Breath Magic here', but some sense of loyalty to those she had met, those who had been kind, held her back. Maybe there would be a time for that note, but she was hesitant to say it yet. She moved to her next point. "Breath Magic's core is subtlety, stealth. If a Breath Mage of any skill wanted to influence Ascension, one would not be so clumsy to lead you to think it was Breath. So, my report, delivered in full: I saw nothing in my many days at To'Breath to indicate To'Breath is involved. Yet as the deterioration of Arc Ascension has reached as far as To'Breath, a fact I confirm, I do recommend the Arc Spire seek the source of the tumult with haste and renewed consideration, if you are not already doing so."

Again, she scanned the Mages, watching each one, most with explainable reactions, and only two perhaps off. Jehanne rapped the table and they all turned to face her. Xelle had as much as she would get here. Now, to cover her footprints in the snow and get a clear ticket out of this room. To her friends. To think.

She pretended Jehanne's rapping had not involved her. "With

respect, Spire Mages, I remain curious why I was sent. You said a Study would draw less attention, but a Study has less access, more chores. And of all the Studies, why me? Why the problem Study who is too successful to abandon but who refuses to pledge? I can't discern it."

We'le rose from her chair, looking more agape than Xelle could remember (or imagine) in a high-ranking Mage, let alone a Spire Mage. "Study Xeleanor Du'Tam, we are grateful for your report. Your mission is complete. You will take two weeks of rest and reflection before resuming normal duties." She scanned the table. "Any objections? Good," she said, just a moment later. "I thank the Spire for this late and sudden convergence. Study, you are dismissed."

While that could have sounded rude, Xelle distinctly could not shake the idea that We'le was trying to help her. Anyway, she'd done it. She thought she was going to add some other things too, but it didn't matter. She'd done it. She could go back. She allowed one last look at Jehanne, whose fingers rested together, over her face.

Xelle bowed, then turned and left, allowing the stewards to quickly ensure she made it down to lower levels before leaving her again alone.

Her heart pounded.

It was a little late for the lab, but they often worked beyond now. She spiraled through the Tower, down to the large room. She would not make it weird. Even her repeated idea of a friendly hug dissolved. She pictured it, but not now. Not like this. She just needed to talk.

Walking quickly, then slowing as she entered, she tried to cover her winded breath, glancing around. Several were working, and at least one threw down their pens at her approach.

"Xelle! You're back!"

"Yes!" She walked to armtap each, truly glad to see them but too distracted to say much. "Ay'tea around?"

The Studies fell silent, as in bad silent, and looked at each other trying to decide what to say. Xelle glanced to his desk. Empty. Completely empty. She doubted there was a speck of dust on it.

"Oh, was he reassigned?"

One shook her head. "No. He left. His . . . whole studies. He said goodbye and not to worry about him."

"We . . . we thought you knew," another said. "You seemed so close. It seemed he'd tell you."

Xelle had no energy for it. Not to fake a smile, not to understand. "Long day. I'll see you tomorrow." And she turned and left.

The exhaustion from all her rush-induced running around hit her at the same time, and she wandered aimlessly for quite a while, wandering into spaces she'd barely remembered existed, like a sackroom and weights space, and then past a supply room filled only with vials of ink. An interior garden she'd forgotten was so close, without even snow to hide her tears. Just cold and empty. Alone.

Needing someone, someone who would care, she wiped her face and wandered up to Mage housing. The steward either recognized her or wasn't going to stop her; she ignored xem. And she rapped on the door, surprised by the speed by which it opened.

"Xelle! Holy Fira! It's so good to see you. You look terrible! Are you well?"

"Hey," Xelle answered, needing to get this out. "I'm well. But I'm tired, I've had some things happen, and I need to get to my room and rest. But I really needed a friend, and . . . you're the best one I have here. I hope that's ok."

"Tea? Tea always helps."

Her heart skipped. Leaves. Drink. Not . . .

Helia looked her up and down. "Or I've got a good wine."

Numbly, she nodded, and walked in, her senses returning as she watched Helia hurry to wipe two glasses, setting next to it a tall bottle with some sort of charm sparkling from the top.

Xelle couldn't keep two wood joints set half the time, but she sure made some friends with expensive alcohol. As she went to sit, she remembered the book still in her pocket. "I enjoyed this on the way back, and thought you might like it."

"Oh, thank you!" Helia held the book as though it had not been curved in Xelle's pants, and set it on a ledge. She paused a minute, then got their glasses situated around her low talking table.

"Do you want to talk about anything?" Helia asked, as they both sat down.

She didn't. "I really don't. Not today? Later? I'm just grateful you had me in."

Mmmraaau!

Xelle jumped in her seat as a furry per practically leapt over her, roughly landing four feet onto the fine wood table, before running away. It was then she noticed there were significant changes to the space: items removed, new blankets. She raised her eyebrows.

"Bear!" Helia shouted, then lowering her voice. "Yes, this is Beryl, well I call aem that. Ae bonded to me when I was gathering winter herbs, and how could I say no to a cat bond?"

Xelle could make some arguments. But, fire, that was a beautiful cat. Maroon hair, almost as if ae were showing crownhair. She wondered what mood maroon would signify for a cat, if the concept even applied.

Bear jumped back onto the table, between them.

"Cats are very protective," Helia said. "Ae thinks ae's protecting me."

With another silent nod, Xelle realized she had some respect for the cat. She reached her hand out tentatively. Beryl sniffed it, huffed, and then left to curl in a corner.

And Xelle had no idea what they'd just been saying. "Anyway, I didn't get what they wanted on the mission," she said, rather blurting it out. "But I've thought about it and . . . have some new ideas."

Realizing that she'd just suggested she might be working Spire issues covertly and that Helia would certainly pick that up, she glanced away.

"Honestly? I trust you, Xelle. I have no idea what your plans are, but . . ." this next bit came out more wistful than Xelle was comfortable with or ready for with her mind racing and her heart unsealed . . . "you will always have an Arc Mage on your side. Always."

"What if I do something horrible?" She tried to break the tension.

"You wouldn't." Helia matter-of-factly reached for a set of crackers she'd just laid out. "Not knowingly."

Xelle sat a moment, unable to even find a relevant thought. "Helia?"

The Mage looked up, somehow able to eat crackers and spread against a pillow while remaining absolutely elegant in form. She could be on a painted advertisement in Vattam. Xelle kept that thought to herself.

"Can we just hang out for a while? My candle's low, but—"

Helia waved off whatever Xelle had been about to say, which was good because she wasn't sure either.

Within minutes, there was a shimmery set of rose glass dice on a velvet mat, and Helia was teaching a dice and token game designed to be low-stress so people could not be too distracted to network and negotiate while playing it.

Despite the rather weak sell, it was calming and pleasant, and the moonstones were out in full glow, shining through the sheer inner curtain hung in front of her Mage-room balcony, when Xelle realized Helia probably had reasons to sleep. Helia set the dice back into a padded box as Xelle fastened back on her boots.

"Thanks again . . . this meant a lot to me. Ok?"

Though she rose, Helia stayed by the couches as Xelle approached the door. "I missed you when you were gone."

"I missed you too." Xelle was still sorting out the tiny void that had opened inside her at the news Ay'tea had left, but this was truthful. She had missed her. She hoped it was ok to say that. She wasn't in a place to be here, but she had needed a place. It was all too confusing.

"Look, Xelle, I know you're dealing with things, but at some point we should talk about it. I really enjoyed our dates together. If you were willing, I'd like to try again."

Ash, she hoped she hadn't messed things up by coming here. She *did* like Helia, and maybe they should go out, but Xelle didn't want to hurt her. Maybe like how she felt now. "I . . . I don't know. I'm working through a lot." She fumbled for what else to say.

Helia waved her, not an Arc, but a common sign for 'later'. Relieved, she nodded and turned to open the door.

"Xelle?"

She turned around.

"I will always be your friend. Please don't worry."

The thought warmed her, even through her confusion. "Thank you, Hellie." She tapped her chest twice, then glided back into the hallway. Anyway, that's how she felt.

Her bag was waiting on the ground floor, and laughingly in the way that one does when they are entirely spent, she whispered to it that this was hopefully the last time either of them would have to endure this much weight.

It took nearly all her remaining energy to focus, pass through the stone wall, and enter her garden room, where she was met by the same glow of inkbloom buds she had left. Oh, how she had missed it. And surely, she'd be spending most of the day here tomorrow, with something new to try.

She unloaded the obsidian, still in its own bag, whispered that she'd be back soon, and left again to find her abandoned bed and sleep in it for as long as she could.

16 – the Enchanted Forest

A long while had passed since the last time Xelle had two important things to do, requiring actual prioritization and thought. Ash, she almost felt a sense of purpose. Maybe being sent on nonsense missions was a thing everyone could try. Guaranteed to send one swimming for the ladders.

She wanted to care for the inkblooms, but she also wanted to act on her hunch. Her own mission. Xelle laughed; she was not calling it that.

Her decision was to at least get the obsidian out of the bag, see if it caused any changes just through its presence, and then return for magic or research when she had more time, as she would when she was back to her day-in day-out life as a Tower Study.

It brought immeasurable comfort to be back in her little space (and not aching and half asleep). Sure, her space was strange and oddly shaped, with a partially-tiled floor worked around a few curved protruding roots, her spinning chair, two livewalls and a tall cabinet— all roofed by a decrepit moveroom ramp with an artisan guardrail, but it was her space. And it was magic.

She gazed across the dormant buds of the inkblooms, their vines spread everywhere they found soil. She was fine with their lack of growth; having them decline during her absence would have been a much larger worry. Nerves suddenly striking her, she opened her backpack and eased out the drawstring bag. Taking the obsidian pieces out handful by handful, she scattered them in all the beds on both of the room's livewalls. "I hope you like this," she said. "I put a lot of effort into this total guess so let's make it happen."

Maybe she shouldn't tell them it was a guess, but if they were going to be friends, honesty seemed the best cast. Speaking of which, she'd considered spreading the stones on one side only, both as a test case and to be sure she didn't harm them all, but these phyta were special, and if this was really her gut, she wouldn't let one half sit and sense the other either thrive or struggle. Sure, phyta did not have anima senses, but their magic was special and Xelle had learned not to underestimate it.

She finally pulled the last, larger stone out, unwrapping it, excited to see that it looked unscratched. Though . . . she really didn't know if obsidian would scratch? So much to learn, once she could get back at it. She laid the dark stone down on her main seat; when she had a chance she'd build a wire harness for it and mount it to the back wall. A mysterious mirror for the darkness.

Coals, I didn't thank Helia for the mirror. She'd have to do that soon.

With mirrors on her mind, she couldn't help but pick the stone up. Her own face appeared in the shiny black, looking older than she'd remembered. The bottom of her cap ribboned across the top, covering the dampened moods of her crownhair beneath. The strange mark on her forehead. A crooked mouth, somehow unable to smile. He had mentioned the stone. He had said it, then immediately left. Why? Why then? Why not a conversation? After all the time they'd worked together, hour after hour, not even a conversation? She hadn't even understood if something was really there, she'd grasped—a tiny tendril, reaching to see if it found land, and he'd thrown this at her and then left.

"Why did you leave?" She called into it, tears streaming suddenly down her face, as if they rolled down the black surface as well. Resisting the urge to throw the item as far as she could, she set it back on the platform surrounding her chair, cradling it in the bandage where it had been wrapped these last weeks.

She stepped back.

If this was how she really felt, no, she couldn't right now. She would think about it later.

Curse Fira.

Later.

~

She took the next Tower taxi to Mytil, then walked the stretch to the Enchanted Forest.

Her reasons for going to Mytil were two-fold. First, the only thing she really knew about Kern offhand, was what everyone knew—about his famous cura here, Tenne. Second, or maybe this was first, there was someone here she wanted to talk to first.

Perhaps it was very Xelle to run first to the person remaining she felt she could tell everything to without giving xem burden, but with everything upside down, she simply needed the grounding of someone who never could be. Ever. And to his place—a place that always felt right.

Now, Xelle loved many places, to the extent she often wished she could make copies of herself to simultaneously live lives in each, but this place was unique. A place out of world, out of time, where she could simply be. She loved To'Arc, she loved Vi'Arc, she loved the places she had traveled. Each with expectations she couldn't seem to meet. She loved places she'd never been but had heard only wonder about. Places that would only leave more behind. She loved her homevillage of Tam. Deeply. Even there, waited expectations, and culture, and traditions that Xelle couldn't quite make fit.

All those years of her childhood, Mytil, the big city, biggest this side of the lake, had developed in her mind as a wondrous treasure. A city of art and expression and even glamour, she'd revered the very idea of it, certainly on those trips when she could convince her parents to accompany her, when they'd find a shop of such whimsy it could never find home in Tam, or when they'd eat from a new and exciting style, one that took different pots, pans, stoves, or oils—or even items served semi-prepared on the table. Sometimes even different types of tables!

And so, the first time she'd been old enough to manage her Basic, she'd saved some money and traveled back to the city, first happening upon a tavern she'd always admired when passing by, but her parents never wanted to visit, called *the Enchanted Forest*. Yes, on the painted wooden sign, the first word was not capitalized. A mystery that Xelle could interpret a hundred ways when her mind got spinning around it, but which she preferred to simply let be.

She'd spent the better part of an evening there, meeting a bartender who had seemed to take an interest in her. The per had struck her as more of a rainbow gender (private thoughts only) so she'd been a little surprised to hear him take he. Klein, he'd introduced himself, but never added a placename, not even Du'Mytil. Turned out, he was more than a bartender, but also the proprietor, who seemed to enjoy tending bar as well.

Xelle liked that. If she ever had a tavern, she'd like to work at it too. Coin was nice, but passion was better.

In fact, when Klein had heard she was a Study (To'Ever at the time), he'd offered her a room there—said it was a loft over the kitchen, but with angled ceilings and creaky floors and without a night view of the glowing Mytil galleries down the hill, it wasn't much interest to traveling patrons. Then, he said, with an honesty that she appreciated, having access to a caster was always a good deal in a large city that often breathed on wealth and influence. That said, he insisted, there were no strings attached, and she could keep the room as long as she wanted, for a nominal fee, paid annually, no matter how often she used it.

It might seem an odd arrangement, but Xelle had seen odder things in Tam. Pers liked connections, they liked stability. Sometimes they just liked to be nice. If she could maintain a tiny room at her favorite nook in the world off of Basic, without taking advantage, she wasn't going to argue it. So at the bend of each year, she always made sure her room was paid.

Klein had grown only dearer in the time passed. And it was an immense relief when, after so many weeks and days of worry and sadness, she felt—just happiness—surge through her at the familiar surroundings. As always, as she saw the colorful sign on the wall and the dark-stained wood, tears gathered in her eyes. She shook them away.

"Xeleanor!" he greeted, wiping off her favorite stool at the bar. "I'm so glad to see you."

That was another thing about Klein. He never threw in "it's been a while" or any of the other phrases that made Xelle worry whether they were barbs.

"You're looking good. Interested in something new?"

"Not today." She placed a coin on the counter. "An enchanted forest of my own." The drink, something he'd concocted just for her one time, was her favorite. It involved a generous amount of Ever Spirit. Almost as much rare mountain wine, which almost tasted like a spirit in its concentration. A drizzle of pine syrup. Those were stirred and strained with ice, pulled fresh from the chiller. Then it was served in a conical glass, given a quick shake of cocoa and chili powder, and one frozen blueberry.

Though she hadn't admitted this to Klein, she'd even attempted it in the Tower once, substituting what she could for the more expensive ingredients, and she swore she would never do it again. The balance was more subtle than a cast.

As he garnished the drink and slid it in front of her, she let her nose hover over a moment before taking a slow sip.

"You're too good to me," she said.

"I'm working on that," he answered, tapping the counter.

Xelle laughed. Oh, another thing about Klein. Back to that sense of trusting pers, she'd long ago concluded that if trusting a friend was going to be her downfall, then so be it. And her trust of Klein was inherent.

She did throw a quick thought of detection (Klein wouldn't tell) to make sure someone wasn't casually listening in. No one was. It was . . . a bit early in the day and the only table occupied was nowhere near the bar.

"So I met with the Arc Spire. About a month ago." Another great thing about Klein. She could say something like that and he didn't react. She could probably bring up the dragons (she wasn't ready for that yet) and he'd keep drying with his towel.

It always seemed odd to her that others didn't talk to Klein the way she did. They'd get their drink, then act like he didn't exist. She figured it was like a lot of special things in life, if they're just there, one gets used to them. Like how phyta generate the life energy for all magic, and most of the populace toss their images around for any old purpose, or just to like the look. Whereas Mages were so sensitive to the meaning of phyta, what magic they hold, what they can do.

"Have you been away?" he asked, pulling her from her distraction.

"Yes, I went to To'Breath. Lovely Tower, kindly pers there. I have a new appreciation for Breath Magic now."

"That's always good," he said, now pulling out some small drink spears and running them through a thick clothie.

"Someone is undermining trust in Pelir. Who is planning on ascending to the Crown when Jehanne retires. I'm sure you've heard all that here by now. The Arc Spire thought that someone at To'Breath was causing this, or they said they did. So they sent me there to check it out."

"What do you think?"

Xelle looked up, but Klein still wasn't looking her way. Should she walk through it or just go?

"I think Kern is involved. I watched the Spire Mages as I made my points. His reaction was the one that felt wrong every step of the way. Nothing obvious, more all wrong. He avoided looking at me when I sounded urgent, then when I made it sound like I had nothing, he relaxed, and then when I started in again, his whole body tensed, and he wasn't looking at anyone else either. I can't be sure, yet . . . I really feel it. An instinct? Or just what I saw? But what do I do about it is the question. He's not going to just tell me if he's involved in something nefarious. And if I start asking around the Tower someone would report it. Pers get downright reverent about their ranking Mages. And eyes might be on me anyway, if word got around that the Spire sent me on a mission, which it probably did.

"Klein, I have no idea how any of this works." She took another sip of her drink. Fira, that was good. "I did not sign up to be a spy."

He smiled, and now looked right at her. "Then why are you doing it?"

"Well, I'm the only per with the lead. And it's sensitive. And the few pers I'd trust with this sort of information, I don't want to put at risk. And it's not information. It's a hunch. And this is important. And I . . . I set the whole thing up in the first place—busting in on the Spire, then saying things designed to see how they reacted. I don't know. I have a sense of pers. Or maybe it was that storyteller, all his talk about heroes. Trying what you have."

"Storyteller?"

"Yeah, in Vattam. Jimmi . . ." She tried to remember his placename.

"Jimmi Du'Ard?"

"Yes, that was it. You know him?"

"We run in the same circles, you could say." He chuckled, as if he'd made a joke. "I would recommend his inspirations anyday. Plus. You do have a sense of pers," he added, though Xelle wasn't sure why he sounded hesitant.

"I think that's proven by how much I like you." She tilted her head.

He laughed more fully, the kind of natural, joyful laugh, that made a per feel good.

Xelle grinned back. "I do!"

"It is entirely appreciated. And I will give you the best advice that I can. In questions of motivation, find what a per cares about."

Xelle leaned in, after all this mystery, grateful to have someone to give her advice. "Then what?"

"Then go from there."

She shook her head at the bartender, who was tossing the wet clothie back into a bin. It landed solidly in the middle.

"Nice toss," she remarked.

"You'd be surprised how hard that is for me." He stopped and turned around, but said nothing.

Xelle stopped, locking eyes with Klein. "What he cares about . . ." She took another sip of the drink.

17 - Bon Tenne Du'Mytil

It felt nice to be back, and so Xelle accepted with ease when someone asked if she'd join a knockball game. The three players were visiting from an Ever Region village, so they had a lovely time sharing forest stories, and sometimes simply waiting silently as the next hu lined up a play. As the night crowd grew and the game ended, they invited her to share a meal, but she was getting tired and was still full from a toasted sandwich Klein had made her. So with pleasant regards, she bid them goodnight.

Xelle's little tavern room was just how she'd left it. A simple change of clothes, a few lace overlays she'd picked up at a crochet shop, and her one splurge: a sturdy stained glass lamp, for which she used good, soft colored salt so the lightpod would not overpower the tiny, angled room.

Its equally tiny washroom sat otherwise unused on the main floor, long ago replaced by larger ones off the main entrance. She'd stopped there on her way up, so all that was left was to fall into sleep until sunrise through the tiny window awoke her.

When it did, Klein wasn't at the bar, but he'd left a small pot heating on the stove, and she was delighted to smell a light, savory broth wafting her way. Grateful, she poured a mug, knowing that it would keep her warm long into the cold day.

Her plan, initially, had been to chat her way about the art district. Perhaps learning more about Kern's family could give her some leads. Now was a good time for it, as she was off of her duties for a couple weeks. Besides, asking about a celebrity would not arouse the suspicion asking about a Mage would (even if this celebrity had a Mage parent).

Yet after her conversation with Klein, she'd decided to change the plan. Sure, she could spend the day wandering the art galleries and asking around, but what she'd told Klein was true. She hadn't signed up to be a spy; it wasn't in her nature. Look what she'd done at To'Breath: sit and read old books, and then listen to Mages unload about random facts and theories in a small conference room.

All her life, pers had been consistent on what she was good at—directness, honesty, empathy, sometimes new ideas. A few offhand suggestions that raised her eyebrows, but none of them 'have you considered espionage'.

She was going to go talk to the Mage's cura. Yes, she considered what could happen if it went wrong, and shuddered a bit at the unknown of what if Kern (or this Tenne too) really was working for someone with ill-intent, but anyway, she'd been pulled into this, and she didn't think she could just go back to her lab (a darkness hit her) and pretend she didn't know.

A tiny, stabbing moment made her realize she didn't want to go into that lab again, but unable to cope with that thought, she pushed it in. Today—she had something to do.

Everyone she knew, with a few very-buried-in-their-thing exceptions, had heard of Bon Tenne Du'Mytil, latest winner of the E'lle Prize, named after Bon E'lleame Du'Mytil, the primary original architect of the Mytil art district center. Xelle wouldn't have questioned the name before, but after reading (fine, sometimes scanning) countless history books, she'd learned that placenames could be manipulated over time, especially those from earlier history. Just as now, pers might change their placename because they changed their identification of home, they might also change it for a perceived increase in status. Not just a Mage taking on one's Tower, but non-Mages, taking a placename perceived as wealthier, harder to move to, or more historic.

There was an early-era per who'd changed her name to 'Du'Gold' and gathered the resources to found an entire town, still called 'Gold' just because pers had thought she must be from somewhere of tremendous wealth, and still attracting the types who wanted the name themselves.

What she'd learned was, this idea of a per changing their own name extended to historians tweaking the names of peacefully deceased pers for the same reasons. In fact, placenames had not been so extensively used in earlier times, that second names had traditionally come from different sources, including family links or professions, and that under Alyssian unification, placenames had been standardized. In fact, E'lleame may not have preferred a second name at all.

Really, this appeared to be what happened when one spent weeks in the history library. Total doubt in everything.

Something to consider further on a day when she was not trying to meet up with one of the biggest celebrities of the moment and then ask about his potentially nefarious parent.

So, the E'lle Prize. Awarded every five years by a conglomeration of sponsors, the winner received a full-year residency in the E'lle Gallery, with fairly wide range to create, inspire, perform—whatever xe preferred.

Awardees always received fame in Mytil, a city that thrived on art and culture (and the perception of it), but Tenne, said to be charming and quirky, had transfixed Mytil in a way not seen in years. Beyond Mytil, his art had become known throughout Alyssia—said to transcend the space between painting and sculpture, created as artfully in the palm of his hand as done sweeping across a gallery garden. In addition, and this was not Xelle's concern but particular to Tenne's fame, he was known to be perfectly handsome.

Xelle walked up the low gallery stairs, the chill wind funneling down them. Whatever else had been in E'lleame's portfolio of expertise, air dynamics had not. Glad for her cloak, she pulled it tighter.

"Hello," a steward said, standing by a large, metal doorway, one side propped open. "Welcome to E'lle Gallery. We have two exhibits open for winter, plus a today-only tent section, with—"

"Pardon," she said. "I may see the exhibits later. Today I'm here wondering if it's possible to speak with Bon Tenne Du'Mytil." Xelle loved art exhibits, but only when she didn't have something time-sensitive on her mind. Which meant she didn't go to art exhibits nearly often enough.

The hu scrunched xyr face in irritation. She knew some pers didn't like being interrupted, but from another view, she hadn't asked xem a question and was trying to save xem some time. No one ever saw it like that.

"I presume you have no appointment with Bon Tenne?"

"It's a private matter. And I believe one of importance. Is there a way to ask if he'd see me? I could provide information."

Xe sighed. "You seem reasonable, and that's not a given, with some of the pers we see. But you must understand, with the number of admis who try to meet Bon Tenne under some auspice or the other, he'd never get anything else done. I'm sorry. If he's not expecting you, you must leave. You can always send him a note through Gallery Post," xe offered.

So much for direct. But now was the time to do this, returning again would raise suspicion or, worse, put Tenne on alert. At least now, the steward barely looked at her, repeating the part about Gallery Post like a tour guide.

Xelle glanced around. The domed facility stretched above them, but not terribly high. Not like a blockbuilt or a Tower. But like a Tower, she'd bet the layout was predictable.

She let out a breathy sigh. "I understand. The exhibits— Do either of them feature Bon Tenne's recent work? Or even . . . the awarded works?"

The steward's face lightened. Xe did proceed to fully explain both exhibits plus the tent day, and this time Xelle waited patiently. With xyr blessing, she walked past the donation box, dropped in a coin, and then followed the arrows to the first Exhibit Hall, at the end of which rested (xe'd excitedly told her) Tenne's award-winning piece: *The Mud Stares Back.*

The gallery was well attended, with visitors quietly gasping about, and early morning regulars arranged on benches, fixed on the pieces before them. Art stewards waited in every space, providing background on the art, or warning pers when they stepped too close.

Xelle rounded each section, item by item, imagining where she was on the building's map as she wound through. Given the pattern she could see in the rooms, her closest approach would be about midway, and unless the layout was more complicated than it appeared, there would likely be doors, probably heavy and closed, connecting to the central section. She'd have to get there and see.

While her pace of meandering had felt tedious through each room, she was glad she'd had the patience as she reached what she believed to be the inner middle of the hall. There were indeed doors toward the center of the complex—two in this room. The wide, thick-framed doors were not shut, to her surprise, but they were attended, with a steward in each, and views of a wide, mostly empty space beyond. Not wanting to draw the attendants' attention, she milled over to a small piece on an adjacent wall.

Xelle loved art and especially appreciated its diversity of forms—and Tenne's were certainly interesting. This one was mostly flat like a painting, and then on one side the image rose outward from the presumed canvas, reminding her of a mountain rising from the land. The colors, other than one clear section (which was cool) were a sequence of muted land tones. She searched for a hidden pop of a brighter color, but couldn't find one. On the flatter side, a clear mixture had been formed and dried, so that a piece of solid substance arcing from it, painted black, reached, floating, toward the mountain part.

This is why she wasn't an art critic. 'Literal Art Critic' was a job posting nowhere, she thought.

Yet nothing in it moved her. Of course, art was personal. Perhaps she just wasn't Tenne's audience. She looked for a title, but didn't see one. The frame, plain like a take-apart molding bin, suspended from thin wires, no other plaque or label.

"Is Bon Tenne this way?" a voice squeaked behind her.

"This is authorized access only," one said. "The exhibit continues that way." Xelle imagined xe was pointing to a door to Xelle's back, the intended path through.

The hu, who sounded young, began to argue.

"Please continue through the exhibit, or you'll need to leave."

Out of the corner of her eye, Xelle saw that the two stewards had moved together, closing in to convince the young hu to move along, that Bon Tenne could not be seen and xe really didn't want trouble with the government of Mytil.

Ashes, this wasn't the clean throw she wanted. But they were distracted, and how long could she look at this painting?

For a second, she considered whether she should reach into some of her most advanced magic, and travel past the guards, into the hallway. Not only was it a cast she hadn't recently practiced, it'd go well beyond the strict measures on magic use for Studies. She *was* still a Study, if even by her own doing. And she wasn't looking for trouble from the Tower. But that hadn't stopped her from making her garden. She'd done it then.

. . .

She couldn't. Not outside the Tower. She had one throw at doing this the simple way, and she had to take it. Quickly, she slid past the guards, both turned away from her.

"Why does xe get to do it?" the voice squealed.

Fira.

Hurrying now, she pictured the likely map and wound up and around to where she would put the private gallery, not in the dome itself, but probably in that blocky area behind it. She whipped around a corner, and nearly ran into a hu.

Was this him? As she snapped her eyes up to assess, xe scanned across her cape, as if for credentials.

"Stop! You are under order from the authority of the City of Mytil to stop in place." Xe folded xyr arms.

Aaaaaash.

"Hello." She forced a low smile. "I mean no disrespect. I have a private conversation for Bon Tenne, one of importance. If you could only ask him if he would be willing to speak wi—"

"This isn't some village where they smile and give you a cookie, Hu. This is Mytil. And if you don't immediately follow me out of this building and put your regs down for temporary suspension, we will take you to the Frond Magery and then, Hu, you can tell them what's going on."

Fira, she'd forgotten that the populace used terms like 'Magery'; she'd never heard that stuff from her parents. And Frond? Already? She thought, as long as she didn't disobey or cast, they'd escort her out with a stern warning. They were certainly serious in the art district!

Sure, she could drop that she'd studied at To'Frond herself. Spook the per into letting her go. Frond's societal charge of managing individual harm was something she knew was important, but one of the reasons she'd not lasted very long there. It was for someone to work, but not Xeleanor Du'Tam.

Ash, the local Mage who would determine her course of rehabilitation was probably one of the teachers whose classes she'd fallen asleep during. Not really; few professors would be reassigned to transgressions, but weirder things had happened. (Everything was weird lately.)

Xelle did not like to drop status. She didn't even like status. She thought all pers should be respected for who they were, and that systems of titles were too simple, too influenced, and too restrictive to the unseen pers who stomped their own paths. And she didn't need the trouble with Arc—or certainly Frond!

So she bit her lip. About the four Towers that knew her. How xe could call her 'Study' not 'Hu'. About the fact that she was trying to burning protect them from something that felt very scary without alerting the whole city to her search. She kept her voice calm. "Would it trouble you, saving you the trip to the Magery, to at least ask Bon Tenne if he'd talk to me?" The hu scowled, and she heard footsteps behind. "If he tells you that I am welcome, you can return to your duties. And if not, I will leave straightaway."

Her calmness had only riled xem. "I don't think you know where you are!"

More stewards poured into the room, and she was now surrounded by at least eight. "Come along with us," another said. "Go ahead." Xe gestured in front.

"Shouldn't some of you be watching the art?" she blurted.

It was so unwise to antagonize them, but the whole last month had been really odd, and she'd behaved and went along, and something was starting to slip on that.

The stewards didn't respond to her jab; they'd started debating what to do with her. Apparently, pers usually argued a bit, but never actually refused to leave once confronted with a steward or two or certainly not the threat of being taken to the Mages.

Mages. Plop. She was caught surrounded by harrumphing stewards because she didn't just ash-fall use her magic down in the gallery. The thing she'd been working on for a whole burned out decade, and more. Because she was only a Study and she was so firefalled controlled. Maybe it was time to stop making that mistake.

What could she do now? With her storm racing up and no time to think? Reaching in, again glad her material was so well, she pulled a thread and stitched it, quickly like a child was late for school, onto her own voice.

Hoping the stewards wouldn't notice the wee addition, she called over them, "Tenne! Tenne! Please help!" and throwing the little dart up and around, toward her best guess of where the artist chambers would be.

"Hey! That's enough of that!" A steward choked out, clearly losing xyr patience. "He can't hear down here; see the stone in these walls? Now, you'll come with us."

"To Frond Mages? I just wanted to see the artist," she stalled, trying to sound nervous. "What will happen at the Magery?"

"Xe's right, you know, there's too many of us up here. What if it's a trick? To get more of them up here? Remember the tattoo group? We need xem down. Now. We're going to have to touch xem." They argued amongst themselves a bit, then moved into a formation around her.

The idea of these pers, despite what she could tell were good intentions, pulling on her arms and touching her nice new cape was more than she could tolerate.

"Please, I'm sorry. I'll walk downstairs." She drew back away.

The stewards softened. "Don't be afraid. Everything will be fine. We just need you to follow us for a while."

As Xelle turned, a few of the stewards stopped. Her heart pounded; those who'd stopped were facing back up the stairs.

"Greetings, good stewards," a powerful voice let out.

Relief fell through her as her shoulders relaxed. She still held her body as far from any of the stewards as she could, worried someone would still touch her, even accidentally.

"What's going on?" he said. He, presuming this was of course Bon Tenne.

A flurry of voices broke out, and still nervous to turn around and spook the stewards, she waited as they narrowed down to a single voice.

"Another admi, Bon. Xe's trying to get up to you, unauthorized."

Xelle thought their training should include not confirming that his chambers were, indeed, up.

"Excellent job looking out for me, as always."

He didn't come down here to compliment them. Yet Xelle was nervous to turn around. Any movement with their boss watching could cause them to be more protective. So, she spoke clearly. Ashes, she didn't want to bring up the Tower but she knew no other way to get out of this.

"I'm not here as an admi. I'm from To'Arc and I'm concerned about someone you know there. I think your parent there knows who." She had no idea how many parents Tenne had, but certainly that would drop the clue.

"Please face me when you speak." The tone was harsher than the words. She turned, slowly.

Now, Xelle had heard a lot about the famous artist of Mytil. Handsome, striking, powerful, with art traversing between worlds. Each of those things was in the eye of the beholder, for certain, but the per himself looked quite . . . normal.

His clothing did not. A white suit, with satin accents and fabric that bowed in and out for dramatic effect. A huge, thick, billowing cream cape and a headscarf that wound around and then down past his shoulders. Tall, white boots with elevated heels. Xelle wasn't sure which exact words those in fashion would use to describe clothes like these, but she was certain they would say the clothes wore *him*.

Tenne's face soured. He turned to the steward wearing the largest metal badge. "Worse than an admi. Tower pranks. I know exactly what this is about. Xe will answer for this at To'Arc."

"We'll take xem to Frond, Bon," the steward offered, bowing as xe spoke. "You don't need to deal with it."

"I will deal with it," he said. "You know of my parent, Spire Mage Kern Du'Arc? I can make pers regret making light of Arc business."

The stewards bobbed a bit, as though slapped. Tenne raised a hand, and only then did Xelle realize his white suit had satin wings hanging down from each arm. Absolutely stunning, except who painted in all white? She would have shaken her head if not for the incident in progress.

"Excellent work. I will add to each of your files." A couple of the stewards openly beamed. "With me," Tenne boomed, and Xelle obediently followed him, without looking back.

His words followed too. About his parent being a Spire Mage. He could absolutely upend her life, and that was without something more sinister going on. Something more dangerous, like the feeling she'd had from the Mage back at Breath. She hoped she wasn't in more danger than she'd considered. What else could she do now?

She followed. Up the stairs, around a bend, and through a thick, stone doorway, which Xelle noted had no steward. Tenne closed the huge door with a large *thud*. Xelle had the impression it wasn't often closed.

If Tenne's costuming was amazing, his office was moreso. She'd need hours to take it in. Stone, paintings, mosaic glass, yet not overdone, at least more than it was meant to be. Everything with flow. Everything in its place. Then, she remembered, this was one of Mytil's grandest spaces. A Tower Atrium of the populace, if one would. What a place to win as one's office. Realizing her mouth was open, she shut it.

"Are you offended by crownhair?" he asked.

"Um . . . no . . ." she said, trying again to get past her Tam cultural influence; there it was simply not shown. She'd seen plenty when in Vattam, but to have someone expose it right in front of her, before a conversation . . . Anyway, why should she care?

Yet, she blinked a few times as Tenne removed the huge, squarish hat, and a medium tousle of hair spilled out. She avoided looking directly at it, and crownhair and its colors grew differently for different pers, but she could immediately see the yellow band across, maybe half a year old, when he'd received the E'lle Prize. Bright, bold, and incredibly excited. Above that, a mix of duller tones, not unlike the lighter shades of his art.

Tenne also looked young. Not young, maybe a few years younger than she was. Xelle was going to have to get used to pers being younger than her, especially ranking ones.

At least, though, at least he did not seem upset. She moved slightly in place, letting some of her tension relax.

"It's so heavy," he said, scratching around the sides of his head. "Also, hi. Sorry about all that. Everything is intense here. Tradition, and rules, and here I thought I got *away* from that refusing to do magic." He laughed, nervously, then stopped. "I couldn't do it anyway." He stared at the wall. "I think they all know."

"I'm not offended," Xelle answered, trying to smile reassuringly through her own settling gales. "I get it. I'd show mine but," she waggled her hands around her cap, "it's complicated. No one needs all that. And . . . thank you for helping me, back there. I'm sorry for all the drama. Maybe I should have thought it through more, but I was trying to not be noticed."

He raised an eyebrow, and she chuckled. "You have very serious stewards!"

"They're good pers. Well, most of them. A few I'd buy tickets to Getouttahere if I could. Can I get you anything?"

"Water would be nice," she said, gratefully accepting a cup he pulled from a side cabinet. He pointed to a pitcher, and she went to fill it up.

"I think you got my message, anyway, which is why I'm assuming you don't think I was pretending to be from To'Arc to talk to you."

Tenne sat back on a bench, his legs jutting to the sides in a posture much less elegant than his dress. "Uh, pers have pretended to be Mages to see me. We get everything here. That's why the stewards have to be so strict. Anyway, they always say Charm to see me, not Arc, and they def don't invoke my Da. So, I don't mean to sound blunt, but why are you here?"

She'd thought a lot this morning about what she'd say to him. She'd already decided she wasn't the operative type, but if she barged in all Xelle, would she risk tipping Kern off to her suspicions? That she was working this still? Whatever this was?

There were stories she could pull from to cover for mentioning

Kern on the stairs. Invent a third per, an overheard conversation, say she was worried only for Kern and not also about him. But Xelle just didn't want to deceive. Ever, if she could get away with it. Perhaps there were some who had to deceive, even for essential reasons. Xelle could respect that, even respect how hard it had to be. But it wasn't who Xelle was, and it wasn't who she was going to become.

The world was turning out to be a complicated puzzle, and Xelle only hoped there was a place for her in it.

"I'm Xeleanor Du'Tam, she or e." Noting his surprise, she added. "I'm not a Mage, I'm a Study."

"You threw a solid cast for a Study. Went right in my ear like my Ga was still here."

"Thanks." Xelle half grinned, that losing the grip on the handle sort of grin where anything starts to go. She tried to collect herself. "I don't want to get into everything, but someone is discrediting one of the Spire Mages."

"Which one?"

Xelle remembered with a start that he probably knew them all. Like, knew them. Ok, then. "Pelir. Who is favored to be Crown Mage once Jehanne retires."

"Pelir is great, though not lord of the party. My Da likes Pelir."

Discomfort rose in her chest. She had no idea whether Kern was even involved. Except, she'd been convinced just yesterday. "I know very little," she said. "All I know is when I asked some basic questions about it, I thought Mage Kern acted strange. First, he wouldn't look at me. Then he did. Then he got weirdly rigid." This didn't sound like solid evidence once she listed it out. What was she doing?

But Tenne nodded, strangely unsurprised. "I don't know anything, but I agree something's up. But, look, he'd never hurt Sa Pelir." His face tensed. "I don't know. I just know he hasn't been himself. I mean, I know him. Plus, it's just everything— He hasn't thrown me a call for months. I send him messages, the non-magic way, and weeks later I get a brief response . . . I don't know. That's what I've got. Sorry if that's not worth your trip up here. But at least I could help you not go to the Fronds?" He shrugged.

Ignoring that last bit, Xelle thought what more she could ask. "Is there anything else? Anything that might seem unrelated but could be?"

When he didn't answer, Xelle realized how little they'd actually discussed, which reminded her how little she had to discuss. She had to say something. Why was she here? "I'm not trying to harm anyone, not your Da either. I just . . . if I can help, I'd like to. Even if I'm just the one thrown into it, I'm there now. You know? So I tried here."

Oddly, Tenne smiled, as if understanding, then opened his hands upward. "See, I don't know." He flopped them back to his side. "I'm not there. I'm busy all the time now with art projects, and meeting with artists, and arranged meet and greets, which is why I had to ask the stewards not to send other admis up. I'm sorry about that. I'd love to hear from pers but it gets really hard to sort it. And that's when I'm here. I honestly try to avoid the place. I love my art but I really love it making pers happy. Laugh and smile happy. So mostly what I've been doing with the grant is finding new villages to visit, and creating projects in them. When I can get away. I'm supposed to be here."

That sounded interesting. "As in, your sculptures? Are they outside?"

"Yes, outside; I'm inside enough." He glanced around. "No to my sculptures. It's more like, what do pers need?" He sat up straighter. "Sometimes an old trashyard that no one's bothered to clean; we just get a group and clean it. If I dress a certain way they don't recognize me, and afterward I pay someone to add in a playground. Other times there is a place without brightness, so we find it. Like a yard where people work, or a drab old wall. We paint things across them. Not prize-winning things, but sunshines, and rainbows, and magical pers, like flying frogs wearing long veils."

Specific. "That sounds nice."

Tenne glanced away, and suddenly Xelle could see Kern's same expression in his face. The one that holds trouble in, all the while expressing it. "I thought he'd be more excited. You know how . . . massive this is. And he knows how much this means to me. Whatever's going on has to be big, right? Or he'd . . . Honestly, I'm relieved you're here, because I can't sit and wonder what's wrong with him anymore. Even if I don't have anything to help you." He spun back. "May I ask you something? If you find out what's going on, will you tell me? Would you promise?"

Xelle tensed. She'd learned a long time ago about open-ended promises. She hesitated, thinking how to say no, very much aware of the power differential between them, yet he hadn't been playing that on her. But this could go a real bad way, especially with the tickle that had just started in her mind.

"Please?" he pleaded. "Hey. I grew up around Mages. I get it. Caution and respect, and, well, mostly that. But one thing I learned from them is that Mages aren't supposed to go around barging in other pers' lives."

That stabbed at Xelle's mind, already flaring at the updrafting thought she'd just had. She wasn't a Mage, but this seemed a direct swipe on her intrusion here. And there were codes and reasons; she'd learned all about them. He wasn't stopping.

"What I mean is, he's my parent—my only parent now—and if something's going on, maybe I can help. Maybe we could work together. Or I can put the cube back on my head and make the request sound more impressive."

Normally she'd appreciate the humor but it was a rather bladed humor and her mind was spinning and the attempt fell flat. "What you're asking could put me in a tough spot," she managed to say. "It could put *you* in a tough spot. We don't know if this is nothing. Or if it's more."

"You came here?" Tenne shrugged. When Xelle didn't respond, he added, his voice low, "I have to know."

There was a sadness, an earnestness, a worry in the elaborately cloaked figure with the artist's demeanor and poorly played authority, that—very much against her better judgment, Xelle said yes. "If I find anything out, I'll tell you. But nothing about anyone else. Just about your parent. Kern," she clarified. "But you have to tell me how to contact you, so we can save the whole complex some stress."

18 - A Tickle and an Itch

Xelle didn't return to the Enchanted Forest. She was too bothered, and too galecaught to resolve the mix of worry, fear, and unknowns swirling inside her. She didn't do well with unresolved interactions—they created a column of heat and wavering pressure in her core that wouldn't let her go, no matter how much she tried to ignore it. In particular with this one, for if the tickle she'd had during her conversation was pointing correctly, this was going to be a very difficult and *complicated* conversation. Not one she could leave waiting around.

Unlike her recent travels, she knew her way around the Mytil taxi system (including how much to tip), and was glad the vroom that picked her up was friendly, and fine enough for a low-pressure, no-conversation jaunt up to To'Arc. As the conn pulled up the road and through the trellised gardens toward the tall, vine-covered Tower, Xelle went over her plan. Hopefully simpler, and without so much trying of stewards.

The clerks at the Front Desk always knew her unless they were quite new, and so, unsealed, Xelle passed the clerk on duty a simple note:

Spire Mage Kern Du'Arc,

I visited Bon Tenne Du'Mytil. I request a private conversation with you.

Respectfully,

Study Xeleanor Du'Tam

"Study, did you mean to address this to Spire Mage Kern?"
Xelle nodded. A Study would never get away with a sealed note

to a ranking Mage, but she thought that this could work. "Yes, when should it go out?"

He tapped around a little before answering, "There's a cart going soon, but the next with high floors, about an hour."

The clerk returned her friendly acknowledgment as Xelle turned and headed back into the main Tower. Not stopping until she was safely in the Atrium, she took a seat for a moment, pressing her fingers against her temples, trying to place another odd feeling she'd first noticed on the way here. More than her normal distress pinched at her; she'd not felt anything like this before. An itch, maybe, in her head but leaning to one side of it. She fought a sudden updraft. With the little she knew of medicine, the idea of something inside her mind was terrifying, whatever its source. She hoped it wasn't that.

Itch was just a reference she'd grasped. The sensation was stranger than an itch, like outside of her head, against it, and inside it all at once. Her gut told her, then, it was something magical, not a headache or other ill, and definitely not from her own casts, including the one she'd tied to the phyta.

It had started on her way back from Mytil, so was it related to her visit? Someone who didn't want her to see Tenne? Tenne himself? Someone at the gallery? Had someone turned the magic on her? Or tried?

The idea of being intentionally harmed was new, and awful. Yet over the past weeks, she'd tread more carefully, watched pers with new eyes. While she wanted whatever was going on to be over and resolved, she couldn't reconcile it as a simple rumor or angry citysper. She had a sense, a strong sense, that the world was changing. Too many things going on at once.

She should see a healer. There was likely a Frond Mage somewhere in To'Arc, on assignment. Xe would draw runes on her and sing and maybe give her some really rough news. If it got bad enough. But she'd already sent the note. She had to focus on Kern.

What if Tenne was the source of her itch, perhaps in sensing her tickle? Back to that. How would it impact her discussion with Kern, if Tenne had somehow deceived her? How could he've, though? She'd not sensed magic at the gallery, none at all. Ashes, he straight-out said he couldn't do it. And Tenne had seemed genuine; she wanted to trust him.

Xelle couldn't start mistrusting everyone. And this was all too much to consider on top of waiting on Kern to call, or summon, or whatever he would do.

Rising, she decided to return to her room. The regular one. Which apparently had not been cleaned on rotation as there was an impressive layer of dust over all her unimportant supplies and Tower issue items, those she had not stashed in her garden.

After a bout of half-sanded dusting, she went for dinner, and when there was no response, no note on her door, she wondered if she should have said more in the note. Or perhaps, Kern was still at dinner too.

Finally, seeing the moons out her small window, she realized that without a story better than she had, no nighttime Front Desk clerk would send a message to a Spire Mage from a Study. She pulled off her undercap, brushed her crownhair in the mirror (which could use a wipedown but later), and snuggled into the lackluster covers. Tomorrow, she would reach Mage Kern no matter how many stewards might be flustered along the way.

The Front Desk clerk was the same from the day before. "I did you a favor yesterday," he said. "I don't normally send to the high floors from Studies. But I'd seen you around a while so it seemed legit. However," he licked his thumb before turning over some piece of paper, "I am not sending a second one."

Xelle put on her most reassuring smile, the one she'd seen Helia use. She borrowed her tone of voice as well. "Yes, thank you, but this is a new note. This message is of importance and must be sent nondelay.

Thank you." Mages never explained their mail, they never justified it. And she hoped the boldness of claiming a nondelay delivery would at least make the clerk worry that he was missing something important. "Spire Mage Kern should be expecting it." *He should.*

Checking that the seal was affixed—yes, she'd sealed it this time—she handed over the note.

> Spire Mage Kern Du'Arc,
>
> I must speak with you regarding a personal matter, and the more privacy you can provide, the better. If you can arrange it, it will draw less attention than if I do. I'll be in my room the next hour.
>
> Xeleanor

Xelle turned away with confidence, striding on through the arch.

After not long sitting blankly in her room, she was relieved when a clerk rapped on the door, informing her that Spire Mage Kern wished to see her and xe would accompany her to the location. She sighed, her breath coming out shaky enough that the clerk tried not to act like xe'd noticed.

The itch had grown since last night and it continued on as they walked together to the Spire floors. She didn't mean to keep calling it an itch when that wasn't right at all, but it troubled her, troubled her mind. And Xelle already had a troubled mind, so describing something more was a bit beyond her. It could be stress, she reasoned. She'd been through so many changes over these weeks. Maybe those things combined. Her mind was already so crowded with tumult and spin, that a new stress would have to compete.

She didn't really believe this, but compared to a new ailment, or a magical imprint, or intentional harm, a little extra worry was something she could handle. The idea that it had arrived after seeing Tenne stayed with her of course, but like any knot, there were threads one could hold and others one could move. And right now, she was focused on Kern.

Once the door was closed and the clerk outside, she could feel the Mage throwing a series of casts. She didn't recognize them all, but she felt certain the conversation would not be overheard. Perhaps her words could be recorded, though she hoped not, for without her consent that would be turning the magic. She couldn't worry about it. She couldn't worry about everything.

A Mage walked into her view. Velvet, forest green robes, an embroidered Arc sash, and a tall cap that twisted around to a point. He stood straight, slender but with a strong build, punctuated by huge rings on several of his fingers. Even without his more ceremonial items, Spire Mage Kern looked every bit a force of power. Xelle silently remarked how when she'd been in front of the whole Spire, she'd processed the moment as a surreal part of generally-surreal Tower life. Here, alone with one very powerful per, she found herself in awe. And more than a little nervous.

"Xeleanor," he said, calmly as if they were old contacts, he a trusted mentor. "You don't want to be part of this."

He's a per, she told herself. "In fairness, you made me part of this," she reminded.

"And you ended it. Now you can leave. Please, trust me, and leave it." His tone was too steady, as if forced.

She raised her eyebrows. She'd love to leave. She'd love to banter cleverly and decide her interest was misplaced. But she was increasingly convinced her tickle was correct. Something was amiss with that prize. With this Mage. And now that itch, that itch wouldn't stop. She pushed it all down like calling over a room of toddlers, ensuring the words got out.

"Spire Mage Kern—"

"When my door is shut, please call me Kern," he interrupted.

"*Kern.* I believe this is about the art grant. I also believe you, or someone, sent me to Breath to stop the others from asking, or to buy someone time, or maybe to avoid involving someone used to this type of thing. And, first, I need to tell you something, and it's really important. You sent the wrong Study. What, because I've been a Study so long, I was looked down upon? But you don't know me. I love my home. I love Alyssia. And I love the magic that has been built over centuries here, to give all pers better lives. I can't solve all problems, but if something feels threatening to the very structure of my world, there is nothing, *nothing*, that will dissuade me from pursuing it. Not orders, not threats, not expulsion, not anything."

Kern burst into tears.

Stunned and unsure what to do, Xelle waited. Something, though, something must be worse than she'd feared.

"It's better for you if you leave. You need to leave." He took a series of unsteady, short, but deep breaths, and made a quick cast to dry his face. Seeing that Xelle was not leaving, he walked closer, not threateningly but as if a conversation held closer might prove his sincerity.

Then he stopped. And stared for what felt like a very long time, though of course it wasn't. She considered he might not be stable. She considered at what point she would run, what casts she could make.

"How?" he whispered. "How?" He started to step backward, nearly stumbling, as if afraid. His mouth formed the word a third time.

Fira. What the ash. He was not making this easy. The storm in her mind, and the itch, and the tickle, and the fright of watching a per's reactions for possible harm when she wasn't used to doing so.

"Please, give me a minute," he sputtered out. Nearly stumbling, Kern went to a gilded side stand to pour a drink of water.

Sure, take your time. Xelle took the moment to steady herself, to scan the room. She hadn't intended to say all she'd pushed out in setting the tone, but with Kern's reaction, that worry did not catch her.

"No one saw this," he finally said. "No one. And I can't sleep, but what can I do. It's more than my cura now. They are good, Xeleanor. It was we who were not good to them. Maybe . . . maybe we need you."

"Kern," Xelle was surprised to hear it spoken sternly, when her stomach was gurgling and her hands shaking. "I'm sorry. I know much is going on, but you're making me scared. And I want to know what no one saw and who is good, but first I need to know what happened with the art grant. Will you tell me or not?" She took a breath. "I am in so much trouble doing this and being here. Are you going to tell me? Or do I have to leave and then deal with it? I'm not going to just stand here." She couldn't take it.

Kern, with a flick of his arm, cast toward a cushioned armchair, and brought it closer. "Please, take a seat," he offered.

The thought crossed her mind that she should not take a seat, but her limbs were wobbling, and really it might be best. She nearly fell back into the (extremely comfortable) chair.

And as Kern walked around behind his desk and sat, Xelle had a sudden impression that what he'd been drinking was not, indeed, water. So early in the day. Or perhaps still, from last night? Another worry to juggle.

She tried again. "I don't want to keep going back and forth. For both of us. Right? Please answer my question—will you tell me what is going on?"

He rocked, very slightly, in the seat, and cast over to the side table, floating the small, stoppered pitcher onto his desk. He continued to rock, and as Xelle had the impression he was working up to something, she waited. She wondered if he had actual water, as she could use some about now, but it seemed an insensitive question.

"The sigil. It changes everything." He took another swig. "They must be pursuing them," he said. "I . . . sensed this, but denied it. Awake, every night. They are strong. Right? They must be. They left the pact; they can handle this. Right? Right? Do you know?"

"Kern," she said gently. "Whoever started this, maybe we can keep them from hurting others. Tell me, please—who are they? And who are they pursuing? A group of Mages? The art guild? The Mytil government?"

"*Them,*" Kern said, almost hissing as he pointed toward her head and took another drink from the pitcher, its stopper clanking against the glass as he set it in place. He tapped his forehead.

Them.

Them. Her mark. Thunder. She'd been focused on Tenne and Mytil. She raised her own fingers to the mark, letting them sink against her skin. *Oh, and—* Then, the dragons *had* caused it? She had to be sure. She was sure. Still.

"Say it." Xelle lowered her hand. "Who?"

"Dragons," he whispered, like a child, then again changed tone. "They are more powerful than— They are powerful. We reside here only with their tenuous grace."

He slurred, slightly, over the last few words, but Xelle didn't really hear them anyway, as of course the feeling in her head was the mark. It was such a different sensation. When she'd first noticed it, it had hurt . . . more the normal way. But that had settled. It just seemed . . . cosmetic—to her great relief as she'd monitored it at To'Breath. She'd tried to stay focused, but her attention drawn . . . Yes, the mark was her itch. And what was Kern saying, because 'they' were at risk? The dragons? "And whoever is . . . threatening you, may threaten the dragons?" She tried to clarify; she could not misunderstand this.

"I . . . They want something, in the mountains. At first, I thought it was mining. They said it was mining! I have been worried for . . . them. The hu, I don't know what they intend, but they are foul. They are dishonest. You met them?" He gazed again at the mark.

Xelle nodded. "I met one. I saw others." She was going to have to get to the bottom of these theys and thems, but at least now he was talking.

He straightened, his voice regaining strength. "Why would you have gone mountainward, on your way to Breath? What would have given you that idea?"

She wasn't ready to answer that. And he wasn't telling her who these threateners were. "Please, Kern. I want to know what hu are involved with the Ascension and the dragons and the art prize." The words sounded absurd in her own ears but it was all she had. "I want you to tell me what you know."

With another drink, he still affixed her with an unhealthy stare. "We work together," he said, his free hand clenched on the desk.

And maybe too much had changed in the last few days or maybe the reality that a Spire Mage had truly been withholding danger from To'Arc or maybe the tapping in her head and the revelations of it had her cloudy, but she looked right back at him and said, her voice now steady, "We work together if I say we do. First, tell me what you know. *Who are 'they'?*"

Strangely, this seemed to snap him back to the presence of a ranking Mage, and he restraightened, shaking his head in the negative. "I don't know," he answered. "But there is organization. Much more going on than I understood. Than . . . I understand."

There were too many things to figure out all at once, so she sifted through pressing questions as though they were resting in a box, as if her fingers shook, flicking through them. The next question that she saw was why Kern hadn't brought the others in, to help them understand.

That one, she didn't want to ask. Whether it was fear for Tenne, fear for himself, or some noble belief that he was protecting the Spire, she didn't want to hear it. She'd come here with compassion for the Mage in hand, some understanding what he could have been through. But he could have spoken anyway. Could have tried to nip this, before it was already a sprawl of vines with Xelle thrown into its thorns. Even now, if he spoke, it was because of her mark, not her insights and risks in finding Tenne, the risk Tenne had put, himself, in trusting her. Somehow, this came back to Tenne.

She felt for Kern. She did. But she also felt frustrated. Angry. "Kern. Tell me about Tenne."

He hesitated. "Will you promise not to tell anyone?"

Xelle shook her head, no. No. She could not promise that, and, again, she withheld her own thoughts on that matter. "I will do what I can to help. I promise," she added, softly. "He wants to know."

Kern slowly lifted his head. "I know less than you will think or hope."

Resisting the urge to throw her arms to the sides, she tried to give a reassuring smile. It came out rather twisted. Luckily Kern had turned to stare at the wall.

"It was a prospector, meeting about quarry opportunities in the mountains. Casually, she mentioned Tenne applying for the prize. 'Yes,' I said, 'it's his passion.' This would be well-known for anyone trying to influence me." He flicked a hand. "She mentioned that she'd thrown in a good word with the selection board; it should go better for him. I didn't think much of it. Pers seeking favor from Mages often whisper such things, and we've been well-trained to spot it. When I said I'd consider her plans but, without detail and an assigned hearing, they were unlikely to be approved, she mentioned one more thing. 'I told them I was working with you,' she said. 'There is always interest in new quarries.' As I was processing what this per had done, she added that I must not reveal 'our' influence in Mytil, or Tenne would be disqualified."

Kern now spoke as though a waterfall had been let over a crop of rock. "It was a threat, and I should have sought the selection board to tell them, but Tenne would be devastated to be disqualified if they did so out of caution. It could impact his future, his reputation, right when he was trying so hard. The truth is, I saw her threats as a reckless attempt for a land permit I was never going to grant, and . . ." He closed his eyes. "I . . . did not think he could win. I . . . didn't. Please," he now whispered. "Never tell him that."

He gasped in air, as if coming up from the lake he had just flooded. "Then he won. As you know. And another per returned; I never would have let that first one enter the outer paths again, let alone the Tower. This next one told me that he knew about Tenne's award. And if I said anything, they had proof that I was directly involved. The last per had her pass, from the desk, authorizing her to meet with me soon before the awarding of the prize, in addition to her testimony."

He was speaking so quickly; Xelle tried to absorb it.

"Tenne was thrilled. So thrilled. He immediately went to work, devising ways to use the grant coin and access in ways the prize has never seen. His work among the populace made him a star, the fervor spreading to those unaware of it. Even in the Tower, pers pointed at me, not in the way of a Spire Mage, but Tenne's parent. Me! On the Spire!

"I was torn, absolutely torn. Yet I told this next wicked per, you are not getting any land grant; consider this over. With a terrible smile, he said the grant was no longer necessary. They just wanted to call in one last favor, and then they wouldn't see me again. A map of the lands upmountain of Arc, for their future consideration. This was . . . trivial. Maps of that area have little detail, and they are available at the Records Post of any city of size, or even local village, as part of the full mapping of Alyssia as related to land rights. Maps are our social responsibility—not a secret. He could do nothing with this, whatever he thought. I wanted him gone. So I found a copy, and without seeing him again so he could plant no other threats, sent him away."

Kern finally stopped. Xelle could understand. Those words would hurt her to say too, amidst the picture he was painting. "They came back?" she offered.

He nodded. "They demanded a roster of Mages and projects and I said, no, that's Mage business. But then they reminded me I'd given them maps, ones marked as Arc maps, on top of not reporting Tenne's prize. If I backed out now, not only would Tenne suffer even more than he would have, but I'd lose everything I'd ever worked for. My ability to help."

Again, he burst into tears. As he reached for the pitcher, Xelle now tried to warn him off, but he was not done. He was shouting now, though with his casts, Xelle felt sure no one could hear them from the corridor.

"Tenne is the love of my life. He was a sweet child; my spouse loved him more than anything in the world. Do you know how brave he was, in our family—in this family—to leave power behind, to be willing to make arcing little molds, and live off of Basic, only known as a man selling funny paperweights in a tent outside the gallery on a too-chilly day?

"These monsters. These fire-eyed monsters. And now they own me too. First the art, then the tasks, then dear Pelir— I bet you would have stopped them, right? You would have said no. You must think me a weak, awful hu." He threw back the next drink. "Even now, I make excuses. They discredit Pelir, I think that's terrible, but their option is as good. Then they want to put me on the Crown. Me, the fool who fell for the map. Because I didn't want to see. *I'm* the one. I promise you, I do not want it." He waved the glass around. "I didn't want any of this."

Xelle felt sick. But at least now she had something.

"Kern," she said, as softly as she could. "Please set down the glass. They don't have to control you anymore. They don't." He looked unsure, so she added, "We work together now. Tell me what you're doing."

His hand still clenched around the glass, but he dropped his neck just slightly. "Their first goal is to force Pelir out of Ascension. They claim Pelir is part of some shadowed group they call the Amberborn— those are the rumors. A secret group of Mages who wish to hurt the populace rather than assist them. I don't know much else." He held out his free hand, palm up. "I really don't."

"Would Pelir be?" she asked.

Kern shook his head, feebly.

"You'll need to turn on them," she said. "If you're serious about this."

He hesitated, fear across his face.

So unstable. Xelle watched her words. "If you are scared for yourself, I understand. I'm not used to fear, not like this, either. The best way for us to remove this fear is to understand and expose it. Get Alyssia to work against it. Not let it fester. As for Tenne, he got me to promise him I'd tell him. About the influence, not about your thoughts. Those are safe with me." The word jarring her, she didn't also mention something she now realized, that Tenne could be in danger. "So I will go to see him. Discreetly. The question is, can I tell him you're going to do something about it?"

With a swollen face, Kern stood up again, his robes swaying around his legs and elaborate hat reaching upward, and Xelle again saw the power she'd seen just a few minutes ago. The power of Arc Magic, and the spirit of those drawn to wield it. "Yes," he said. "As I said . . . if you will accept it . . . we will work together."

Again jarred by that power, so inherent in his fabric and his sash, Xelle said something extraordinary, something she never conceived she'd say to a Spire Mage. "We work together only as long as I can trust you. Right now, that is tenuous." This next bit, then, was critical. "Tell me about the dragons."

He calmed himself with quick meditations. A breath. Perhaps a mantra. Then opened his eyes. "The dragons must be protected."

Protection. The word settled in her mind. "From what?"

"From anything. Harm, control, manipulation, further relocation. I don't know much; the information is guarded and the little I've heard, I am sworn not to say. I am worried they are in danger from these hu, putting all of us in danger. Everything." He nearly whispered the last part. "I'd doubted myself, but . . ." He pointed a shaking finger at her mark. "It must be so. As for how or why, I will try to learn more. Whatever I can."

"I don't know much about being an operative," Xelle said. "And the whole idea of conflict between Mages has me flailing in new skies." She didn't repeat his vague sense of a threat to the dragons. Frankly, she didn't want him near them. "Here is what we need. If you trust anyone at Breath, I would go there, bring xem in for advice, and maybe a few good potions." She glanced at the pitcher. "Only if you truly trust xem. I think the hardest part is you'll need to convince these other pers that you are still working for them. Anything that is revealed must be blamed on me. Or someone else, just know that you could put pers at risk. If this is really as serious as it feels."

"I have someone," he said, slowly. "I think who can help me, know how to do it."

"Keeping trust with both groups will be critical. They can't suspect you. Whom you tell on the Spire . . . or if you do, I don't know. Your contact. That would be a good question. Stick to that," she added firmly.

Realizing what she'd just said and that with a knowing gaze, he did not argue but relaxed back the slightest touch, Xelle subconsciously exhaled. "If you need to talk to me, you can call? Do I need to give you anything for that?"

"Without a strong connection," he said, "I would need a location."

Xelle had a feeling she wasn't going to be living in her Study room for a while. The best locations, then, were her room in the Enchanted Forest or her secret room here. Her garden, she decided. She was going to start calling it her garden. No, her nightgarden. But she wasn't going to give this Mage, who'd chosen her side only minutes ago, and only because of a mark on her face that he found impressive, the location of either of those.

"I will be moving around." She flashed the Arc, a gentle reminder that an Arc Mage, or a student of Arc Magic, thrived on travel. On change.

Kern gasped, like something had pricked him, and fumbled at his neck. Finally, with what Xelle felt as a tiny hook of magic, he removed a chain. His hand shaking violently across the desk, he handed it to her, clasping his hand over it until, unsettled by the gesture, Xelle pulled it away. A small locket, in metal over which a color changing sheen had been washed, sat in her hand. Xelle was certain what this was. And that it was not enchanted.

"My spouse's. A symbol of my trust. And I promise, if you wear it, I will always be able to find you."

"Are you sure?" she asked. "I can't promise I will always wear it."

"I know," he said, waving an arm, comically dismissive given the circumstances. "Now what?"

"Now, I am going to tell the Front Desk and anyone else standing around that you read me the Study Guide for interrupting you and I guess Bon Tenne's statement that I could go talk to you was a load of ash. Then, you are going to put that away," she gestured to the pitcher, "and send for a potion to help. Tell them it's for an apprentice if you must."

He nodded, awkwardly. "Do you want to try it first? It's from Grand."

Try it? This was not appropriate, nor had she tried a Grand Spirit before, possibly ever. Frankly, about now, she did. If he meant to poison her, he was a skilled Arc Mage in a sound-sealed room. It wasn't a concern.

Kern poured a glass and walked toward her chair. Xelle rose.

As she took the offered glass and made a face in reaction to the slow sip, he chuckled slightly.

"It's so herbal! And strong! How do you drink this? I mean, it's good, but sort of a thousand when a hundred would do!"

Now he laughed, the same way that Tenne did. A bubbly laugh, like even the darkness couldn't drown the joy. "Gloria used to tell me the same thing, e—" He stopped. "I'm sorry. So much I've lost. Because of—"

There would have to be a skilled therapist to deal with Kern's guilt and sought redemption, and Xelle was a tired Study with a storm in her mind and a pounding dragon mark. "I know," she said. "And one of these days you'll look Gloria in the eye"— (Kern was actually tall enough to do it) —"and tell em the whole story. And you will deal with it how it will be."

A memory popped through. "In the formation of the third tier, Spire Mage Martin said to the Gold Brick Rioters, 'The light is always correct to correct your path.'" She'd liked that; it had stuck with her. Not an excuse, but a way.

And while she hoped it would provide a more positive note on which to leave, she saw that the Mage was crying again. She set down the still-full glass.

"Xeleanor," he choked out.

"What?" she replied, her voice low.

"We . . . I picked the right Study." Moving back to his seat and desk, he folded onto his arms. Xelle picked up the glasses and pitcher, closed them back into a cabinet, and walked out through the now-unlatched door.

19 – Mark of a Hero

It was a unique chance to be on the Spire floors without an escort, and so she moved, as quietly as she could, which here meant also without magic, to the personal chambers of the Crown Mage Jehanne.

Her mind spun and swirled, but a couple things had occurred to her. First, Jehanne could not retire, not yet. Second, if Xelle had really been marked by the dragons, then she would need some leeway. This was not the right time to deliver these messages, but she couldn't wait for another chance.

The door automatically opened, and then closed behind her.

Crown Mage Jehanne was seated at her own desk, relatively small but not lacking any detail in the carved and inlaid wood. Her index fingers pressed against her lips and a stack of papers looked pushed to the side. The uniquely shaped black cap sat snugly against her, still, as if never removed.

Xelle bowed. "Crown Mage Jehanne." She walked toward her, down the length of the long room. "You know where I've been?"

Jehanne smiled, like it was an inside joke. "From where I sit, these matters are delicate. Correct moves only, one could say."

Xelle was certain there was more to that, but a Crown Mage allowing her in to casually remark on shared business was surreal enough, had Xelle already not felt dissolved to shadow in the per's quiet presence, which was simply encompassing. If Kern had felt powerful like a mallet, Jehanne felt like a moonstone. Yet the Mage now waited, apparently to hear what Xelle had to say. What had she come here to say? Oh, right.

"I've not learned very much," she started, not thinking an introduction was desired. "The clouds are thick. The discrediting effort sounds larger and more organized than it initially did. More than a whisper, more than a cast. There's layered planning behind it." She took a breath.

"Crown Mage Jehanne, I recommend that you do not retire until we know more, while continuing to tell pers that you plan to. I know that's a hardship after the life you have given, and you shouldn't be asked, but I worry you are the last puzzle block they are waiting to be pulled. I don't know that, but, it makes sense, at least without more time to think about it. I also recommend you keep the Spire as-is until we know more." Xelle cringed, realizing she'd said 'we' and suggested, what, firing Spire Mages?, but Jehanne was regarding her pensively and not with displeasure. "That's . . . that part." She'd wanted to convey that she wasn't going to say more about who might be involved, but she couldn't say it like that. She's said what mattered. Keep the Spire as-is. For now.

Jehanne continued to sit, though it seemed she had raised one leg over the other, and was now tapping her knee with her fingers. "You are a trusting per, and that delights and also concerns me. I have worked with these Spire Mages, in one capacity or another, for decades, and each of them came to this rank because they are genuine, passionate, and perhaps flawed in their sense of balance." She glanced away, not at the bookcase to the side, but in the direction of it.

"We are fortunate here in Arc Tower to have such spirits. Yet see what still happened. What may still. Whatever happens in Alyssia, I must ask you to guard your feelings of trust. They likely speak rightly now, but as you are better known, they will present terrible risk."

Not sure what to say, for this whole concept upset her greatly, Xelle nodded. She did trust pers. Her parents, her friends, Klein, Helia . . . others.

"If you ever need someone to trust here, Study Xeleanor Du'Tam, trust We'le." Oddly, she did not append We'le's title.

Was this a test? Xelle recognized her own short chuckle at the idea, after it had already escaped her.

Jehanne raised one of her fingers, atop her knee, and her head cocked the tiniest bit.

"I'm sorry, Crown Mage Jehanne." Xelle bowed. "It was just if I'm not supposed to trust pers, how do I know I can trust you telling me who to trust?"

She nearly saw herself saying the words, and knew her eyes opened wide. "I'm sorry," she gasped. "I say things and—" No. She was not going to waste one of the seven Crown Mages of Helina's time explaining her own mental challenges and disorders.

Jehanne seemed unbothered, if not even amused. "You already trusted me, because I'm the one you came to."

Xelle quieted at this. "Thank you," she said, bowing again. "The discord, whatever it is . . ." She was trying to remember if she'd said everything. What were the two things? They wouldn't be alone again soon if not ever, and she always remembered what she'd meant to say just after leaving the door. This was not the time for that to happen.

"I don't think the pers involved are Mages." Except Kern was a Mage. "The pers causing this." She moved quickly along. "I could be wrong, but I don't get that feeling from it. I think they want to discredit the Mages, either at To'Arc, or worse: broader, by making it seem like they are fighting internally. Then maybe worse things—" she'd had no time to work out what having Kern on the Crown Spire would do and her mind was in no spot for quick ideas. "The goal? I don't know." She thought what Klein said. "We'll need to find out what's important to them." Why didn't she have time to think this through? She had to be making no sense.

"You spent a lot of time reading in To'Breath?"

An odd segue. Xelle nodded. Then saw the Crown Mage before her. "Yes, Crown Mage Jehanne."

"The history we must seek is the one that does not obscure motivations. Comfort," she added. "Hu are like all nature, whether a bud of ivy or a drop of water, we run to comfort. Our actions lead to comfort."

Xelle wasn't quite sure if she meant good actions or bad.

"All of them," Jehanne answered. "The only difference is whether they seek the comfort of one, a few, some, or all. Which our heart desires. Consider that when you will."

Only comfort? She wasn't sure. What about love, and power—were they comfort too? "Thank you, Crown Mage Jehanne."

"I appreciate you coming to me, and I will consider your counsel."

This worried Xelle. "I know you can only consider, and of course I'm honored that you'd consider it at all, but I would feel better knowing—" She was going to say 'that the Arc Spire will stay as it is for now' but she'd already made that point.

"We are in a delicate moment. Please continue to trust me, Xeleanor, as I am trusting you."

That was strong. She'd have to take that.

"We will continue to investigate here," the Mage continued, looking more elderly as she leaned into the light of her lamp. "I have others working it. For now, I request that you lower your profile."

Xelle felt relieved at this. She'd planned to find more about this organization; it was an obligation. But if these aspects: the Spire and the Ascension, were now being worked here, then she could better commit to the other concern, deeper in her mind. Literally. An idea sprung into that mind. Not an idea, a necessity. Should she do this? Could she? It would provide the lower profile Jehanne had requested. It would give some space, from— Oh, why didn't she have time to think? No, this made sense. She knew it did. Still, the words hurt to say.

"Crown Mage Jehanne, I wish to go to Ever Tower for a while, and resume studies there. May I go with your blessing?"

Unless she misread it, she thought Jehanne's head lowered a touch. "Would my blessing or the lack of it change your plan?"

"It would not," she said, relieved to be so open. "But it would make my appeal there much easier. I used to study there, when I was young. And they will be skeptical of my return, as you could understand."

Jehanne smiled and paused. "Granted." She began to rise.

As that must signal that they were done here, Xelle desperately pulled at a rope in her mind, one that had just shaken loose. She knew this was unwise, but she might not ever get another chance. "Crown Mage? Study Ay'tea Du'Ail. He was my lab partner. We were friends. Do you know where he went?"

She stopped her motion forward, her weight leaning into the hand against the corner of her desk. "I am sorry," she said. "Our paths can be complex, and unlike our actions, they do not lead to comfort. I am sorry, Xeleanor. I know how it feels."

Xelle had no idea what that meant, but Jehanne had stood straight and was walking toward her with a stance that stated that there would be no more said on that. Reaching Xelle, she lifted a finger upward. Toward Xelle's forehead. Toward the mark that still rang in her head, but she'd managed to take its noise and hold it back, with such important tasks at hand. She planned to deal with it later; she knew she'd have to. But of course, if Kern noticed it, Jehanne would too. And she'd been running around Alyssia with it!

Jehanne held her finger steady, her expression now simply unreadable. "You may choose to cover this," she said. "It is a difficult choice either way, and I will not interfere in it. Now, I have something for you. This choice I do not have; the pact is clear." She raised both arms, her wrinkled hands held nearly at face level, and then breathed in deep.

Xelle's being swelled with wonder and awe as Jehanne stood silently, casting magic around them, which built and swirled like thread, or a whirlpool, or a column of wind, or all of those at once. It felt ancient, complex, close to otherworldly, and Xelle shivered in its might. The cast layered and built over what felt like forever, perhaps a minute, perhaps more. And for a moment the chambers turned to frost, and then the most brilliant snow, and when Xelle caught her bearings she was facing Crown Mage Jehanne Du'Arc, holding a long blade, made of what must be obsidian with a clear crystal handle. As she gazed into it, moving closer as if physically drawn, she saw that the obsidian was not smooth black, but etched with a fine pattern of ivy.

The magic fell slowly to a stop, like the falling snow she thought she'd seen, and at last they stood together, in quiet. No longer standing like one of the seven ranking Mages of Alyssia, but a grandparent, letting something go.

"What is it?" Xelle asked. An underwhelming response, but what could she say! She could imagine no use for such an object, though she scoured her mind for suggestions, ranging from practical to magical. It must be enchanted, though she didn't sense Ever Magic from it. Not that she was going to cast detection in front of Jehanne.

"It's called a sword," the Mage said as she handed it over. "Designed to kill."

Xelle almost dropped the blade, but Jehanne did not let go, and soon Xelle held it steadily. Clearly magical in nature, it was not heavy like the bag of obsidian she'd lugged across Alyssia and back, but light. It felt like an instrument of the wind in her hands, and taking the cue from how Jehanne had held it, she stepped back and swooshed it to one side, then the other. In it, she felt peace, and balance. Not death.

"It's old," Xelle said aloud. "And not Arc Magic, and I don't think Ever either. It feels so complicated."

"It is," Jehanne agreed. "Now. Please remember to eat, rest, and sleep. You will need these things. You have lived in presumptively peaceful times, but you must always remember that for a Mage to be caught near one's material limits is a dire risk. Not only for casting, but for energy, interaction, health. Remember what you were taught here about material; it is not academic: it is life or death, and not only for yourself. Now, unless you have any final comments or questions, we both have much to attend."

"It's sharp," she blurted out. "Is there a case?"

Jehanne chuckled. "Not anymore."

Xelle knew, just knew, that as soon as she left, she'd think of everything she meant to say, in addition to fretting about what she did say, and if she'd done it right, and it was like always except with one of the most important pers in the world. Yet she was overwhelmed and needed space to recharge. Forget material limits, Xelle had to worry about her mind limit. Or was that what Jehanne was just saying? She looked at the sword.

"Send it somewhere for now." Jehanne nodded. "Go ahead, I know you can do it."

Gaping back at the Crown Mage, she was surprised to be trusted with such advanced magic. A Study would never be allowed to transport an item, certainly not a sharp one that killed pers. Had this . . . killed pers?

The Crown Mage, expressionless, stared back as if Xelle was wasting her time.

Xelle took a breath. If Jehanne could bring a blizzard in and send it out, certainly she could send a little sword away. She breathed in, breathed out, focusing on her nightgarden, a location she knew intimately from her months training to enter it. She sensed the Arc phyta growing in Jehanne's office. A vine wound over the bookcases. She asked for their help. And with a sensation that felt rough as well as thrilling, the sword collapsed from view. Xelle's hands stayed suspended in the air, until she lowered them.

She turned back and smiled at Jehanne, her eyes alit. Jehanne seemed unable to withhold her own feelings, as she grinned back.

"Good! Now go check that it worked; that's quite a valuable item!"

"Yes, Crown Mage Jehanne." As she stepped backward, she paused, not sure what to say. A normal salutation seemed to fall flat.

"Until we meet again, Mage Xeleanor," Jehanne said, flashing her the most perfect and dignified Arc Xelle had ever seen. Now completely overwhelmed, Xelle returned a shaking and sad Arc, and practically ran out of the Spire floors, and down through the Tower.

Still too much to sort. Her head felt funny, yes she'd forgotten to ask Jehanne about that and whether it would put her at risk to see a Frond healer, she needed to plan, she hadn't had lunch, she needed to empty out her room and lab, and tell the lab she wouldn't be working there anymore, and she needed to tell Tenne what she'd learned, not just because that was a promise, but because she was worried for Tenne's safety. On top of it all, her heart ached at the words that she'd said. She loved Arc Magic with all her heart. Maybe she should have told Jehanne. Maybe she should have just pledged.

The idea had flashed, suddenly. The magic of protection, could she protect the dragons? She couldn't just go back to her lab here, she couldn't. Kern wouldn't want her lurking. Space, she needed space. Why, then, in that moment, had she blurted Ever? Yes, protection? But was that all? The call of her home Region? Had it all been a huge mistake?

She couldn't change any of that now, and there was much to do.

Her first task was easy, at least it felt easier now after everything else. She stopped by the Front Desk and did make quite a lowkey scene about Spire Mage Kern wanting nothing to do with her. The clerk looked intimately annoyed, as she'd been the one to get him to send a nondelay, and so she apologized and said Mage Kern's cura had asked her to say hi, and he'd been way off, and now she just wanted away from all of it. With the throbbing in her head and the swirl of spinning thoughts, at least she was certain she pulled off being upset by the whole ordeal.

Then, making certain she was alone, she walked her way through the stone of her nightgarden. Oddly, after casting Mage-level magic in the presence of a Crown Mage, walking through her wall almost felt commonplace. She had no idea why Jehanne had called her a Mage or if it'd been a slip-up (she didn't think so?) but it had bolstered her confidence.

The sword was there!

Not that she was excited about the sword—a bizarre item and more about that in a minute—but the fact that, under pressure, within the eyes of the Crown Mage, she'd done something that complex. What else could she do?

She walked around to look at the plants, reminding herself they had not been in the reflection of the obsidian chunks for very long. The immediate disappointment was the lack of blooms, or anything that looked like a bloom in progress. Yet she leaned in and walked past, and saw clearly that the small dots of light were brighter; the shiny leaves felt stronger.

Much more to do here, but it couldn't be today. Picking up the sword, she leaned it against the back wall, wiggling the point into the soil in the wedge she hadn't yet tiled, and stood up. "Inkblooms, Giant Knife, I will return."

She thought of what Jehanne had said, about trust, and danger. While ensuring access only from inside had seemed safer when she'd done it, she'd much rather be able to get in now without walking through the Tower. Especially—and her heart pinged with pain she could not yet process—if she was no longer an Arc Study.

She pushed those thoughts aside.

Again, she drew a cast of communication, for safety and warning. They tied off stronger and easier this time. Her door should be secure, as closely as it was tied to her, someone else would more easily doze the bricks around it. She thought about placing heavy objects in front, but that would be more of a sign than just letting the old corner be. Then, how to get in from outside, without time for learning new stones.

With a sigh, she realized she was going to have to leave it until the blooms developed. She'd have to use Frond Magic for connecting runes . . .

What if she combined them?

Rummaging through her cabinet, she found her strongest paint, a deep, gloopy red that had probably now been curing longer than it was supposed to. And positioning it in the largest open space, the area in front of her swiveling chair, but neither right in her old doorway nor on the seat, she painted a connection rune. This was not appropriate (ok, totally forbidden) to do on her own; without the registry she could interfere with some Mage's movement or even bring them here.

It must be unique—unambiguously. Concentrating, and knowing she must go slow, she painted, humming deeply, a complicated rune across a set of the polished tiles. The character for reception here, secrets here, warning here. Remembering she could be crossing magic with a Frond Mage right now, she hurried to add her own elements. She looked across the room, adding the shape of the sword, tilted to the side from where it was stuck into the soil. Remembering the lab she'd shared with Ay'tea, she drew the little figure he'd used to depict himself when he left her notes. And then, caught up in some personal response at that thought, she slashed an 'X' across all of it.

Staring at what was now a complicated and embarrassingly dramatic jumble, she thought—no one in Frond Tower would ever paint that. And if they did, they were welcome to stop by.

"Now my friends," she said to the dots of light. "As you grow, please shine your light on this."

"And sword," she said, waving to the object. "You are extraordinary but I have no idea what I would do with a killing knife. But if you dig, you can help the inkblooms grow. Now, I'll see you all soon."

Xelle walked back through the wall.

20 – Danger

Too nervous to take a Tower vroom to Mytil, even with the shift change at the Front Desk, Xelle instead walked down to the village. It wasn't just her relationship with the desk clerks that had been shaken, she now felt more cognizant of her smallest actions. Of someone knowing, perhaps, that she was going back to see Tenne after talking to Kern. Even walking along the path, she felt exposed, frustrated. Restless.

Normally, she'd reason through her options, but the morning's events had her emboldened. And she really wanted to get to Tenne so that was one less issue on her list. Her steps felt slow. Frustrated. And her material felt frustrated within her, not separate, but like a need. Another way she was holding back. She had to stop holding back.

So, with the Tower out of view, Xelle decided to experiment. Experiment because Arc Mages' reverence for travel made them a bit rigid about how they conducted it. A ranking Arc Mage would use an inkbloom with great need, but most simply took a moveroom, reveling in the journey. Which was fine for other days, but Xelle was in a mood. And she wanted to see if she could make an idea work.

Humming a tune, she pulled a long thread of travel from her spirit and whipped it out like a frog's tongue catching disrupted pond phyta. She snapped it against a tree ahead, propelling herself forward, lifting from the ground with a howl she could not contain.

It felt good.

Briefly. She hadn't considered how to step back onto the path after such a propulsion and she went rolling over herself, cursing whether she'd scuffed her new cape and checking that her cap hadn't pulled off.

She tried again, smaller pulls, no howls, and gaining confidence in finding the right arc to land safely. After a couple successful glides, or whatever one called them, she sped past a steadily walking moveroom, with a moment of alarm at realizing what she was actually doing, out here on the actual road. Upon landing, she ducked behind a bush as the vroom passed her back, hoping its Tower passengers had not seen her gliding past their windows nor felt the magic emanating from her as she had. After they were out of view, she walked again, the regular way (ok she cast one more time to shortcut a bend) until the low buildings and tents of Vi'Arc came into view.

Fortunately, the conns of the village were used to not asking questions when it came to Studies sneaking incity, so, doing her best to hide a new sense of exhilaration, she found a small taxi, paid enough for privacy, and was soon on her way back, again, to Mytil.

The feeling of her mark—Kern had called it a sigil?—still pressed into her thoughts as the vroom clanked down the road, and Xelle pushed, again, to focus on her destination. Get Tenne off the list, then she could better focus on what else Kern had said. Maybe she should have asked him more, about the mark. But it was so unsettling, and he'd kept saying I don't know. No. For now, focus on Tenne.

She considered getting dropped off nearer the galleries, but settled on the night market (it operated from afternoon through evening but pers liked to sound fancy), offering her a logical destination for the conn, as well as a fairly short walk to the art district.

Holding off on the desire to throw more travel casts, she instead wound her way around to the art gardens, still packed with layers of old snow that had not melted here in the shade of the massive trees or the shadow of the tall, stone building. She trudged on, through a dual-eclipse, glad to be out of view so she didn't have to deal with disapproving views from the Mytil old brigade. Besides, the eclipses were nearly moot in the waning daylight, the moons starting to emerge above.

Stopping, she peered over at the gallery's side, sure this was where he'd told her. "Here we go," she said. Not seeing anyone watching her but thinking in the future she might want to buy a less distinct cloak, she strode to a thick metal door, one which looked like it guarded one of the old Mage vaults in the cellars of each Tower.

She tapped a nearly unrecognizable lever (it looked like part of the metalwork), and a small panel, waist-level for Xelle, opened up, revealing a pane of glass behind. Removing Tenne's numbered seal, she held the coin-like shape against the window. The other side, without a number. If they asked her to flip it over, fine, but for now she'd rather not announce who she was or that she'd only recently received the token.

The window closed shut and the door swung open, stopping at a square angle as if closing out the per who had opened it. In front of her rose a slow, stone staircase (and ramp), turning out of view of the door. Almost forgetting the second lever, she descended a few steps and pulled it. As she did, she could hear the door resealing from below.

The staircase wound up and around, and directly into the artist's chambers. She laughed to herself, wondering what would happen if he wasn't here, or what she was supposed to do if he'd gone out for chips. She supposed, most pers arranged appointments.

Xelle realized that the galleries must be closed this close to evening; perhaps she could have just gone in the front. On second thought, no.

Relieved to see the top door open, she walked into the wide, lofty room, peering in nervously to see Tenne molding a gray chunk with his hands. He had taken off whatever cloak and hat he'd been wearing, and instead wore shiny slate blue pants, a flowing plaincloth shirt, and today a dark undercap over his head. A messy apron was slung over all of it.

"Hello? I'm sorry to interrupt."

He turned around, stopping with his arms still extended. "No, it's fine. I had no idea when you'd be here, of course, and I thought it'd be more than a day? Sorry my hands are covered in sculpto."

Xelle had dated an artist once, when she was younger. There was more language to it than the magesphere.

"I work fast," she said with a light shrug, though the message came out a bit blank. She waited as he went to a tub of water, scrubbed his hands at length, and then dried them. He walked back, gazing at her.

"It's that bad?" He pulled over two stools, the simple devices in stark contrast with the rest of the elaborate space. Apologizing, he pulled a stained rag off of one, then sat on that one himself. She joined him on the other.

"Well," she started. This was complicated. "I have an issue with my mind that I'm figuring out. So I can't stay too long."

"Sorry to hear that. Can I get you anything? Tea? Hot or cold pads? I can call in, like, anything here."

"No thanks. But, no, it's not good news. I'm sorry."

Tenne grew silent, and Xelle's chest began to pound. She would add that he told her to tell him, but he already knew that. Best to rip this off.

"Someone claimed to interfere with the art grant on your behalf in order to hold it over your parent. He didn't understand what was going on until it was too late." The truth creaked a few different ways in that, but she wasn't going to get into the details. "I can't actually say for sure what your status was with the prize, but either they believed they interfered to cause your win, or they were able to convince him. They say they have evidence, but they've also been untruthful. I can't get into how they tried to use him, but he is going to work now to try and help. You must keep silent about it all and not let on that anything's changed. But I knew you'd need to know. That part."

The artist tapped his shoe against the floor. "Da must be wrecked."

"It's hard, but he's doing—" She almost said he was doing well, and then she remembered his drinking and outbursts. The pain in his eyes. Also, hardness. "He's going to get through this. He's terrified how you'll take it."

"I couldn't believe it, you know. When I . . ." He got up, and suddenly slammed the stool across the room. "Inferno! Burned up, eternal inferno."

His reaction was startling, but she understood it. She'd be furious too. The metal of their family locket pressed against her, still. She imagined a spirit in it, listening. Not liking that idea, she instead imagined a spirit who felt no sadness or grief, but only empathized. Sent comfort. She wished she could give Tenne the locket. Not today, though.

Stomping, Tenne pulled the stool up, brushed it off as if it'd accumulated dust by being thrown across the room, and gave it a shake. "Got these at the market. Cheap. They are fire-burned solid." Sitting back down, he started again. "So now I gotta figure out what to do about all this." He looked up at her. "Who would have won?"

Xelle shook her head, realizing she'd reached today's capacity for outbursts from the Kern family. "I don't know anything about the prize or the grant or the process. I just know what they told your parent, which did not include anything about other applications."

"I'm going to find out," he said, gruffly. His face pinched, and Xelle was unsure whether it was anger, or determination? Thing was, she didn't know this per at all. She'd done what she promised; it was time to wrap up and get out of here.

"I don't know if that's a good idea or not, but I do need to warn you. Mage Kern is still in danger. You are now in danger. I need you to keep silent about everything I've said. You asked a favor of me; this is what I need of you."

He nodded, looking right in her eyes.

"And I would tread lightly in interfering before you understand where the pieces lie. And, as for your Da, while I think knowing you were handling this would comfort him immensely, I also think you should use caution contacting him openly." Surely a Spire Mage and the hottest celebrity in Mytil could work that out without Xelle's help. "I implore you both to use caution. Things are . . . changing. Maybe it's a little problem and we'll get through it, or maybe it's—" She wasn't sure how to frame this.

"A shift in vogue," he offered. "Maybe you've painted in one style your whole life but you see a new trend emerge and have a feeling your paintings aren't going to sell for maybe a real long time."

Arguable, but better than what she'd got out. "Sure, but what I'm trying to say is maybe a bad trend. Maybe we've gotten used to our lives, that nothing can happen here. When maybe it already has."

Tenne's face still held tension, but otherwise, he had settled into a stance of calm. Or, sadness, perhaps. "Sometimes," he said, "when things change for the bad, we can pull from it change for the good. Maybe they weren't what we thought they were. Maybe we can sculpt something new."

Grateful for a clear out, she stood, yet perhaps both a bit dazed, they exchanged brief pleasantries a minute longer. Xelle could barely remember it. She remembered he said something kind about her mental issues, and it was all she could do not to throw the other stool. Whatever was happening with her mark, it was one issue on another on another. Why did no one understand?

Her mind tried to answer her and she shouted back, *No one who is here.*

She did not throw any stools. Instead, she rose, walked back down the marbled steps, and into the now dark garden, beautiful in the way the moonslight reflected back and forth like she was walking on ribbons in between the fabric of life. Until she was by herself and she could collapse onto the ground clasping her head in agony.

21 - *Sigil*

She was not well. Were the gardens closed? She hoped they were closed. The idea of being seen here, against the ground, and having to explain it to a stranger was too much for Xelle right now.

There was no dinner, nor catching a moveroom like this either, and so she stumbled, repeating a small lyric as she made her way through the city. She could not go on this way, but she'd confronted Mages, she'd learned about danger to the dragons, she'd delivered awful news— she'd subjected herself to so much stress. If she could get somewhere to rest, then she'd see where she was in the morning.

At least she knew there were Frond Mages incity. If it came to that. She laughed out loud, at least thinking it was laughter and not liking the strange and pained sounds that she heard. She returned to her little song, not liking the repetition but knowing her mind would do this at times, she could likely not fight it.

The moonslight reflected gently on the cobbled streets, and she used the beauty of the glowing silvers, the lines between them, to try and soothe her as she made her way to her tavern loft.

She had to walk through the bar, but the crowd that was there did not seem to see her, and she hurried through, to the narrow stairs and directly onto the top blanket of her small bed.

Desperate for rest, she sank into the night ivy, traveling without sleep for a few minutes, then probably an hour, then more, replaying the conversation with Kern, with Jehanne, with Tenne. Thinking again about Thyra and Kwillen. Avoiding thoughts of her old life, her old friends, terrified to remember what it was she'd just given up. Given up, when she could have just pledged. When everything could be different now.

No. Maybe sleep would find her soon. It always did, eventually.

Jehanne. She'd called her a Mage, had that been an accident or a sign? A sign to pledge at To'Ever? Did she know she'd been with Kern? Did she suspect him as the one who'd turned? Maybe she already knew? Maybe Xelle really was just a flatcap sent to stall, and she had nothing to do with any of it. Jehanne was being polite. But then she wouldn't have the sword. She wouldn't have met a dragon.

Protection. She needed to protect the dragons. That should be her focus. Help the dragons. Protect them.

Dragons.

Dragon mark. It was a dragon mark, that's what was hurting. Kern had confirmed it and Jehanne had seemed to know it. She hadn't told them of its ache. Should she have? But what would they have said? That the dragons were in her mind? Why would the dragons get into her mind?

"Burns," she hissed far too loudly, rolling over and falling onto the hard floor with a thump she barely felt.

Springing to her feet, she rushed to gather her cap and cloak, and pull back on her boots. How had she not realized it? Dragons read minds. However that worked, were they pushing it back the other way? And Xelle only resisted them, like a toddler with ripe greens? The mark hadn't been inflicted on her, she'd consented to it at least in Thunder's mind; she'd specifically asked if they could meet again. Thunder was crying out, and she was bobbing between Arc and Mytil, chatting and plotting.

Her last clip snapped into place, and she did use magic this time, once through the now-empty bar and out into the cold. She whisked herself away, in the direction of the mountains, seeing the very faintest outline in the moonslight. Settling into her mark, no, Kern had called it a sigil, she could feel it, feel their direction, feel the emotion of worry. She needed to go.

Xelle had skipped lunch, skipped dinner, and she didn't even have a bag, just Essie clipped to a grommet on her waist. The one thing Essie didn't have was food.

She could go back and wake Klein but what would he think, her grasping at her head and asking for foldcrisps? She had to go. She'd find out what was going on, then get the help she needed, including a healer then, even a Frond one.

Now casting with urgency, she pressed on, back up the road toward To'Arc. Pulling ahead, cast by cast, slowed by the need for caution in the moonslight. When, without knowing, perhaps she'd reached a thousand steps, she was glad for the progress she'd made. Then, at ten thousand, she couldn't imagine how she'd had morale at only one, how she hadn't collapsed then. On and on, the trials of the last days building in her already exhausted mind, she focused only on pulling herself, with the magic, each new step.

Finally, as she passed the Tower and reached a point of exhaustion, she realized the feeling in her head was less blurry, less pressing. More focused, it now felt like a beacon, and pulling herself up again, she followed it.

She would not have taken this path through the mountains—it was thick, with tall inclines. But with Arc Magic to pull her she whipped the threads over and over, pulling herself forward, up the sides of hills, or even up cliffs, winding at times to find a section with a clearer path.

Magic coursed through her limbs like the very Arcs it represented, and she wondered why she'd never drawn this deep. Years of training, years of caution and practice, and now she soared up tufts of mountain snow, a small speck against the moonslight.

A familiar rhythm stopped her. Fuelstones. Huge fuelstones, by the sound of them, clanked and pushed, even now, through the night, through the icy mountain terrain where winter still held fast. How was it possible that they had not been detected by the Tower? How that they even accessed stones this size?

Her senses sparked at the edges, subtle and prickly, like how an eclipse might feel if one couldn't see it. She paused and threw the strongest detection she could, almost knocking out her own wind, but still she could only feel the sparkle, like burrs of light stuck to the edge of nothing.

She tried to remember the Breath version that Kwill had taught her. It used the Mage's own breath as the inhalant, and she had giggled the whole time e'd tried to show it to her, as she swore she could never be a Breath Mage. She tried it now, imagining there must be small plants here in the forest, repeating in her mind the exact sequence e'd taught her, the poetry e'd recited to place the images in her mind.

A sense got in her nose, like a scent but without fragrance. Magic. Amidst the fuelstones sat powerful magic. It was not active, nor so much an enchantment, it felt like it was . . . waiting. Had it been wrapped? From whom was it meant to be hidden? There was too much here Xelle did not understand, and her Breath Magic was not keen enough to discern more.

Wanting a visual, she pulled herself into a tall tree, large enough that she could find a branch to support her weight, and peered, through the needles, down at the moonslit scene below. She ignored the pricks of the rough branch and the thick sap that must be caking her gloves, glad at least that her Arc wristtubes were covered; she'd wanted to save those.

Below her cranked a massive machine. The concept of a move-room: fuelstones propelling feet upon which cargo sat. But this was no vroom. A set of bladed rollers chopped and then stomped anything in its path, slowly creating a flat swath of passable road, like a rusted stitching tool ripping through fine embroidery. Behind it waited two huge vehicles, flat, forged platforms with rings, chains, and clips. And behind that, a large passenger vroom, covered, with only tiny, circular windows.

What were these monstrous objects? How had they obtained such fuelstones? Were the quarries involved as well? How was this happening, out of view, while the Mages fretted about Pelir? What did Pelir have to do with machines and mountains? Nothing here was right.

Carefully now, and taking whatever sense of Breath Magic she'd just imbued, she swung over the machines below, pulling around them and past as her cape flapped behind her. Where was Thunder? If zhey were worried about the machines, zhey must be close. No, Xelle knew zhey were close. Hopefully enough to hear her thoughts directly. *I'm sorry for being late! I didn't know. But I know now!*

Xelle grasped onto a tree, overwhelmed by a sudden sadness. While she'd worried about time before, it had all been in the course of business—a fast Ascension could take months. She wished she could start again. Start everything again, but this time without absurd choices in between periods of doing nothing but the ordinary. If she could start again, everything would be different. She'd be more direct in investigating what pers were hearing of Pelir, not spend weeks sitting around the library reading, not practicing magic, not really doing anything. Relaxing for hours, chatting with Kwill. She would have learned more about her sigil instead of simply noting it. She might not have agreed to go to Breath at all. Just because they'd asked her to, that had really been a reason?

All she could do now was find the dragons and offer herself to help. Finding that the moment of rest had wearied her further, Xelle pulled harder, willing herself to cast again—away from the machines and toward the dragons.

She did not remember where the dragons had been before. Thunder had taken her there and flown her around and she hadn't had the steady perspective to build a map in her mind. But with the sigil, she could sense them, the direct location. Them or Thunder specifically, she wasn't sure. It was stronger now, more pointed. She turned that way, and with each effort, found herself closer. Only once nearly upon it, the gap in the trees against the stone was visible, and she lunged herself its way.

As she slung down into the huge area she'd only glimpsed before, she stumbled over, and up onto her knees. Before and around her, the magnificent pers slowly turned her way. They were even more glorious than she'd remembered. The streaks of color in their stretched and smooth skin were finer than art, and the shape of their bodies rose in stark angles and curves unlike any of the other anima of Alyssia. From closer now, she could see more detail, variations between them: ear shapes and sizes, and spikes, on their head or running down their backs. Each distinct. Each faced her way. A few moved toward her, their voices warning, in low growls.

They were agitated. The air buzzed between them. Did they speak in thought? Had they seen the machines, crushing their way in what she now knew was toward them? How much time did they have?

She scanned, quickly, for Thunder, but here, a tiny hu kneeling in the hard dirt, she could only see the few that approached her, their eyes filled with intensity.

Xelle was not afraid of the dragons.

E gazed directly at them. Something in their stance, their colors, the unease in their eyes—Xelle knew then that e was forever dedicated to these pers. E would do anything to assist them, anything to protect them. If it was crawling back to Ever Tower, then that was what e'd do. If it was staying here, in the frozen mud and snow, and repelling every invading Mage, Machine, or Monster, then e would. E would never, ever, abandon them, as long as they would welcome eir help.

Two of the dragons now rose, and one screeched. Xelle's reflexes reacted. E sensed no harm, but in zheir size and the strength of the call, there was immense power. And to create the sigil, e now considered, there must be other powers as well. Perhaps the approaching hu knew that too.

What now? The dragons must know of the danger; Xelle was sure of it. What could Xelle do that they could not? Did they wait for a confrontation? Was e interfering?

But what could e do? Nothing could go well if these hu made it here. And the dragons could not know all that was going on, even if they knew more than Xelle. These hu, on their way, whoever they were—all Xelle knew is that they hurt pers—these Hurts—had turned a Spire

Mage. All bets were now off. And Thunder, Xelle was sure zhey were here somewhere. Listening to em.

That's right. Thunder had called em here. That was enough.

E didn't need to speak; the dragons could read minds. But saying it aloud helped em clarify these words from the other thoughts bouncing around, putting all the other regrets and worries and tasks that kept her from crafting a clear message into background noise.

Trying to stand, her arm jerked, and she fell down into a patch of frozen soil, grating against her already worn gloves. Gasping, a leg convulsed and she turned sideward.

In all of her studies, she'd never come close to her material limits. She'd not known what it was, or what it felt like, she'd just taken care to keep her casts modest, proper, and in balance. She'd considered it that: balance, an ethics pledge. Always check your material. Don't take more than one gives. Life or death in the spiritual sense. But now, wrenching on the ground, her mind screamed with what might happen if she'd pushed too far. Or the other thing—what she didn't want to think but she could hear them saying it, hear it echo—that she could burn her magic out. Shuddering, she tried to control her limbs which twitched violently away from her. If she made it through this, she *would* help her inkblooms. And she would always, always watch her material.

She rolled onto her arm, fighting feelings of shock through her body as well as the storm in her mind. "Hello," she said, waiting for no diplomacy. "I am Xeleanor. I know magic but am not a Mage. There is a group of hu approaching from the next valley and I believe these hu could mean you harm. I don't know if anyone else has a sigil, but if you sense any that way, I believe they were brought along for deceit."

Several dragons growled, but she must keep going.

"They will be here soon, and I worry they have methods to contain or control you. I . . . hope they couldn't, or wouldn't, but I don't think you should take that chance.

"I believe you should fly farther away, higher into the mountains, until the hu can learn what is going on."

There was a huge flapping of wings at this, the percussion sweeping across the ground and through her and drowning any cries that may have accompanied it. Her sigil pinged, giving Xelle the idea that maybe Thunder had tried to tell them the same thing. Thunder seemed the youngest; they may have ignored zhem.

"I'm sorry, you must have a hoard here. You've built homes, structures. Everything is unclear, but something is changing, and until we know what, I think you should move farther away. If you'll allow me, I'll reach for Thunder"—she hoped the name she'd given the dragon conveyed the correct dragon in her thoughts—"and zhey can find me. I am sorry that hu bother you so. There must be more to it. I'll learn it. And I'll find out what is going on and help you in any way that I can, with your welcome. I promise. I *swear* it. But for now, get away from them. Please."

The body language of dragon pers was not so different from hu pers, in that if this had been a room of elder Mages, she would have known every sentiment without hearing a word. Some urged the group to consider the dirt-covered hu, others insisted this was their home, they should not be driven from it (again . . . it felt like). That it was time.

One, a sleek yellow dragon that moved like the lightning in Xelle's legs, rushed toward her like a darting river lizard seeing a spot of sun, and screeched, so loud Xelle had to cover her ears. Zhey had stared right at her sigil, clearly displeased that it had been done. For a moment, Xelle almost shouted that she'd not known of it, but that wasn't true, she'd asked Thunder to meet again, and this is how Thunder had done it. She wasn't going to blame her friend. Who was just trying to help, whether they got that or not.

With a second furious screech, fire came searing out of Lightning's mouth—zhey could argue about zheir name when zhey weren't confusing Xelle with a carrot—and unable to roll, Xelle threw an arm out casting Arc Magic to bend the plume away, where it dissipated upward.

Curse all mind-reading dragons. She remembered they could hear all of this, at least it seemed they could. Including that.

Stung by the strength of her cast, Xelle flopped over on her back. She was in agony and they didn't need to see her mouth move. "I do not know what hu have done to you. It is kept a secret from us. I will find out. I will learn. And you know what, I'm sorry. I'm not going to tell you to move. Fire-fall if I know. I'm just saying, I ran really hard to get here because my friend wanted me here, and those pers with the machines that are very much almost here are not authorized by any element of the Mages that I know, and some pers have been threatening Mages at To'Arc, really powerful Mages, and those pers over there—I get a *really bad vibe* from them. Maybe it'll be fine. Maybe they're curious. Maybe they'll just take your hoard and go. Maybe they can capture or mind-control you. All they really need is one, right, and if you got mind-controlled you could fly off with them? I don't know. If you leave, I will do whatever I can to make sure you can come back. I will do this as long as my heart beats. I will. My body hurts . . ." she finally whimpered.

As she turned over, she could see the dragons gathered in conference. Some drew close, while others flew up, to get a broader view. No, they wouldn't see it, the path was made around the turn, they'd need a specific angle. She thought.

Lightning came running toward her again, and in the flash that Xelle was worried about reacting, zhey lifted her up, inelegantly, and Xelle hung down, painfully, by the seat of her pants. Thankfully the discomfort was short-lived, and the dragon put her down as if painting the ground with her, perhaps intending to ease the fall, and Xelle went rolling back, away from the encampment. The village. The city. She didn't know the right term.

Heaving herself to face upward, she could see the other dragons had risen into the sky also. Their silhouettes cast eerie shapes in the moonslight and she could hear the flapping of wings, like a chorus of drums. Among them, a huge, cracking noise nearly split her mind in two and she realized, slowly, what the dragons had done. The cliff was falling down in huge swaths, over where the obsidian wall had been, over what had looked like a cave across on the other side, and over the area she'd just been.

Covering it. They're covering it!

She could hear the hu shouting now, on their way, and unable now to travel by Magic or any way at all, Xelle scooted herself across the rumbling ground, shoving her butt backward with her hands and heels, toward a tree where she could at least lean back. One by one, the dragons took off across the mountains and away, and tears fell down Xelle's frozen face, carrying dirt and sap down onto Xelle's cloak.

"That was my good cloak," she squeaked, pulling it around her for warmth.

Now, she sat silently against the tree. The pers—these Hurts—had abandoned their vehicles, running through the trees at the flight of the dragons. She waited, exhausted and numb, as they ran into the clearing, shouting, and howling at each other, in words Xelle could not understand. Hoping at least she could maybe learn something that might help her find them later, she watched, willing her drooping eyes to stay open, her legs leaden beneath her.

One, a silhouette from where she sat, stared at the mess of stone where the wall had been. Others spread out, and she willed them not to see her, not to come her way. Then, she felt magic. Detection, she felt sure, but in her weakened state she got no more than that. Not even which prong. There was nothing she could do.

"There xe is!" a strained voice shouted. "Go hard, xe's a Mage."

"Xe's injured," a smaller voice called from further back. "Just go!"

Xelle almost cast.

She almost reached up and used her Arc Magic in ways she had never considered but were clear to her now. Jehanne stopped her. In her mind.

There was no victory worth hitting her limits. She could not risk it. Her material would recharge. She had to wait. She could not do it.

Several hu rushed toward her, their boots thudding in the snow, and before she could see much more than a glimpse, a rough sensation scraped her face, shutting out the view of the moons, and the tall trees over them. Her hands were pulled behind her, the gloves roughly removed, and the feel of burlap brushed her lips.

She'd never heard of such a thing, and her lips burned with fury which spread down her arms and through her boots and Xelle had not felt anything like this in her life, and a voice flamed up, not out loud but through the storm of her mind: *You **will** regret this.* Rough arms slung her up, over a shoulder perhaps, and she could not listen in on the conversations as there were too many, too stilted. Mostly, to go, to hurry. This way, that way. Xelle bounced in numb agony, yet she felt no more casts, not even a shield to block her, in case she regained strength. Finally a door was opened, like a moveroom or something on the machinery, and then there was a furious screech, and her sides were pinched and she could feel she was rising upward, her bound legs dangling beneath her.

She could not see who held her, but it was clear in her sigil, and amidst her pain her heart leapt with joy.

Thunder! I was looking for you. I hope you're not upset; I didn't want to call to you and put you in any danger.

Thunder let a low warble, and Xelle could feel them lowering, together, onto a cool sheet of rock. She felt a long shape, what she realized must be a tooth, against each arm, and she held as still as her shaking body would let her, as Thunder snapped the ropes from her arms and then legs.

Updrafted and scared and angry, she fumbled with her freed hands and ripped the bag off of her head, not caring what magical evidence it might hold and just throwing it, tossing it, dropping it, who the flame cared, that bag went flopping off of the cliff on which it slumped down into the trees like the failure that it was. She spun around, covering her eyes as the sunrise broke over the mountains, bathing Thunder in golden light. A huge face drew forward, as Thunder nudged Xelle's own, nearly knocking her backward.

"Careful! And thank you! I should say thank you! I missed you, too. And I'm sorry about your call. I understand it better now."

Thunder started to chip away at the rock as if making Xelle a seat.

"Thunder. I promise we can talk later, but right now I really want you to go with the others. I don't want the hu to catch you; they may have Mages. And I don't want you to get in trouble, either! We can talk later; I promise. You know how to reach me."

The dragon stomped a foot, and a feeling pinged in her sigil. *Protection.* Zhey wanted her safe too, Xelle suddenly understood. "Ok! I hit my material limits, or I strained one, I'm not really sure yet. Drop me off at Arc Tower. I promise if I get there, I'll be fine. They can take care of me. For now. Please? And, hey, I'll find you. I promise."

Xelle screamed once, by instinct, as Thunder pinched her up, soared down the small cliff, and darted down the mountains, toward the Tower, its peak gleaming bright gold in the emerging morning light. She worried, with zhem now heading the wrong direction, whether Thunder would be able to catch the fleeing dragons, but then realized an awareness of where the others were, perhaps Thunder's own sense. The throbbing of her sigil had stopped, thank Fira it had stopped, and she could sense the dragons flying higher into the sharp peaks. Xelle felt fury at this; they should not be forced to harsher lands, less to eat, longer and more dangerous journeys for food. And she had asked them to go!

As Thunder screeched and circled To'Arc, Xelle looked down to see hu rushing outside, pooling into groups like melting snow. She grew dizzy as her friend circled and descended, and then set Xelle down onto the steep peak of the Tower itself.

Confused, Xelle grabbed on to the wood shingles and held tight, as Thunder, zheir streaks of color shining in the sunlight, raced away, throwing her a final bundle of upset and unsorted emotions on zheir way to find the rest.

And Xelle was on the roof. Her reaction to heights kept her from doing anything but clinging and squeezing her eyes as closed as possible, freezing her in a moment of howling wind and all-consuming fear, where Xelle could not hear the shouts she was certain were echoing from below. Her hands shook, even moreso against the cold wood, and she could not hang on. Only one thought clarified. Material limits or not, she was not going to fall freely from the highest peak of To'Arc, plummeting into the watching crowds.

She was meant to trust, but that was an exercise too far. With a furious pull of Arc Magic—no not of it but with it—she drew the longest thread she'd ever made, slashed it toward the ground, and let go, allowing her form to flow along it, her cape billowing up over her head and flapping against her view of cloud and sky, as she floated unsteadily, story after story, to the ground.

With a final twist, she wrenched over to land on hands and feet. Both slipped from under her and she collapsed. The cast snapped away.

Shaking, she heard words. *Dragon. Study. Healer.* She did not want a healer. Not now, not for this. She would take care of it herself.

On her bare hands and shaking knees against the ice, and stumbling to attempt a rise to her feet, she pulled herself away from the feet and legs around her, nearly hissing at the hands reaching to touch her without consent.

Everyone around her talked about Thunder as if Xelle wasn't right there, her heart pounding and body shaking. "The dragons are real," voices said. "They are back," another said. "What about . . ." An older, whispered voice trailed off.

So much for my low profile. Sorry, Jehanne.

As voices overwhelmed her, and Xelle considered what cast she could do to get away—get away and think, a familiar voice soared over all the others.

"Stand. Back."

Bejeweled hands reached down but did not touch her. Why the jewels caught her eyes, she couldn't say. They sparkled and glistened. So many colors.

Reaching out, she took them, and Helia slowly pulled Xelle to her feet, wrapping an arm around her. "I will take care of her. She needs you to back away. Please! And stop staring! She's our family! You! You're leering. Want to see my favorite cast? Go!"

This went on a minute or two, with a few "Yes, Mage Helia" from what must be staff or Studies, until Xelle groggily noticed that the crowds now kept their distance, others filtering inside, perhaps to resume their breakfast or get to their class.

As they also walked slowly toward the entrance, Helia did not loosen her grip. "Do not cast again. You are so close to burnout; to cast so little then attempt this. I'm horrified."

She was making it sound like alcohol tolerance, she thought, eager to distract herself. Well, she didn't have that either. Even the Emerald Forest was in moderation. Why hadn't she taken Helia to the Emerald Forest? Maybe they should go. Klein had a pink flower drink with actual flower petals that she knew Helia would love.

"I heard you'd been ordered," Helia said, her voice as calm as any. "I tried to find you but there was no sign."

Ordered? Like, with transgressions? Her mind spun to discern it. "Oh, the art gallery thing? I had no idea they'd figure out who I was so quickly. Fira. We should hire those stewards." Tenne. She hoped he was safe. "I've been in Mytil. You know that, I guess, if they are trying to order me."

"Art gallery? What are you talking about? If you have multiple transgressions, Xelle, I cannot break you out of Frond Residence. And I'm not going myself. No, I heard in the mid-floor café that you were part of this Amberborn movement."

"Me? Like me me, by name?"

"You you."

Low profile, check. She wondered if this started before or after she talked to Kern, what, yesterday? Someone was really working fast.

Xelle stopped, almost flipping head-first over Helia's arm. But she needed to stop. She pulled her face up, surprised to realize she was now directly in Helia's. "If you trust me, I will tell you I have only the interest of Alyssia in mind, and since that can be warped in POV, to clarify, I remain dedicated to the mission and purity of the magesphere."

"That wasn't the whole accusation."

"Whatever. We have bigger problems, Hellie. Something is going on. I'll tell you . . . only if you're willing."

"Study Xeleanor, I am dragging around a double transgressor at a material limit who just got tossed onto our Tower via dragon. Do I burning look like I'm willing? Like I trust you?"

They were so close. She was so kind. Leaning forward, she locked—they locked—in a long, slow, gentle kiss. Xelle blinked and pulled away, her heart pounding. What had she done? "I don't know what that was," she whispered.

"I'll explain it to you sometime. We've got to get you inside; I can't do much if a ranking Mage decides to take over. I'm like, a level one player here, remember?"

"Oh! I forgot to thank you for the mirror. It was really nice. I will use it."

"Is there more?" Helia looked half-ready to push Xelle back into the packed, melting snow.

"Uh, there is. I sort flash-decided to go to To'Ever for a while. Jehanne has blessed it."

"First name basis; I guess pledging is for rookies." Helia heaved her hands up, reminding Xelle that for Helia's build, hauling a grown hu must be a chore. She tried to stand upright, but only stumbled.

"I can go with you," Helia said, "for a little while. Or I could request assignment there."

"I'm sorry. About . . . what I just did. I . . ."

"We did that, technically."

"I initiated it; you know what I mean."

"Xeleanor, I missed you when you were gone. And now you're going away again. I know, I'm supposed to say bye, have fun. But I can see a future with . . . us, if you were willing to try it. And," Xelle could feel her smiling weakly from the side, "I am an Arc Mage, so seeing the future? It's what I do."

Arc Mages seeing time was one of those Mage jokes like Grand Mages transforming into trees. Not the first time it would be used to pick someone up. Slowly, they continued the trudge toward the door. She felt Helia's arms against her. Soft. Strong.

"I think I need some time," Xelle finally said. There was so much in her mind. "I'll come back, and maybe we can have dinner. I've got a place in Mytil that I bet you haven't been, and the galleries are gorgeous in the Spring."

"Sure, if you're not on the Gallery Wanted List."

Xelle would have laughed, but what was left of her feelings felt something was very important right now. "I . . . I can't be what you want."

"Just be you," Helia answered. "And I will deal with the rest."

Her sigil no longer felt, not specifically. The itch, as she'd termed it, had left almost the moment she'd realized what it meant, and instead a sense settled into her mind. A connection with Thunder, as she believed it to be.

For now, it felt distant.

Taking a stretch alone in an enclosed garden, she tried to send a message back. *If you can give me time to see what's going on here, I promise I'll see you soon.*

There had been no response.

She checked on her room, the Tower-issue one, a final time. With everything that had happened, she didn't expect a writeup for smudged walls, but she'd been here for many years, and she did want to make sure some small item hadn't slid under a dresser or jammed in a drawer.

Yes, she knew the adage that if one didn't miss something one didn't need it, but that didn't mean one might not want it. Or find it embarrassing to leave around.

Her last visit to the lab had been particularly painful, and she was sure she'd not visit that specific space again, even if she were to return to To'Arc. Painful in all the normalcy she'd had to squeeze from her already worn mind, especially without showing she'd had to squeeze it.

The space had been crowded with well-wishers as she gathered her things. One Study had put in for a corner workspace and she was glad to hear that the new lab lead had already promised him Xelle's desk once she packed up. Which had been difficult with the stream of Studies stopping to wish her well.

That respect made it harder, in the ways that were more difficult to describe than they might seem. The fact that her desk had been untouched all this time, down to the three scratch papers she'd casually folded into standing fans, all now fallen over with pencils rolled into them.

In those last moments, she'd tried to give a small speech. Whatever looks of displeasure or avoidance she'd seen walking back through the Tower after what had been a long and painful rest, here she saw wonder, admiration. The fact that their lab lead had been "put on the roof by a dragon"—*their* lab lead.

Without much else to go on, she'd drawn on that energy. They already knew this lab was more about logistics and data than magic, that the project was looked down by some in that regard; she didn't repeat that or emphasize its value. What she told them was that life was measured in how you lived it: love, kindness, passion—they made the fire that burned and illuminated everything else. "Never forget that," she said, before turning out into the corridor, to enthusiastic applause.

Squeezing back tears, she wound around and again trying to ignore pers hoping to get a look at her, until finally she felt safe enough to approach her nightgarden one last time. Not last. Last for now.

Though Tower rules would prohibit her from occupying Arc space while studying at Ever, she was not about to give this project up. It wasn't even in the Tower, just a side garden.

Of course it was not. Not just, she meant.

The blue light of her lamps showed the rune she had drawn, shining dark purple in the light, hopefully providing her access from outside when she could better connect it. The little inkblooms had kept the touch of brightness she'd thought she'd noticed since spreading the obsidian. Still no signs of flowering, but their little glowing dots gave her hope that maybe she was getting closer, or at least on the right track. Though use of the blooms was deep Arc Magic, there could be resources at Ever that might help. Having access to their libraries, though still not Mage-level access (she was going to have to reckon with that at some point), which might let slip details that would be more protected here.

Before she realized she was giving her inkblooms a speech like the lab, she was already halfway through it. Yet she kept on, pledging her commitment to them, telling them she'd figure it out, and she'd return to them when she could.

The sword was still there. It had fallen just a little but what she'd learned was called a hilt had stuck on one of the bumps in the block wall. She resolved to build it a better stand as she tilted it the other way; the extraordinary object deserved that rather than leaning against her scrapwood storage cabinet.

Perhaps some redesign was in order.

The little space had taken on a lot more glam than it had had before she'd left for To'Breath. The obsidian blade with crystal hilt almost disappeared into somewhere between pure dark and pure light in the darkness of the room. Not the hilt versus the blade, she meant all of it. It all drank the darkness as if there was a hole in space itself just waiting to be filled, and at the same time it looked as though it hid the light of eternity, bursting in a surreal white glow from its edges.

And her livewalls, built with a secret inspiration—a fringe challenge—to see if she could grow her own inkblooms, sparkled in the darkness with the chunks of obsidian covering the narrow stretches of soil. Not sparkled, so much but . . . dazzled. No, not dazzled. Like black diamonds that illuminated the hollows they created with light brighter than the universe yet calmer than the darkest void.

Her mind returned to think about him, here in the prismatic darkness, to weight his departure with finality so she could move forward without that weight herself. She unwrapped the large section of obsidian. Then, not ready to see it again, she wrapped it up and slid it onto a high shelf of the cabinet. Returning into her seat, she swiveled around and closed her eyes.

Why did she think about someone who seemed gone from her life? More than a month, and still he took her thoughts. Or she gave them; it wasn't clear. When would it stop? Now? Maybe now. He was a partner, that was certain. A partner who took and gave humor, care, and earnestness in return. That was real, very real, even if he didn't share the other growth that had emerged like the ivy they'd both loved. Even if he'd seen it, and decided to leave.

He hadn't said goodbye. Not even a note. She couldn't deny the confliction in that feeling. If she had overstepped, if she had shown herself, the truth of herself, then perhaps he needed to leave. Yet it made her rage like the fire she'd discussed there, in the lab. She burned and screamed over the uncertainty of it. The embarrassment. The emptiness. Yes, empty. Not overall, but a section. Like the way she'd tried to describe the darkness around the sword.

Perhaps she could not fully shed the weight. That empty space . . . was also real.

If one were to ask her, would she see him again?

No. She wouldn't. She knew that.

But knowing it couldn't make her believe it. Yet she did now need to accept it.

She breathed, in and out, and the darkness of the room calmed her. Darker than night, as they said.

"Darker than night," she whispered.

~

"You're going to be fine, Xeleanor," Helia said.

The space between them felt extended, yet it eased Xelle's tension. "I'm not going to run there and pledge if that's what you think."

"I know," she said, rolling her eyes a bit.

"I don't know why I said it, but I can't talk myself out of it either. I think it's my best bet for . . . learning things I need to learn." She turned the letter from Jehanne in her hands. It was to soothe the Front Desk, anyway, she was certain Jehanne had already contacted the Tower. She hadn't talked to the Crown Mage—she hadn't talked to any of them, not since that morning.

She'd thought more about what Jehanne had said before, about a low profile. She wondered, and hopefully this wasn't a pretentious thing to wonder, whether the low profile was for herself, or from them.

Either way, maybe this time she'd use the space correctly. Learn new magic. Investigate these Hurts—the name had stuck in her head—find what she could learn about these Amberborn Mages. Reconnect, more privately this time, with the dragons.

"But I'm worried too." She glanced away, tracing her finger over a wandering vine of the carved column.

"As a Mage, I'm probably supposed to tell you not to trace the column," Helia said. "I know you are," she added when Xelle didn't answer. "You don't know if this is the right choice. You love it here, you love Arc Magic; anyone can see that. Honestly, Xelle, I'd tell you to trust yourself but at this point who the flame knows. I'd even tell you trust your instinct but I'm starting to think our instincts are even gambles on their best days."

Xelle looked over. Helia was always so intentional; hearing her otherwise was a shock. Yet her words reassured her. Who did know? About anything, really.

"So how about just pick and do your best to make it work? And if it doesn't work, play Mountains & Motes and know you tried." She fixed on Xelle's face. "I'm always here."

"Thank you." Not knowing what else to do, Xelle made the Arc, holding it out, like she was carrying a torch. Helia returned it, and then bowed. Xelle returned that, and when she rose, Helia was walking away.

Sighing at too much weight for not enough reasons, Xelle wandered into the Atrium one last time. Blocking out the crowds which passed and watched her and pointed as though she couldn't see them, she sat a moment, taking in the space, the latticed windows, the vines, and the air and the life. *I love you,* she thought to the spacious room.

She ignored the pers watching her, chattering about her, whether exalting her contact with the dragons or judging her inability to pledge, or admonishing her supposed transgressions, or whatever else was on their lips. Yet, as she checked out at the Front Desk and arranged a moveroom, the reality finally settled in. If she was not going to be a Mage, she at least could never be a Study again.

They would continue to whisper. The question was, would they be over it tomorrow, in a few weeks, or would this continue? Would it stay at Arc, or would it follow her? Unsure what her future held, she decided to do the only thing she could do.

Be herself.

Night Ivy: The End

About the Author

E.D.E. Bell (she or e) was born in the year of the fire dragon during a Cleveland blizzard. After a youth in the Mitten, an MSE in Electrical Engineering from the University of Michigan, three wonderful children, and nearly two decades in Northern Virginia and Southwest Ohio developing technical intelligence strategy, she started the indie press Atthis Arts. Working through mental disorders and an ever-complicated world, she now tries to bring light and love as she can through storytelling, as a proud part of the Detroit arts community.

A passionate vegan, radiant bi, and earnest progressive, Bell feels strongly about issues related to equality and compassion and loves fantasy as a way to perceive them while offering our minds lovingly crafted worlds in which to settle. Her works are quiet and queer, and often explore conceptions of identity, community, friendship, family, and connection. She lives in Ferndale, Michigan, where she writes stories and revels in garlic.

E hopes to write many more stories with Xeleanor Du'Tam and perhaps you will join em in them. You can follow eir adventures at edebell.com.